Ace In The Hole 1

By: Moody Shula

Instagram: @Moody_Shula

Ace in the Hole 1: The Untold Story of Blue, Smiley, And Ralo Copyright @ Skyboxx Publications LLC

All rights reserved printed in The United States of America

This is a work of fiction. All of the characters, organizations, names, and events portrayed in this story are either products of the author's imagination or are used fictitiously. First published in The United States by Skyboxx Publications LLC.

"Story" By Assata Shakur

You died

I cried

And kept getting up

A little slower

And a lot more deadly

To my many supporters up and down no matter what you never switched up. Loyalty b4 Love! To my beautiful daughters Malika and Maliah only you 2 motivate me to take the righteous way. If you fwm #100 if not fukk ya!

This book is dedicated to my neighborhood role models. And the ones I love & lost to the streets. Rest Up Bossgoon & Bossgoon Jr. And Ralo, Mobey, Freeman, Chop, Poohbear, Shawn, Boogie, Dirt Lee.

In Loving Memory Of Cherry Wilson!

To everybody on a joce from the State to the Feds. Never be complacent, always think outside the box. They can cage your body. But never submit your mind to bondage. I've been there and still am as I'm writing this.

"All I need in this life of sin is me and my girlfriend." Blue sung along to Tupac's lyrics as he dropped a stack of money in his money counter.

"Fffddddddd! Beep!

He looked at the digital screen and scribbled the numbers on a small writing pad.

"That's two-hundred and fifty thou-wow. I just counted up. I still gotta drop these bricks off to the hood, and we gone eat good girl." Blue said to his two Malawa's that stood erect on each side of his desk. He zipped the bag up and said something in German. Then the bags of money were dragged by each dog to the hallway.

Watching his surveillance cameras, Blue was thinking about if it all failed. Who would he leave everything to. He had double digit babymomma's. And was still finding out daily he had more kids on the way. Either way it went he had enough money buried in the ground to send every single one to college.

When the dogs returned to the office, blue tossed them each a doggy snack. And they sat back erect on each side of his desk. He was backing away from the desk getting ready to leave when the phone on his desk began to ring.

This was not a regular for him to receive calls. Ever since they've cut ties with Waldon. Blue did take heed not to be the first hand in the mix. He sent everyone to Ralo to grab their drugs. So, he wasn't expecting any calls.

He looked at the caller ID as the phone kept ringing. "Who the fuck could this be calling the spot." Blue mumbled to himself.

The phone stopped ringing and the only thing Blue could hear was the bear like Maliwas breathing. A part of him was paranoid and somewhat scared. Who the fuck could be calling his house phone? If they were calling his phone, that meant they knew where he lived as well.

A few minutes later, the phone began ringing again. This time it was a different number. He was receiving way too many calls on his phone today. This time he decided to answer it.

"Yo, who this?" He spoke calmly as possible. Trying to disguise the worry in his voice.

"I just called, why the hell you ain't answer?"

"I didn't make it to the phone in time."

"Okay, we'll check this out. Take a look at your cameras. Blocka spoke in an urgent voice. "Hurry up and look!"

"For what?" Blue asked in a paranoid voice. "What's going on daddy."

"Just listen! Blocka snapped at him." Now is not the time to be bullshittin. Now, stop asking so many fucking questions, and do as you're told."

Blue walked back over to the desk where five security cameras were. He searched the cameras for anything abnormal.

"What am I looking for?"

"I just got word danger is heading your way." Blocka warned Blue.

"Danger!!" Blue began to grit his teeth. "Tell them send their best man, I'ma kill em all."

"Kill who? What the fuck is you speaking about? It's the alphabet boys.

"Well let they ass come." Blue shot back all while grabbing his 2.23.

"Calm your happy go lucky ass down." Blocka spoke in a calm voice. "I know you's a fighter, but this time is different. This time you gotta think your way out of this one on your own. Meanwhile grab anything you not supposed to have and place it across the fence in your neighbor's yard."

Blue removed the 2.23 soldier strap from around his shoulder, and he reached down and chambered a round inside the rifle.

"Son, You still on here?" Blocka asked hearing silence on the line "say something."

"Yeah, I'm here. I need time to process this for a minute."

A part of blue wanted to go out like Tony Montana in the end. Jail wasn't an option. He took his time to build his empire from the ground up. He was almost to his set goal. Where he would be able to leave the streets alone. Visions of his kids ran through his mind. If he filled out and went out like Tony who would raise his kids?

"This is do or die!" Blocka snapped through the phone getting Blues' attention.

"God Dammit!!" Hearing Blues tone both Maliwa's perked up hungry for action. Following Blues' every move, they began to grab duffel bags with Blue. Some were filled with money others were filled with bricks. Blue did as he was told and started to toss them in the neighbor's yard.

Making it back to his office, blue picked up the phone. "Hello."

"Yes, son you need to make wudu (ablution) and go wash your hands, face, head, arms, feet, of the sins you've committed. Make two rakats (cycles) or salat (prayer) ask Allah for forgiveness."

"I gotta call Smiley and Ralo, let them know to be on beat."

"At this point it's every man for himself. Salamu alaykum." Blocka ended the call.

Blue made wudu then placed his prayer rug to the direction of the east. A lonely tear crept down his right cheek as he recited Surah (chapter) 3, ayat (verse) 160. "If Allah helps you, there is none that can overcome you: and if he forsakes you, who is there that can help after him? And in Allah should the believers put their trust."

As blue finished reciting the front door of the house came crashing in. Hearing the sound of intruders. The Maliwa's jumped into action. They were shot quickly. DEA agents flooded the house flipping any and everything in their way. The only room they didn't search for some odd reason, was the office. Where Blue sat in prostration with his face at the front of his prayer rug. Hearing footsteps nearby. He ended his prayer. Walked over to his desk and took a seat in his office chair. He opened the cigar box and grabbed a Cuban cigar and fired it up. Watching the security cameras as they swarmed the house and his subdivision like a parade.

Chapter 1

("Back In The G")

The sun was rising early morning. As the sounds of car doors opening and closing could be heard throughout Flag Street Apartments.

"I found something!" Blue said aloud, removing the MCM duffle bag from the backseat of the 96 Chevy Impala, causing the car alarm to go off.

Instantly, Smiley and Ralo came running to view the prize of their late night early morning car hopping spree. Usually they only found a few dollars, guns, and car keys. But tonight seems different.

Blue started unzipping the designer bag anticipating to see what it held.

Boca! Boca! Boca! Gunshots echoed.

Oh Shit! They shooting! Smiley screamed.

Then the three struck out like runners at a track meet at the sounds of the gunshots. Bullets begin hitting windows, breaking them as car alarms started screaming. Warning them the shooter was aiming towards their direction. The faster they ran, the closer the shots came. "Whoosh!" A bullet could be heard nearby. Boca! Boca! Boca! Boca!

Soon as they made it out the apartments. The shots came to a cease. Never slowing down they jumped fence after fence. Until realizing they were in Angel's backyard.

Blue tapped lightly on the back window, trying not to awaken his son. Seeing the blinds move. He spoke, "come open the door, hurry up!"

Right before opening the door with nothing but a t-shirt on. Angel peeped through the peephole. Noticing the three had a duffle bag, then smiled. She made sure to lift her shirt in the back to show off her 150-pound frame. She had a small waist, small breast, with a horse behind that had stretch marks that made them look like tiger stripes.

Unlocking the door, she began to fake snap. "Uun! Uun! What the fuck yall problem coming to my house this late, this is not a trap." She said walking away knowing they could see her tiger stripes. Adding more twist in her walk than usual.

Stepping inside, Blue cut the lights on. Smiley and Ralo said nothing until they heard Angels room door shut. Nobody wanted an argument; this was not the time. They all were anticipating the contents of the duffle bag. Especially being they almost lost their lives over it.

Entering the kitchen, the three huddled around the bag like a football play. Blue dropped the duffle bag and slowly unzipped it. First removing two white squares wrapped in plastic with a Cuban flag stamp on both.

Viewing this they all looked at one another and gasped. Still seeing a black grocery bag inside the duffle. Blue removed it and pulled it apart, causing stacks of rubber banded bills to scatter all over the kitchen floor. They all begin to celebrate slapping and dapping each other's hands.

"I need to smoke something" Ralo said.

2

Blue walked over to the kitchen drawer and pulled out a ounce of exotic weed. And some backwoods. "Roll up",

They all began unwrapping the leaf blunts and dumping its tobacco guts in the trash can. Each grabbed 2 grams of bud and refilled the now empty blunts with some of the earth's best weed.

Smoking a wood a piece the three sat back puffing taking on the sight of their new found fortune.

"I think we should lay low". Blue spoke first.

"Fuck that we been broke for too long." Ralo chimed in.

Smiley just nodded his head in agreement.

"We buy all the guns we need and whoever want smoke we can take it there." You heard 2Pac don't go war unless yo money right." It's right!"

"Who we gone use em on, if we don't know who shit this is Ralo? We can't beat what we can't see." Blue explained.

"Fuck all dat! Let's count this paper." Smiley finally spoke, cutting the conversation short. They begin to unleash the stack of bills out of its rubber bands. It was all twenties, fifties, and hundreds. Ralo took the twenties and started to count. And Blue took the fifties and Smiley counted the hundreds.

After they each finished counting their stacks. Smiley counted up $25,000, Blue counted up $15,000, and Ralo counted up $20,000. Seeing they had $60,000, they split it 3 ways. Leaving them with 20 thousand a piece.

The clock on the stove showed it was 6:03 am. 20 thousand sat in front of each of them on the table and in the middle of the table 2 bricks of cocaine. Blunts being passed around and plans to buy everything imaginable were discussed. But the only real plan that stuck out more than others, was a aspiring career in the dope game. With the amount of weight and money they had, the only way was up from the bottom.

"How we gone sale this shit? We don't even know how to cook or got no customers." Ralo spoke of the process cooking cocaine from soft into hard. It was the 90's so the crack cocaine era was in its youth. But the money to be made was on a grown man level.

"Pass me one of them keys" Blue said pulling out a pocketknife and sliced a small hole in the plastic the cocaine was in, placing the blade of the knife inside returning it with the white powder. He put it to his nose sniffing it immediately, giving the substance time to take its effect. Instantly he felt his nose become numb then the famous cocaine drain. "I can't feel my face", he expressed as Smiley and Ralo smiled watching him geek." This some good shit we bout to sow the hood up."

Good as it sounded, they all knew in reality they didn't have an ounce of hustle in either of them. They were robbers and thieves not hustlers.

Blue only knew one other person he could go to for guidance. And hope it won't affect his judgment on him, his father Blocka. Next, they all changed outfits. Being at Angels Blue kept spare clothes that Ralo and Smiley borrowed. They went their separate ways. Before Blue left Angels to go home to his father's house. He went back in the backyard and buried the coke inside the "MCM" duffel bag under a doghouse leaving afterwards.

Blue entered the house very quietly. Hearing his father up early wasn't a surprise, he was a Devout Muslim. And knew he stayed up often after making the morning prayer of (FAJR) for Muslims.

Ring! Ring! Ring! Ring!

"Salamu Alaykum Ahki, How's the brother?" He listened as his father began to speak. "You've heard correctly, yes, I'm out brother. This game is a young man's game, it's been good to me, and Florida is a snow state, the boy isn't as strong as it is in New York. And I'm not tryna be the one to break the ground down here. I'ma leave you both spots, the one in Harlem and the one in Walter Winchell houses, they both do numbers. I just started a non-profit organization. It's time for me to give back to the world instead of taking it away. I got a councilman dinner I'm going to in about 2 weeks. I don't need to be caught up with the feds before I start. I'll be in touch. Yes sir, Wa Alaykum Salam." Blocka ended the call by putting the phone down on the night stand.

If Blue had just heard correctly. He now confirmed the thought he always wondered. He had seen his father countless number of times with a lot of money. And assuming his father had something illegal going on or was a drug dealer. But by him making moves out of state in New York. He never could figure them out. After overhearing his conversation. Everything was confirmed and he saw his father in a new light. Hearing him mention snow(coke) and boy(heroin).

Approaching the room door, the nervousness he felt caused his stomach to rumble. It was time to have this talk about the newfound fortune. And his idea of becoming a drug dealer.

Knock! Knock! Knock!

"Salamu Alaykum father"

Come in, Wa Alaykum as Salam son, where were you this morning? You missed fajr prayer."

"Angel's house," Blue lied.

"As Salatu Karun Manana-um," his father spoke in Arabic. Letting him know (prayer is better than sleep."

"I know father, but I came to speak with you about my next moves in life."

"What about them?" his father asked sternly.

"Well, college is just not me and I wanna be like you."

"What do you mean, be like me?" He paused, looking his son in the eyes. Seeing the same look, he once had in his eyes as a young hustler. Choosing his words wisely. He started to explain to his son. He was opening up a shoe store. But was cut off.

"I wanna be a boss and a cocaine cowboy", staring deeply in his eyes.

"Ha! Ha! Ha! Ha! Co-Ha! Caine-Ha! Cowboy! His father barely got the words out through laughter.

It was the 90s, so the cocaine Cowboys was a term turning around Florida. It was half myth half reality. Down in

Miami Florida a war was ongoing about the cocaine control. One reality that all knew was the numerous murders being shown on the news every week. Word was a Spanish narco Trafficante by the name of Griselda Blonco had come from Columbia to Miami to flood the streets of Florida with cocaine from the "Ochoa Family." Being around the same time Castro let a bunch of Cubans leave Cuba, who headed right to Miami with coke of their own. This started numerous of Cuban on Columbian murders. This mayhem with the cocaine created the term Cocaine Cowboys.

So Blocka was fully aware of the term. Also, in shock of this coming from his son fresh out of high school.

"So how you gone be a cocaine cowboy with no cocaine", Blocka asked. Reaching in his pocket Blue pulled out the $20,000 he came up on earlier. "And I got 2 keys of coke". I heard your conversation and I'm not asking you to be a part of what I have going on. But I need guidance and help along the way."

Blocka inhaled and exhaled, psst! "Astafirallah" (May Allah Forgive Me) Blocka said aloud.

He knew it was no way out of this. He was retiring after 15 years of drug running China White Heroin. Now his son was professing his newfound obsession. So, he decided to give him jewels only a father could give to his son without being judged.

"Son, listen," he spoke while looking into the eyes of his son. I'm going to give you the forbidden fruit of this game, this is from me to you. If this is the game you wanna play, remember you gotta do anything to win, the bigger you become in the drug game, the more careful you got to be. To stay clean, you gotta stay away from the drugs and you gotta line people up to take the fall when it goes down. And always and I repeat son, always keep an ace in the hole or get out before it's too late.

Blue sat there digesting the street knowledge he'd just given him. And he was having second thoughts about the game. He assumed in his mind it was just about making money, sexing women, and reaping the benefits of the major profit of tax-free money. But the way his father made it sound was like playing a game of chess. Every piece had to be protected by another piece just to take the fall for the king, to do anything to win. As cruel as it sounded it was what it was. And that day he accepted it. Making sure never to forget his first teachings of the game.

Blocka snapped his fingers taking him out of his thoughts. "Do you have a team?"

"Yes, It's me, Ralo, and Smiley."

"Okay, before starting your run in the game, I wanna take yall to New York. And show yall around to give you a model of how things are run in the Mecca of America. Go get your team ready and let them know we fly out tomorrow." Blocka instructed.

Leaving the house with a vision and promise to himself to be rich. He was brought to a halt. By the "85" Cutlas on 26's with the candy blue paint that shined like a diamond in the summer sun.

Before he crossed the street walking down 12th and Canal to head to Tom's Corner Store. Where he was sure to find Ralo and Smiley. It was the neighborhood hangout store that sat on the end of 12th and Palafox. He had to see who was driving this classic piece of car. Being close enough where he could view its driver and passenger. Paying close attention, he seen the blonde headed female going up and down on the driver side that he swore looked like Angel's head through the windshield. As the car came closer, he noticed it was Caesar driving the Cutlas smiling showing his golds. Word had been spread Caesar who went to the same high school as Blue. Lost his college football scholarship from being shot in the leg. And turned to the streets to start getting money. From the look of the car and what he was doing looked like he wasn't doing too bad for himself.

Blue begins to feel the perspiration under his armpits as the situation unfolded in his mind. Walking to see can he find his homeboys. The 2-block walk felt like a marathon. His mind wondered was that Angel or not. Should he confront her or not. Being he had his first son with her "BJ". He felt like the child solidified his spot in her life. But Angel was full of herself and felt like her looks could buy her whatever. It was a time and place for everything, and he vowed to handle it one way or another.

Finally, making it to Tom's Store. Blue seen Smiley and Ralo shooting dice. Ralo in the main shooting dice, Smiley side betting.

"I like whatever Ralo throw", Smiley said throwing another 20 down. "What cha say", Blue spat to no one in particular, causing everyone to turn around acknowledging him with head nods.

Ralo crapped out rolling a seven. "Bad luck ass dice". "Smiley check this out", He begin walking in Blues direction. Viewing his facial expression.

"What's wrong MainMan?" Smiley replied.

"It's Angel I think she fuckin with that nigga Caesar. You know they say he getting money now."

"Well, you know it's like this, you got niggas that got it and niggas that want it." He spoke while still watching the dice. "Right now, we got it, but until we show and prove. We just some niggas that want it. We got all this paper and coke with no plan. You know proper planning, prevents poor performance." Smiley concluded.

"That's changing", as Blue began to speak Ralo entered the conversation. "What's the play?" Ralo spoke up.

"Look, I spoke with my pops I told him what it was and everything, from the bricks to the money." Blue shared.

"For real!" Ralo and Smiley said in unison hanging on to every word Blue spoke.

"Yeah, he with the move and asked me if I had a team. I told him about yall. Then he said we was flying out to New York Friday."

"Wait! That's tomorrow and I'on got nothing to wear." Ralo said. "We good, we just gone go with the flow. He supposed to be showing us how things operate at a couple spots so we can learn a thing or two."

They all exchanged daps and agreed to meet the next day at 7:30 in the morning to get ready to board their first flight to learn their first lessons as a team together.

Chapter 2

(Jacksonville International Airport)

At 8:45am Blocka, Ralo, Smiley, and Blue entered the crowded airport and boarded their flight at terminal 7.

The flight from Jacksonville, Florida to New York City was filled with silence between the four. None of Blue's friends could actually say they had seen his father. He was raised in New York during the mafia era. So, he stood on mafia principals. He believed in making a way for the family and stayed out of the way. He didn't believe in being seen unless he had to. He didn't even hustle where he stayed. All his business was in New York. So, he lived his life on a half and half weekly schedule. One half in Jacksonville other half in New York. When he came home it was family time. Knowing every time, he left could be his last time seeing them. But by him backing away from the game. He planned to move on to politics in the community. That is more promising with also guaranteed longevity. Then here he was with his son and his two most trusted comrades. He observed them and liked what he seen. But still held resentment in his heart towards himself. Because he knew that what he was about to show them only led to two places hell and jail. He also knew as well if he didn't give them his expertise firsthand knowledge. They would learn their own way then quicker would be their demise. He thought while staring out the plane window at the formless clouds.

(Hours later at John F. Kennedy Airport)

Once the three exited the plane. They followed Blockas lead as he led them around the crowd of other flyers. Who was waiting in the baggage claim section. The crowded airport was full to capacity making it hard to move forward with a swarm of people moving in the opposite direction.

Finally, they made it outside viewing what looked like a million yellow taxi cabs. Blocka was used to this, so he began to wave his hands and arms and whistle until he got the attention of a cab driver. Then the four entered the backseat.

"Don't be afraid to ask questions and pay attention to every detail. This will be my first and last time ever doing this." Blocka spoke for the first time. "Cabbie take us to 116th and Lenox Ave."

"Harlem Aye." The Arabian cab driver said while pulling out the crowded airport at the same time.

Taking in the new sight of New York. Smiley, Ralo, and Blue sat staring out the cabs window in amazement as the Big Apple became alive. The heavy traffic, the people's movement, was like an ant bed after a footprint. Pedestrians were headed everywhere in every direction. Sometimes a trip in New York could take hours only to a short destination. So, the long trip in addition to the jet lag from their first time flying, caused the three of them to doze off.

The taxicab came to a quick halt a hour and thirty minutes later awaking Blue, Ralo, then Smiley. Awakened taking in their new surroundings they quickly noticed men and women blocking the street walking in one direction, looking as they were dressed in sheets.

"Right here." Blocka addressed the cabbie handing him a hundred-dollar bill. They'd just arrived at Jumuah the Friday service for Muslims. In the religion of Islam Friday was observed as the holy day. So, all the men and women were headed to go pray and worship on their sacred day of Friday.

"Gentleman, this is the El-Hajj Malik Shabazz Masjid. Named after Malcolm X. When he took his pilgrimage to the holy city of Mecca in Saudi Arabian he came back and changed his name to El-Hajj Malik Shabazz." Blocka expressed pointing at the building that was now visible as the four of them began to walk in its direction.

"Every time I enter a city, I go make prayer for guidance and protection." Blocka gestured Islamic prayer hands, palms open and together than continued.

"No matter what you all do, always remember God has the last say so in all matters. We can do as we please, but it's through God's grace and mercy God wills things to happen. So, if you wanna be in this game you gotta have faith and believe in something."

The closer they got to the building a chant like melody could be heard over the intercom at the top of the building.

"Allahu Akbar, Allahu Akbar", (God is the greatest).

"Ashadu Anla Illaha Ill Allah", (I testify there's no God but Allah.)

"Ashadu Anna Muhammadun Rasulilah" (I testify Muhammad is the messenger of Allah)

"Haya Alal Salah" (Hasten to prayer)

"Haya Alal Falah" (Hasten to success)

"Qakamah Tu Salat, Qakamah Tu Salat", (come to prayer)

"Allahu Akbar, Allahu Akbar", (God is the greatest)

"La Ilaha Ill Allah", (Theres no God but Allah)

After the chant like melody stopped. Blocka continued to speak. "That was the call to prayer to let everyone who hears it, that the time for prayer has come."

When entering the building the first thing they seen was a pile of shoes lined up neatly in all sizes. They all removed their shoes and Blocka led the way down the hallway to the restroom so they could get ready to enter the prayer area.

Once entering the restroom different ages of males could be seen running water over their hands, face, arms, head, then feet. Blocka started to go through the motions as Ralo, Blue, Smiley followed each step he took. Purifying themselves before they entered the prayer area. In the sacred religion of Muslims. They believe that anytime you approach God you should be clean, and this was one of the ways that Muslims purified themselves. (Wudu)

"The prophet Muhammad said, in Islam purity is half of your faith. So, any obligation or duty must be done in purity". Blocka whispered as the four sat amongst the congregation of male Muslims in the ranks of the neatly sat rows on the floor.

Ralo, Smiley, and Blue smiled at each other as they watched along with the rest. A man with a big beard had everyone's attention as he spoke wisdom standing up behind the podium. Smiley and Ralo was impressed how neat and organized the Muslims carried themselves. Everything about these people showed they had discipline. The call to prayer was called again. Hearing it Blue and Blocka joined the rest of the men, as they stood in lines ankle to ankle from right to left to perform prayer. Ralo and Smiley sat to the side as the prayer leader spoke in a foreign language of Arabic and went into different positions until they all were prostrated face down and repeated the cycle again. Eventually they all were sitting on the ground repeating after the prayer leader in unison "As-Salamu Alaykum Wa Rahmatullah", starting over their right shoulder than over their left shoulder.

After the prayer was over the speaker turned around and faced the rest of the men. And smiled before speaking.

"As-Salamu Alaykum" he greeted the congregation.

"Wa alaykum as-salam" they responded in unison.

"I'm Brother Imam Sai, does anybody in here want to submit to the will of Allah and proclaim their Shahada?" Imam Sai asked. Upon hearing the Imam's words Ralo and Smiley looked at one another as they both rose to their feet and went to the front of the congregation.

When everyone noticed how young the two were somebody in the crowd screamed. "TAKBIR!!!"

"Allahu Akbar!!!" The crowd replied in unison. Shouting God is the greatest giving praise for the two stepping forward.

Blue and Blocka sat in shock upon viewing Smiley and Ralo stepping forward making the first move to become Muslims.

"Alhamdulihah, surely all praises are due to Allah." Imam Sai praised. "I need you two brothers to repeat after me, I testify there's no God, but Allah and I testify Muhammad is the messenger of Allah."

15

The both of them repeated after Imam and professed their faith in Islam for the first time with their tongues.

"You can speak it with your tongue young brothers, but see the faith is here." Imam Sai explained while pointing at the left side of his chest. Showing them that just because you proclaim the Shahada, also known as the declaration of faith with your tongue, you must believe it inside your heart. And only God knows what's in the heart.

Before the four left Mosjid. A group of Muslims escorted them to the Islamic store inside. To purchase Ralo and Smiley gifts they would need to start their spiritual journey as Muslims. Also, as believers of the religion of Islam. They were given prayer rugs, kufi caps, and prayer beads. The love they felt from the Muslims gave them a new sense of loyalty. The brotherly love they were receiving was hypnotizing to the two newly converts.

Back on the streets, Blocka led the way to 125th Street to the infamous Dapper Dans Clothing Store.

"See this the same spot Alpo and Rich Porter when they were getting money came to get fly, or anybody in the game in New York." Blocka explained.

Dapper Dans was known for bringing Paris, Italy, and France to the hood. He was an expert at taking the high price foreign designers patents such as Gucci, Louie, Versace, Prada, and many more. Using them to swag out anything you gave him from clothes, shoes, to bags. Give it to him and it prolly would look better or as if it was made by the brand. He had it going and that's what made Blocka want to bring them here to give them the image of bosses before they became bosses.

"In this game you gotta look like money to attract money, it's all about the presentation Robert Greene said it best. Blocka finished speaking as they walked up to Dappers.

Now entering Dapper Dans, they were approached by a light skinned young woman named Malika. She has shoulder length dreads with red at the end of each dread looking exotic and like she had some type of Spanish descent.

"Welcome to Dapper Dans and Salamu Alaykum Brothers." She stated noticing the Islamic goods inside the bags that read the name of the Mosjid. "How was Jumuah?" she asked assuming they were just leaving Jumuah seeing it was Friday.

"It was great and Wa Alaykum as Salam." Blocka replied smirking at how the three young men were mesmerized by Malika's beauty. And shook his head before he continued speaking.

"Can you grab us a catalog and get the tailor man" Blocka asked. Malika left in a hurry to get Habibi the Arabian fabric guy. Who measured everything from the suits to the outfits to shoes.

"Hey! It's you again with the money." Habibi lit up as he noticed the familiar face of Blocka. "And these must be your son's?"

Blocka nodded his head up and down "measurements for the three please." He pointed.

Habibi looked, "measurements? 28, 30, for you 32, 34 and 36 and 33." He spoke in his accent sizing Ralo, Smiley, and Blue up with his eyes.

All 3 begin to smile at how he had their waist sizes correct. They'd never been measured from hip to ankle nor had ever had expensive clothing.

Malika arrived with the catalogs of suits, coats, and shoes. Their eyes almost popped out their sockets. When they noticed nothing was under $1,000.

"Yall pick some suits not none of that lil boy shit" Blocka suggested. After flipping through the catalog, they all picked the same Gucci patented suit just in different colors. The suit was made like a tuxedo but with Dapper Dans sauce, all over the collar, wrist, the vest, inside the blazer was covered in the Double G Gucci logo in white. Ralo suit was red with the white Double G's. Blue suit was royal blue with the white Double G's. And Smiley suit was black with the white Double G's. Each had picked matching Alexander McQueen hard bottoms same color as the suit. From ones viewing outside looking in they appeared as they were getting ready for a wedding or GQ Magazine photo spread. But in reality, they were like Tony Montana when he went to visit Sosa in Columbia. Today was just another day with the plug.

"The total is $8,657 and 82 cents." Malika said, batting her lashes. Blocka removed 90 one-hundred-dollar bills and handed them to Malika. "Keep the change baby girl." He spared no expense. He wanted to show them what it felt like to be a boss.

Once Smiley, Blue, and Ralo had put the suits on and was impressed by how the tailor-made suits made them feel and look, they took a photo for Dapper Dans wall. The 3 optioned for the picture.

The four men exited Dapper Dans. Not to long after they were on the streets. They instantly beginned to receive attention from the compliments, to pats on the back. They loved the attention they were receiving. When they seen Blocka approaching a Yukon Denali begin signaling them to get in as he hopped in the back of the truck. They followed to see it was 2 others in the front seat.

"This is my right hand Supreme and his son Major." Blocka said both nodded their heads at the young men in the backseat. They had already known they were coming and why. Blocka had made the call to Supreme, his best friend for over 25 years and told him about the conversation he had with Blue. Supreme was from the old skool with beliefs in the same ideologies as Blocka. He'd rather teach his son than let the streets teach him. Nothing but silence was heard inside the vehicle as it got lost in the sea of cars.

It was Blue and the guys first time in New York. But also, the first time they had a feel of how it was to be around bosses. Judging from Supreme and Major's jewels, they were getting money as both of their necks were glistening in the New York sun. They each were a little bit nervous. But still looked confident at the same time in their tailor-made suits.

The wind was blowing as the sun began to set. When the Denali pulled in front of the Walter Winchell houses. Out front was a group of three dressed if they were homeless in front of the buildings entrance. Soon they seen the truck doors opening and the four getting out crossing the street. One mumbled something to the others. All the men arose quickly as if the bailiff in a courtroom said, "All Rise." The group of three homeless men went to producing guns. Two of them had 38 specials and one held a Uzi at waist level pointing towards Blocka, Blue, Smiley, and Ralo.

"Stay right here, I'll be back." Blocka addressed the 3 as he crossed the street towards the armed homeless men.

They begin watching anticipating the worst to happen to Blocka. Until they seen the three men conceal their guns again. They begin smiling and hugging Blocka. Blocka turned around waving at the 3 across the street letting them know it was all good.

Once they were across the street. Blocka introduced them to the men who they now realized were not homeless. Up close you could see the gold ropes tucked in each of their shirts, with shiny gold teeth as they spoke with Blocka. These were lookouts for the heroin spot upstairs. Which they communicated to through walkie talkies. So, anything that happened up top would be handled down low. And anything that happened down low would be handled up top. Being it was sunset nobody was allowed in the building unless you were a resident. Everything was done through a window. Before entering the building, they noticed an old frail lady placed something inside a can, watching closely as the can disappeared up, returning to the ground again. The lady grabbed something out of the can and began to show a snaggle tooth smile walking off quickly.

Entering the building, the four of them went to the elevator and took it to the top floor. Walking behind Blocka the three followed him until he stopped at the last door in the hallway. He begins to tap lightly in what sounded like a coded knock. The door opened slightly than fully exposing a light skinned woman with a sports bra with baggie jeans sagging holding a Tec-9. This was Ruby she had the body of a stripper with the heart of a Russian. She was a known blood member who didn't mind putting in work. Her or her little sister Chanel who was the total opposite in appearance. She was all girly and wouldn't break a nail, but her trigger was vicious. Her slim figure was dressed in an all-blue body suit. These two had earned a name and reputation on the streets of New York. And was referred to Blocka who hired them on the spot. They ran the spot well; it was never robbed and never came up short.

They both immediately ran to Blocka giving him a fatherly hug as he tried to break their tight embrace.

"Nope, nope, nope, nope" they both giggled and protested until they noticed the other 3 dressed in suits.

"Pops who the fuck is this" Ruby asked.

"These are my sons they came with me from Florida. They tryna get they feet wet in the game so I'm showing them around." Blocka stated.

"This might be too fast for them country boys" Ruby said.

"Only thing moving too fast for me is yo lips" Smiley countered.

"Oh, you got big balls huh?" Ruby questioned Smiley.

"Gotta big dick that'll turn them briefs to thongs" Smiley answered making everybody laugh except Ruby laugh.

"Knock it off, knock it off," Blocka interrupted the moment.

"Let's focus on this paper and the bullshit later yall show them how you run the spot."

While Ruby and Blocka made small talk Chanel showed Smiley, Ralo, and Blue around the plush apartment.

"This is my office", she pointed at the window and laughed at her own joke.

Sitting by the window was a leather office chair, several cans, black elastic rope, a blue Chanel bag, next to a 5-gallon metal lined bucket with hazard signs and skulls all over the bucket.

"I don't see anything to spectacular" Ralo voiced his thoughts.

"Of course, you don't, you don't know what you're looking at." Chanel said while stepping towards the window picking up the blue Chanel designer bag. Unzipping it pouring the contents on the seat of the plush office chair. The Chanel bag held bagged up heroin, 50 bundles with 100 $10 bags in each. Each bundle was made of glassine bags that were pre-stamped with Blockas brand name Shocker and his logo, a yellow electric bolt.

"That's 50 stacks you are looking at" Chanel bragged. During the daytime we let the pitchers run the block and at nighttime we work out the window. Our job is to collect the money as each bundle is sold and give them a new bundle."

"So, what's with the rope and can?" Blue questioned.

"At night the pitchers turn to lookouts, once the kids are at home, we shut down the building no traffic comes through. They call on the walkie talkie, and I drop the can. Up comes the money down comes the product" Chanel answered.

The 3 shook their heads in approval of the operation in the small one-bedroom apartment.

"The fuck is this?" Smiley acted as if he was about to kick the bucket. But seeing Chanel panic he stopped.

"This is Sulfuric Acid anything placed inside you'll never see again; this is only for in case of emergencies. Ever since the number of overdoses rise in New York. The pigs been giving' out major time for dogfood." Chanel explained, as she removed the lid while placing a bundle inside. The four watched closely observing as it sizzled a little and the glassine bags turned to small bubbles as they disappeared in the liquid acid.

"Sorry I can't stay long, we gotta get going." Blocka expressed to Chanel he never spent to much time in one spot.

"Yeah, yeah we know." Ruby and Chanel said playfully. They knew how their boss man moved. They both loved him and wanted him to be more than their boss. But he was all business no play.

Before exiting Blocka embraced them both and they shook everyone's hand. Smiley even grabbed Ruby's plump ass cheeks, causing her to throw a temper tantrum. Angry she pointed the Tec-9 at him as he left out last. He winked and kept it moving.

Excitedly, they entered the truck behind Blocka. When the truck accelerated to the next spot in Harlem, just off a 118th in a small duplex. From the modest looking surroundings and fancy cars. This would never have been thought of what was really going on inside.

The truck came to a halt. Then Blocka jumped out of the truck approaching the speaker outside the building. He pressed the number #7 button.

"Buzz!" The speaker made a noise.

"Sorry you have the wrong house" somebody immediately answered.

"Is that right Mustafa" Blocka responded.

"What the hell are you doing here?" Mustafa said in a voice of distress nobody called or knew him by his real name except one person and that was Blocka. So, he thought if he was here unexpectantly it must've been some kinda trouble.

"I brought my sons to show them around." Blocka laughed as he spoke sensing Mustafa's fear. Nobody knew he was coming but Supreme. He believed in the element of surprise. No matter when he came, he felt as everything should be on point.

After the others came out of the truck. They were buzzed in and made it up the flight of stairs.

Entering the apartment, they instantly smelled a foreign smell. Mustafa greeted the four as he gave them a medical mask.

"Salamu alaykum" Mustafa greeted "Follow me."

They all placed their masks on their faces and followed as Mustafa led the way around the empty apartment. In the living room was where they seen what the apartment was used for. Sitting around the glass table were 6 naked Spanish women. Three sat on each side of the glass table. Each had a job of its own.

This was called the milling process. Cutting the heroin consisted of adding milk, sugar, quinine to double the weight of the heroin. The cut heroin was then passed along to be weighed precisely, then passed across the table to be spooned into thousands of glassine bags with stamps on them, and distributed to the other spots of numerous workers who would get served double of whatever they spent.

Watching the process and how focused the women were, impressed Blue, Ralo, and Smiley. The apartment was run like a factory of some sort. Every time somebody else finished the opposite was done with the task and ready for the next.

"What you all are seeing is the cutting process, see the money is in how many times you can cut the dope. I make sure to leave room for the next man." Blocka spoke to the three who was paying attention to the Spanish women breast more than his words.

"How's that?" Smiley asked.

"I buy straight from the source never a middleman. Cause he might step on it and then I'ma do the same. But if I go to the main source I'ma be the 1st one to dilute the potency and that's room for the next."

"Okay I see, so whatever you buy you make triple?" Ralo said.

"Exactly and I still leave room for them to make money." Blocka explained it's time we move out." He headed towards the door with the 3 not far behind.

Leaving Harlem, they headed back to the airport. Where the four dined at Santino's a small Italian Steakhouse. As they waited for their food, they sipped Pinot Gregio and White Zinfandel.

"So, what did you all think about this trip?" Blocka asked.

"I aint gone lie I'm at a loss for words" Ralo said.

"I just appreciate you daddy for showing us this side of things and for the suits and lessons." Blue complimented.

"Yeah thanks", Smiley and Ralo said in unison.

"My question is how you stay in Jacksonville and have all this going on in New York?" Smiley asked.

"Reason being is I never confuse my profession with my business, when I first started, I worked my own spots. But once I got enough money. I put people in position to work them for me. So, it's no longer my profession, it's a business. I own the work in the spots. But they are managed and ran by OTHER PEOPLE." Blocka put extra emphasis on other people then winked at Blue.

It all made sense now to Blue from him and his father talk in the bedroom days prior. He stayed away from the spots and lined other people up to take the fall. If anything ever happened at one of the spots his father wouldn't be responsible, the others would take the fall. Blue thought as he started to smirk. Smiley and Ralo were lost at the father and son connection.

"New Years is hours away and I believe this year is going to be a good year for you young bucks. Blocka spoke changing the subject and energy of the conversation.

But Smiley caught the drift and made sure to pay more attention to the father and son if this is what he was going to be dealing with. The steaks and mashed potatoes were served. Then everybody enjoyed their meals, until they heard the announcer come over the intercom and call their flight back to Jacksonville airport.

Chapter 3

Back in Jacksonville Florida, things felt differently for Smiley, Blue, and Ralo. The feelings felt unreal that they had seen so much in so little time. From the lick in Jacksonville to the heroin spots in New York. Blocka left the 3 by themselves as he went to tend to business of his own. They stayed at the airport and rented a Jeep Cherokee. None of them owned a car so they decided to rent a truck and move together as one.

"It's levels to this shit, we bout to be on the next level", Ralo said while whipping the rented Jeep through the I-95 South traffic in the rearview mirror at the same time.

"We gotta just find a way to open up shop and take over the hood then the entire city." Smiley stated.

"It's a party tonight for New Years and I'm tryna get fresh, it's a party tonight at Club 904. Let's slide to Orange Park Mall." Blue interrupted from the front seat.

"Yea it's time we fuck up some comma's and start dressing like bosses." Ralo said.

Since being back from New York and seeing what they saw. They wanted to approach the game like bosses. So, the coke was still buried at Angel's house buried in the backyard. They were laying low seeing if any information surfaced in the streets about the lick. So far, they have heard nothing. They were headed to the mall to spend some of the money.

Upon entering Orange Park shopping mall on Wells Road and Blanding Blvd. They were the center of attention. It was hard to miss the three in their tailor-made suits and what looked like football thigh pads, as they concealed stacks of money in their front pockets. Every bad bitch was lusting, and every street nigga was acting like they weren't looking. But they were the center of attention with the 10 bands they each held in their pockets.

Before they started shopping, they ran into Angel, Kiki, and gold-digging azz Kiesha.

"Hey babydaddy", Angel yelled getting everybody's attention in the mall. She and her friends rushed them soon as they noticed the thigh pads. "Gimme some money, yo son need some clothes and shoes."

Blue complied, pulling out one pocket full of money and giving Angel a thousand. She gave him a hug grabbing his dick at the same time. He hated how she made him feel. But couldn't do anything about it.

Kiki and gold-digging azz Kiesha, hit Ralo and Smiley with the glossy puppy eyes.

"Bitch I rather see a monkey with a diamond ring than see you hoes with anything." Smiley said.

"Back then they didn't want me, now I'm hot hoes all on me," Ralo said bursting out laughing.

They flicked birds and followed behind Angel. Making sure to make each azz cheek bounce as they walked away with their stank walks.

Finally making it to Designer Factory. They were star struck as they seen all the different designer labels. This was the stuff they heard rappers rapping about. Half of the names were foreign to them.

"Welcome to Designer Factory", the store clerk said. Who was a white, blonde amazon with sky blue eyes and a peach shaped azz. You could tell she was getting money or came from money. How she dressed and carried herself. Her slender but thick frame was tightly wrapped in a crème Mason Margiela sundress, with Gucci open toe slides that showed off her perfectly pedicured toes. Everything about this store screamed money.

Soon as she seen the bulges of money on them. She started to pull down her dress at the bottom to show more cleavage than needed. She was putting on a show as she always did for the rich customers.

"Hi, my name's Mystery", she looked at the 3 and bent down grabbing a shoebox knowing she didn't have on any panties. So, her fat azz was eating the sundress between her azz cheeks.

"Let me show you all around." She begins giving them a tour of the store. "This is the flashy section best sellers Versace and Louis Vuitton silk wear." "Everything has the logo's all over hard to not know what you're wearing." As she continued moving through the store. "This is the conservative section no logos or brand names are showing." "A person would really have to know fashion to know the designs of the clothing line," "Best sellers are Giorgio Armani and Emilio Pucci." Pointing at the different shelves.

"You mean Gucci", Ralo said.

Mystery begins to blush at the fact Ralo didn't know the difference between Gucci and Pucci. "How about you just give me your number and I explain the difference." She shot her shot.

"I call", Ralo stated.

"And this section right here is designer but not high in price designer. This is your Ralph Lauren Polo Collection, Tommy Hilfiger, Lacoste casual, are usually the best sellers." She continued.

They all began to roam the store as Mystery helped a new customer. Blue went to the flashy section. While Smiley to the not high price designer and Ralo to the conservative section.

Blue was tryna go for a Biggie Smalls Silk Versace look. Hard but casual at the same time. So, he picked a white silk long sleeve $1,000 shirt with the big Medusa head on the front with gold trim on the sleeves and collars. For the pants and shoes, he got the all-white pants with Versace going down the right pants leg and the gold medusa head covering the left one. The high-top shoes set it off. They were high top with a strap going across both shoes with the Medusa head on each strap and tongue. As he stared into the dressing room mirror, he felt impressed by the 4 thousand dollars' worth of clothes.

Meanwhile, Smiley settled for a Ralph Lauren Polo all red with the blue horse. And the red shorts with the blue polo horse all over the shorts. He could've purchased whatever he wanted to, but he was the low-key type. And wasn't a freak for fame or attention. Long as he had the money, he didn't care what nobody said. He was trying on a pair of all white air force ones. When he noticed Ralo and Mystery getting a little too touchy. Suddenly he seen her tell the other clerk something and disappeared into the dressing room with Ralo. Shaking his head all he could do was think about how wild Ralo was.

Ralo for some reason was infatuated with the black Emilio Pucci sweatsuit. It wasn't flashy or anything, he just liked the name and how it fit him differently from it being handmade. When leaving the dressing room to show Mystery to get her opinion. All he got was eyes full of lust. It wasn't how it looked on him or how he looked. It was about the $3500 price tag. She wasted no time pushing him back into the dressing room.

Mystery had no intention of playing. This was her everyday hustle at Designer Factory. She moved Ralo's clothes to the front of her as he took off the Emilio Pucci sweatsuit. She begins to nibble on his lips like her life depended on it. Her tender kisses traveled down to his neck, to his shoulders, chest and abs, then finally to the head of his dick. She twisted her tongue all around it, then opened wide and took every inch to the back of her throat. Mmmmm! Mystery moaned with a mouthful of black dick.

"Oh my Gawd!" Ralo groaned. He closed his eyes and leaned his head back. Her mouth was so warm and wet it felt like a pussy.

She kissed his head once more and glanced at her watch. "We need to hurry before my daddy comes back. He's the store owner he'll be back here in 15 minutes." She bent over grabbing her ankles towards Ralo's pants and went to making her phat azz and thick thighs clap mesmerizing him.

He gave her white cheeks 2 hard smacks and pushed himself inside of her and Mystery gasped.

"Oh my God you feel so fucking good", she moaned throwing her ass back extra hard looking him in the eyes at the same time." "Fuck me daddy! Fuck me!"

Ralo obliged long stroking her so deep and wide looking into her blue eyes. He couldn't take the sight any longer and closed his eyes.

At that moment he fucked up. Mystery went to bucking like a horse at the Kentucky Derby. All at the same time going in Ralos pants pocket in the front of her grabbing a wad of $100 dollar bills. Placing them in the front of her bra.

"Umm, Fuck!" Ralo moaned trying to fight the urge and keep his composure. Her pussy was so creamy and moist, that it began talking, sopping, popping, and gasping for air. "Shit!" His balls began to tingle and before he knew it, he pulled out and put his seeds all over the dressing room floor.

"Damn you got the type of pussy niggas will pay for." Ralo spoke.

"Oh yeah," Mystery turned around smiling pulling her sundress down.

"Let's get from back here so I can ring you guys up and give you a discount for that bomb ass dick."

Ralo put his clothes back on and grabbed the sweatsuit and headed to the front of the store meeting Blue and Smiley.

"Boy how much you paid for that pussy?" Smiley asked.

"Aint pay nothing and we bout to get a discount," "I got that magic stick." Ralo bragged.

Mystery began scanning Blues Versace merch up first which came up to $4,252.06 after taxes but she let him pay $4,000 even. Ralo Emilio Pucci sweatsuit came up to $3,875.53 which she let him pay for $3,500. Smiley paid $500 even and declined the discount. Ralo pulled out $100 and wrote his name and number on it and gave it to Mystery. She took it with ease, adding it to the $1,200 she took earlier out of his pants in the dressing room. Satisfied with their services they left Designers Closet and were ready to bring the New Year in boss status.

(Later That Night)

Pulling up in front of Club 904 was a show within itself. Everybody brought out the toys tonight. Lined along the entrance was a fleet of foreign cars in front was a all-red Mercedes-Benz G-Wagon. Sitting behind that was an all-white Audi Q7, and behind those were 3 black on black Cayenne Porshe trucks. Each vehicle had a large "F" on each rim. They all were tinted and sitting on Forgiotos. A group of dread heads were standing in front. The first 2 led the way inside the club as they walked past the long line of pedestrians waiting in line to get in.

Ralo driving the rented Jeep pulled in a parking spot across from the club. From where they parked, they could see the club was lit. The music was bumping, the people out front were dancing. It was New Years Eve; fireworks could be seen up above in the sky. As they walked to the club they went directly to the front door, skipping the long line, each had a gold money clip in hand with big faces in between. Seeing the 3 dressed like entertainers or somebody. Security begins to search them, as they all handed him $500 apiece.

"V.I.P Status!" The bouncer announced pointing at the 3.

Once entering the threshold of the club. Boss sized bottles of champagne with shiny bright sparklers were being rolled out on solid gold carts to any and everyone who wanted to drink like a boss. Before heading up to V.I.P they noticed 3 good looking women, standing by the bar waiting on their drinks. The first was Nia who was shaped like a glass coke bottle with long black hair tied in a bun. Her red Prada bodysuit was skintight and showing every curve. Everybody in the city knew her from her business in bangles. And she was getting attention from all the different customized shiny bangles she wore. Her friend Liya was light skinned with long curly hair in Chanel 2 piece with double C's and Chanel spelled all over the shirt and skirt. Her well shaped voluptuous bottom was playing peek a boo with the bottom of her skirt as she kept trying to pull it down in the back.

As Nia was showing off her bangles. Liya Was showing off her nails being the owner of her nail salon. They were mingling with the people at the bar as they exchanged numbers with different people who wanted to get either accessories or nail sets. While their tag along friend Cici who was a known thot, was leaving little to the imagination. She was twerking on the bar stool with no panties on showing everything below her Fendi dress tried to conceal. Her long Malaysian weave was in between her cheeks, when everybody began crowding round the triple threat. A guy went to throwing money on Cici and she kept making her ass and pussy lips clap to the beat. All the attention was on them.

Smiley and Ralo went to be seated in V.I.P to occupy their booth. While Blue approached the triple threat of fine women. Making it through the mini fan club they had around. He approached Nia and Liyah.

"Ladies y'all too bossed up to be waiting at the bar." I say y'all slide to V.I.P. We got everything already on the way." Blue spoke.

Nia and Liyah Glanced at each other and both shrugged. Looking at Cici in embarrassment.

Come on bitch, "We can't take you nowhere without you showing your ass." Nia spat.

"Literally!" Liyah Blurted.

Making it up stairs to the second floor where all the Ballers and somebodies were. Everybody was popping bottles and smoking blunts. Blue spotted Smiley and Ralo in the corner. At the same time noticing Caesar with the same exact Versace silk button up shirt on. He put his head down as he recognized him surrounded by some group of dread heads who hopped out the foreigns earlier in front of the club. Blue was mad he spent $4,000 just to be dressed like another nigga.

Caesar was dipped from neck up in Buggette diamonds. The Medusa head buttons on the front of his shirt were unfastened, showing off the iced out 30-inch chain was smothered in diamonds and topped off with an iced-out

F.M.B charm. Both chain and charm were smothered in diamonds.

A diamond studded bracelet was glistening on his wrist against the iced-out bezel and solitaire diamonds in his earlobes were shining even brighter. His crew were even flooded in buggettes with F.M.B charms as well.

Blue, Liyah, Nia, and Cici entered the V.I.P booth with Smiley and Ralo. Who both held a bottle of champagne in the air. Liyah went and sat next to Ralo and Nia sat next to Smiley. While Blue and Cici took the back corner. Liyah pulled out a bag of lime green exotic weed. And began to roll up a backwood. The party went well. Until Smiley nudged Blues arm interrupting his conversation when he noticed Smiley pointing below at Angel, Kiki, and Kiesha entering the club at the entrance.

Blue reached for the blunt Liyah rolled and lit. Needing something to calm his nerves. Here he was in the same building as Angel and Caesar. He wanted to avoid this ever in life. He had already swept it under the rug when he seen her inside Caesar's Cutlas. The loud smoke clouds were thick inside the V.I.P booth. But the tension was thicker as Blue watched from Caesar to Angels every move.

Blue adrenalin went from zero to 100 real quick. Just sitting back watching Caesar's charisma and the F.M.B controlled the crowd popping bottle after bottle of the expensive champagne. They were from the same neighborhood but had never seen eye to eye. Blue was from the top streets of the Flag St. area around 12th St. Caesar was around 16th St. The bottom and top streets didn't get along. Also, with Blue trying to find his way in the dope game and Caesar having the neighborhood on lock. Was all playing tricks with his mind.

   Caesar and his baby cousin G money were too caught up in the limelight to notice anybody. On top of that they kept hittas on standby. They drove in separate vehicles Caesar having a red Benz G wagon and G-Money drove the Audi Q7. While the hittas drove in black-on-black Cayenne Porsche trucks. Feeling themselves Caesar and G money pulled out neatly stacks of $100 bills and began making it rain on the crowded lower level first floor in the club. Money began raining from above on Angel Kiki and Keisha falling from Caesar's hands. Getting their attention instantly.

   Big faces begin to scatter on the heads of Angel Kiki and Keisha. Making gold digging ass Keisha dive for the money like a fumble in the end zone. Oh, this caused Angel and Kiki to look above at the center of attention tonight Caesar and G money. The bright light in the club had bugette diamonds dancing on Caesar and the rest of his crews' chains. All the gold diggers and sack chasers were tryna get in the spotlight. Viewing all this caused the ladies to pick up as much money they could. And began making their way upstairs, until they were stopped by the red rope and a big muscle-bound bouncer who favored Damon off Friday after the next. Seeing it was no option or way of getting Caesar and his team's attention. Angel began throwing the same money she just picked up back at Caesar's booth as Kiki followed. Of course, gold digging ass Keisha just watched.

   Them throwing money back at Caesar's booth worked like a charm. At first, he felt insulted until he sees it was Angel

Kiki and Keisha. So, he approached the red rope and invited them to his V.I.P booth.

Soon as they entered Keisha grabbed a bottle of champagne from Rich one of the dread heads with Caesar. And began to turn it up to her lips. Angel and Kiki shyly slid in between G money and Caesar. They weren't used to this type of attention. So, they were enjoying the spotlight, while blushing the whole time.

The lights went out in the club at 11:59 PM. The DJ began speaking and advising everybody to find somebody to start this year off with so they could spend it with them. Caught up in the moment Caesar and Angel both closed their eyes beginning to tongue fight in a intimate French kiss.

"**10!! 9!! 8!! 7!! 6!! 5!! 4!! 3!! 2!! 1!!**" The crowd screamed together.

"Happpyy Neewww Yearrss!!!" They yelled in unison the entire club.

Once the lights turned on, Tupac, "Ambitions as a rider", begin blasting through the speakers.

Smiley and Ralo looked on in shock. Noticing Caesar and Angel still in the lip lock. Blue was high off the exotic weed and his guard was let down. Until he looked at Caesar's booth and seen what he didn't want to see. His heart was blown instantly at the sight. And his legs begin to have a mind of their own. Rushing towards Caesar's booth. Before he could make it to the two. Ronnie and Demon stopped him in his tracks. Coming off the hip pointing different caliber of handguns in his face.

Blue threw his hands up immediately to the sign of danger. Smiley stepped in the middle staring down several barrels. Ralo followed suit. Everybody was affiliated one way or another then they were all from the same neighborhood just different parts. Smiley was from the east side but had much respect because of his murder game and heart with situations as such. So, seeing him coming to Blues aid. Eased everybody's trigger fingers.

A long intense stare down took place until the DJ cut the music and began to speak on the mic.

"Don't make us get them crackers in here Nah!" The DJ said over the mic this statement got everybody's attention. Including Caesar and Angel who were still caught up in their embrace. Caught like a deer in a set of headlights. Angel began to turn red at the sight of all the guns and situation that was unfolding about her.

"Yall fall back! This shit aint that serious." Caesar said breaking the tension in the air like ice.

Guns began to lower as the bouncers moved in announcing the party was over.

Ralo and Smiley begin pulling Blue away. He never removed his eyes off Caesar, Angel, or the rest of the goons in the booth. They moved swiftly through the crowd holding one another's shirts. They wanted to make sure nobody got lost and they stayed together. They were outnumbered and outgunned.

Nobody in Caesar's crew left the V.I.P. They stayed behind waiting for the club to empty.

Leaving the club the three felt the New Year's breeze as they heard gunshots. And began to duck low and jog to the Jeep they arrived in. Hitting the alarm made the headlights cut on. Each reaching up under one of the car seats, each grabbing a Glock. They armed themselves.

Ralo begins to make the truck come to life. Pulling into the Jacksonville downtown traffic on east Adams Street, headed back towards the Flag Street neighborhood.

"Them niggas made us look bad back there." Blue said.

"Us! They made you look bad!" Ralo barked.

"You need to leave that bitch Angel alone, Smiley said while staring out the black window." "I think we're being followed." As he continued. Cocking the Glock pistol putting one in the head.

"I'm about to hit this corner ahead jump out Smiley and knock the motor out that bitch." Ralo instructed.

"Nawl, Nawl, just run all these red lights and lose them" Blue said.

Shaking his head, Ralo complied turning up the speed in the V-6. Smiley was a hot head who was certified, and Ralo was down for whatever. Cause he knew Smiley's gangster was official. Blue on the other hand was a gangster too. But also, the thinker, they all knew it was about who could outthink the opponent.

"So, what we gone do bout this shyt." Blue spoke once he noticed they lost whoever was following him.

"We gotta get our money." Boc! Boc! Boc! Boc! Boc! Boc! Boc! The sounds of an automatic handgun sounded off. Interrupting their conversation. As the back glass broke to the truck. Smiley began to stick his arm out the window and began shooting back. Boom! Boom! Boom! Boom! The bullets were exiting the chamber so fast it sounded like only a few from the echoed shots. But he shot the whole "30" clip into empty and the gun began to click. And the headlights turned off the one-way downtown street.

"Everybody good" Ralo sighed.

"Yeah, I'm good, Blue said" "Yall pass me another Glock," Smiley replied.

They pulled over to inspect the damage done to the Jeep. "Damn they hit this bitch up", Smiley said inspecting the back of the jeep. The back bumper and trunk were covered with small bullet holes.

"That was a close call", Smiley said.

"I told you we should've struck first this nigga on that second guessing shit", Ralo replied pointing at Blue.

"Call Shaq to come pick us up and we need to wipe everything down and report the truck stolen", Blue stressed holding his head in his palms.

Scuurrrr! The tires began to screech as Shaq came to a halt. "Yall good!" Shaq stated in disbelief looking at the bullet riddled truck.

Nobody replied they all just entered the vehicle with their game faces on, "Tonight somebody gotta die", Shaq mumbled to no one in particular.

"Go around to 19th Street", Blue directed.

They began to take the trip down Kings Road as the others politic about what they wanted to do to Caesar and his crew. The only thing Blue could think about is Angel and the mistake he made by seeing her in the club and letting his emotions get the best of him. But his mind kept making excuses for the actions of his babymomma. And begin to make him question, did the shots come from Caesar or could it be about the coke and money they came up on.

Lost in thoughts as they turned the corner on the dead end of 19th Street. It looked like a drive through outside the small duplex. From the looks of the traffic Caesar's trap house was doing numbers. Here it was 2:00 in the morning and the neighborhood was quiet and sleep. This side of the hood went from the 13th to 19th. 19th being the last street and a pair of railroad tracks separating it from Martin Luther King Expressway. So, the heavy traffic was unnoticed.

Shaq hit the headlights and began to let the car lurk. He pulled the car over on the opposite side of the trap spot. And everyone began slouching in their seats. Seeing the traffic leave and more cars coming.

After sitting for 30 minutes Smiley and Ralo were ready for action.

"I say we get out and run up on that bitch", Smiley said speaking of the small duplex.

The spark of a lighter struck instantly on the side of the small duplex. Revealing the smoker slack and gunman watching the trap. As he held the water steady on the crack pipe.

"Look at this shit", Shaq begin pointing. Then they all noticed the 2.23. resting on his shoulders.

They had a look out on the side of the house. That one would notice only if they were walking up. He was to keep the robbers away, be alert if any police activity happened, and for situations like this. But due to the heavy traffic he missed the black Nissan Maxima with Shaq, Blue, Ralo, and Smiley inside of it.

"Whenever the traffic calms down I say we send a message and pop buddy on the side. Ain't no telling what kind of guns they got in there or how many of them there are. And we definitely ain't shooting up no houses," Smiley spoke in a whispering like tone.

They waited for the traffic to cease an hour or so later. The car they were in was one of Shaq's girlfriends. So, while sitting in the backseat Smiley found a dress and a human hair long wig. He began to change into a wig and sundress. Everybody else didn't say nothing, because they knew with the amount of male ego and masculinity he had, for him to be doing something like this meant he was graveyard serious.

Finally, when the street was empty of any customers or occupied cars. Except the one they sat in for the last 2 and a half hours. Smiley begins to give Shaq the directions he needed him to follow. This was a dead end it was no way to make a quick exit if they drove forward and turned around.

Smiley got out the backseat of the car in a low to the ground posture. And begin to creep away from the car so if he was noticed as the female he was dressed as. He wouldn't be seen getting out of the vehicle, or cause suspicion ruining the element of surprise. Once on the same side as the trap spot. He begins to add a little twist in his walk and wave his hair back and forth, which was shoulder length from the wig. Slack seeing the figure became alert and stood up walking to the sidewalk clutching the 223. rifle. When he seen the light pink sundress with sunflowers covering it and the white tennis shoes. He became at ease. It was normal in the hood to see a crack-whore with a dress and tennis-shoes on. Slack went and sat back down and began to light his crack pipe up inhaling the strong smoke.

When Shaq viewed Smiley in shooting distance of Slack. He begins to put the car in reverse and let it creep backwards down the dead-end street headlights turned off.

Smiley looked to the right out of his peripheral vision seeing the car was starting to reverse down the street. And began walking up the driveway like he was headed to one of the front doors. Outta sight of Slack he put his back on the front of the house and begin to slide back in Slacks direction. Slack was so far on the side of the duplex. Smiley wanted to avoid a shoot-out, so he decided to walk past the side of the duplex, and creep on the front of the house getting closer meant getting a better shot. Crouching like a tiger embracing himself for the unexpected. He began to up the gun in the direction and position he felt Slack would be when he popped up around the corner. Soon as he put his right foot behind the left to give himself the thrust, he needed to put himself into action. He heard the door open, and a voice begin speaking. Freezing him in his tracks.

"Bitch I'm on the way home now", The young boy spoke in the phone never noticing Smiley kneeled down walking right past him. Palms sweating, stomach turning, he arose to his feet pointing the gun in the young boy's direction. Boom! Boom! He aimed, squeezed. As he seen him fall as the shots entered his back. He spun around the corner Boom! Boom! Boom! Sending 3 shots into Slack not really caring if he died or lived. Because he was a smoker, and no stripes is earned for killing a smoker. He was just a message to be sent. But now having the opportunity at the youngin this was an answered call. After seeing Slack fall Smiley quickly turned his attention back to the fallen soldier on the ground trying to crawl. He noticed once standing over him, it was one of the same guys from the F.M.B entourage at the club. Same necklace, same outfit. He quickly snatched the F.M.B necklace off of his neck while putting the barrel on his temple removing his last thoughts. Boom! Being satisfied with his work he turned around and begun shooting in the house. With all the action outside he didn't know if anybody in the house would pop out. Sending shots inside would at least buy him a little time to run back to the car.

Adrenaline pumping Smiley begin running full speed around the corner. Seeing the brake lights was the best thing he ever seen in life at this time. Letting him know the plan was complete and he wasn't going to jail or the graveyard tonight.

Back at Blockas house the 3 parted ways with Shaq. It was New Years, and the trio wanted this year to be about getting money. But after tonight the 3 knew things would never be the same. Rather one killed or they all killed. Either way their innocence was gone as Blue & Ralo stared into Smiley's eyes. Noticing a look, they never seen before or would never forget. It was the eyes of a killer. You would have to take a soul to notice them, or just seen what Ralo and Blue had just witnessed. Smiley continued to go over the details and experience he felt. Pulling out the trophy of tonight. They all gloated over the F.M.B chain like it was the fur of a kill out of the safari or jungle.

"Who knows what F.M.B stands for anyways?" Blue asked.

"I heard them making toast inside the club, to fast money boys." Ralo replied.

"Damn them niggas been laying low getting money moving the right way in the hood. Did you see the line of cars and set up how them niggas moving they product," Smiley spat.

Knock! Knock! Knock! A knocking at the door distracted their thoughts. They all looked at one another knowing only one person would be up at 4:30 in the morning.

Blocka entered the room looking into everyone's eyes staring more intensely in Smileys. Noticing he had a pink dress and wig on.

"Salamu Alaykum!" Blocka greeted the 3.

"Wa Alaykum As Salam!" They greeted back in unison.

"You 3 need to make Ghusl and see me up front for Fajr Salat." Ghusl was the only Islamic purification you could make to pure oneself of major impurities. Such as after sex, blood spill, etc.

It was the cleansing of one's entire body. Wudu was the basic purification of one's head, hands, arms, and feet. So, the statement alone of them making Ghusl let them know. He knew they needed purification on a deeper level.

Entering the hallway they noticed 3 sets of sweatpants, shirts, boxers and socks with a open trash bag. They all followed Smiley as he made Ghusl first and placed the dress and wig inside the bag. Ralo and Blue followed.

After taking their showers. They begin to line up in a rank behind Blocka to offer 1 of the 5 daily prayers. After Salaming out indicating the prayer was finished. Blocka made a special (Dua) supplication.

(From you we come to you we must return)

"It's the prayer for the dead." He begins speaking as they all remain seated on their prayer rugs. "War and getting money are like oil and water it doesn't mix. Never will and never have. I don't wanna know what happened and don't care. I just pray to Allah Ta Ila for you all forgiveness." He spoke as he left the 3 sitting speechless.

They tried to fall asleep. But couldn't, their minds were fixed on the outcome of the murder. Just like anybody else in the street. They had to see what the news said. So, they stayed up watching the clock with the channel glued to channel 4. The news in the streets of Jacksonville was like the preacher in the church-house. When it came on and they spoke, granny, auntie, momma, sister, cousin, daddy, cat, dog, frog, they all listened and after that they spread the gossip. Not knowing, rather it was true or false. To most it always was the truth.

At 6 o'clock sharp the morning news begins with the anchor Vanessa Young. All 3 rose to attention when the breaking news in red flashed across the screen.

"Yes!" This is V. Young reporting live from the northwest side of Jacksonville. As you can see, behind me yellow tape and the crime scene technician are processing the scene of what is believed to be a robbery gone bad. Neighbors are saying they heard automatic gunfire and when they came outside seen #2 people wounded. One was transported to Shands of Jacksonville and is fighting for his life with life threatening injuries in the intensive care unit, and the other was dead on arrival. The 2 believed to be these #2. Back to you John for weather.

   Two pictures seen on the tv screen was shown of a 60-year-old man named Odis Jacobs and a 24-year-old man Greg Richards who had died. As they stared at the television it all started to replay in the club. This was the same one sitting next to Caesar the entire night at Club 904. Satisfied with their teamwork the 3 looked at one another and smiled. Mission accomplished.

Chapter 4

Word spread quickly, somebody tried to rob the trap house and only made it off with the F.M.B chain. Once the 60-year-old recovered. He even made the streets buzz harder. When he confirmed the shooter was a woman.

Greg (G-Money) Richards Funeral services were held privately on his mother's asking. It was a closed casket the family didn't want him viewed how they had seen him at the Mortuary. A piece of the top of his head was missing from the impact of the close-range shot. From the Glock.

Music could be heard from the piano being played at Abysinniya Baptist church on Kings Road. While the choir sang the song silver and gold. The cries of G-Money's family were heartbreaking, crying about their loved one. The 20 people were dressed in all black for the occasion. Nobody had an answer or reason for G money's murder. Only suspect they had was a woman and the word of a crackhead. They couldn't trust 100%. But with him also being a victim they had no choice.

The choir stopped singing at the same time Caesar and his F.M.B team entered the church, dressed in all black trench coats with dark shades to hide the pain. Death was in each one of their eyes. Under each trench coat they all carried twin 50 caliber desert Eagles shoulder holsters. The rest stayed behind watching the door and surroundings of the small church. Caesar carried an all-black book bag to the front row to G money's mother with $24,000 in it. To show his condolences and pay for any extra expenses. That he hadn't already paid for. She accepted the book bag, as she stood and gave Caesar a heartful son hug, Removing his shades. To look him in the eyes.

"Son promise me it won't be no more bloodshed", she said tears streaming down her face.

Caesar kept quiet knowing this wasn't the time or place for no empty promises. He wanted his lil homie to rest in peace. And felt this time was for the family to grieve and shed tears. F.M.B wanted to shed blood in the streets. So he just shook his head in response.

Leaving the front row Caesar found a comfortable spot next to Janae, who was G-Money's cousin. Also, his stash spot for his drugs. They hugged and embraced while the preacher gave his eulogy. Janae was solid as it gets. She made sure to hold the drugs down and at the same time took care any other needs Caesar asked. She was there when he got fronted his first brick of coke. And became his backbone once his operation grew. Nobody knew their secrets but them. They weren't officially together, just had an understanding.

After the services, G money was escorted from the church back to the Mortuary, to be cremated. Caesar and his team left early to leave the immediate family to spend their last moments with G-Money. It was a rainy day fitting the mood of the moment.

Janae started the ignition to her Mercedes-Benz sedan. Sitting in the driver seat pondering looking at life reflecting on the past 24 months. Since her three-bedroom 2 bath townhouse on Collins Rd. on the West side of Jacksonville was used to hold Caesars drugs. She didn't want for much, her townhouse and Benz were paid for. She still kept her job at Bank of America. Because she knew living the fast life tomorrow wasn't promised. Tears flooded her face thinking about her favorite cousin G money. A part of her wanted to say fuck the streets and holding Caesars drugs. She felt guilty just knowing the drugs she held could have been a part of the reason behind her cousin's death. At least she thought it was…..

Placing the small Benz in drive. Janae turned on Kings Road heading towards downtown. When the beeping alerted her, she was low on gas "Psst!" She exhaled at the fact she didn't want to stop for gas in the rain or on the north side of Kings Road. Her family stayed over here in the Flag Street, Grand Park area. But this wasn't her stomping grounds.

Stopping at the red light off Kings Road and canal street. Looking to her left she noticed the Texaco gas station and Flag St. Apartments. The light turned green, she pulled in and pulled up to pump two on the right side of the gas station. This wasn't her area, so the surroundings made her feel uncomfortable, and the foreign car stuck out like a sore thumb.

Stepping out of the car trying not to get wet by the rain. Janae walked towards the store and a quick pace, causing her thick frame to jiggle walking into the gas station. Her curves were hypnotizing in the Dolce and Gabbana woman's dress suit. She paid for the fuel, letting the clerk keep the change exiting the gas station all eyes were on her. Causing her to panic. Pressing the button to open her gas tank with more force than needed. But to no avail the small flap on the gas tank did not open. The rain began to pour harder, wetting her hair and making her clothes stick to her. Janae kept trying to get the button to work for her gas tank and at the last try broke down in a crying fit. Washing the remaining eyeliner off her cheeks, leaving what looked like black waterfalls on her butter pecan skin. Today wasn't her day. First the emotional suffering from G-Money's funeral and now she was stuck in the ghetto with no gas.

Vroom! The motor was heard before seeing the white F150 with the limousine tent, pulling in next to Janae's Benz. The tent was so dark it caused her heart to skip a beat. Not knowing what lay behind the dark windows.

Seeing Janae in the rain outside her Benz disturbed Blue and aroused him. He was receiving mixed emotions. Viewing how curvaceous her figure was. Her peanut butter skin was flawlessly smooth, and her silky brown hair was glistening like a fresh bottle of Egyptian Musk oil. Even the crocodile tears she was shedding was making her look sexy. Not being able to take the site in anymore. He began to exit the F150. And approached Janae who was now bent over fondling with the gas tank.

"What you are doing out here in the rain", Blue said while observing how distressed she was.

"I, I, I, just came from the church up the street and was running low on gas, I can't make it home with my gas tank not opening", Janae expressed through tears.

Blue reached into his pocket pulling out a small pocketknife on a set of keys. Causing Janae to step back in fear of danger. He went around to the gas tank placing the knife in the slit of the flap and began moving it side to side until the tank popped open. Removing the pump from the lever inserting the gas nozzle, activating the automatic pump and walked away into the gas station.

Janae lit up like the sun at noon. As soon as she heard the fuel begin pumping into the Benz, then the fuel meter moved, and gaslight cut off. Whoever this man was she thought, she had to repay him.

Walking out of the store seeing the rain calm down to a light drizzle. Blue decided to interact and chop it up with the old school players. Noticing a couple dudes, he went to school with. When he seen the Benz start to pull off. But when he seen it circle around, he got on point then started watching it until it slow creep finally came to a stop. With its driver window rolling down slowly the once miserable distressed looking woman was now glowing making her features more noticeable. She favored Lisa Ray when she played Diamond on "Players Club". Just a light brown version.

"I don't know how I can thank you or repay you", she spoke softly through the window.

"Don't thank me, give all praises to Allah", Blue replied nonchalantly.

"What's your name??"

"Why you the police or something?"

"If I was you would have been in jail for that big ass gun you got on your hip" she shot back rolling her neck acknowledging the fact she had seen the Glock on his hip earlier. Letting him know at the same time she wasn't the law.

Green and he told her partially the truth. "They call me B."

"I'm Janae, B, nice to meet you." She said while extending her hand.

He took her hand, feeling how delicate and soft it was. Feeling the energy sensations through his hands all the way down to his feet.

"Well, listen, I gotta go." "But I'll see you again." Janae said confidently.

"I don't know how to even get in touch with you."

"You can't say that now", Janae handed him her business card. That read Bank of America Accounting Manager.

Blue read the card and looked at her with a raised eyebrow. Watching the car pull off then enter traffic.

Vrrrrrm! Vrrrrrm! Vrrrrrm!

Caesars cell phone had been going off nonstop for the past week. Sitting in his Benz G-Wagon watching the movers move the remaining furniture out of the duplex where G-Money was murdered. His mind was in a deep state of thought. Everything had been running so smoothly until this happened. He could not understand how this happened or why.

Vrrrrrm! Vrrrrrm! Vrrrrrm!

Caesar wanted to throw his phone. The sound of his phone was driving him crazy with every vibration. Until he looked at the screen and seen the name read Hector, his Cuban cocaine connection from Miami.

He glanced out the window to make sure nobody was in earshot. When he saw there wasn't. He picked up the phone and accepted the call. Placing it on speaker phone. "K Ola" He spoke in the little Spanish he knew.

"K Ola Papi", Tou Bi'en" Hector replied.

"Yes, I'm good Papi, just had a little suppressa"

"Me no like suppressa", Hector begins speaking in his broken English.

"It took me a month to call and now Ju tell me about a fuckin surprise!!!"

Caesar looked at the phone like it had lips of its own before responding, "Who the fuck you think you talking to?!!"

"Ju, Juu black piece of shit!! Jomarto Hendey!" Hector repeated.

"Me to, you fucking wet back! I kill people for fun!" Caesar said venomously.

"I been told Ju a long time ago, it's 2 things me no play about. Me money and me family." Hector made clear before ending the call.

Click!!

Caesar slammed down the phone and balled up his fist.

He knew this day would come. He would have to explain why he never made the trip back with the $60,000 he owed Hector. He was trying to buy time and come up with a better story than what actually took place. It was no way he was telling Hector, Rich lost 2 bricks and $60,000. By not following what he said. Instead of Rich going straight to the duplex on 19th to drop the cocaine and money off. He stopped to catch a late-night nut. That cost him more than the milkshake and fries he was originally paying to the young tender staying in Flag Street Apartments. Where his 96 Impala was broken into.

If Caesar told Hector that, that would've just been like signing Rich's death certificate. Now with this phone call and G-Money's death. It seemed like the weight of the world was on his shoulders.

"Damn." Blue said while getting back in the rented truck.

He was stuck in a trance about this woman Janae and the connection he felt after only spending a few minutes around her. He had to have her. She was beautiful not in the typical hoodrat or video vixen type of way. She seemed classier, like a African natural queen in her own right. And seeing the Bank of America card she gave him only made it better.

He put the truck in park once he pulled around back the 2-story house on 13th street. That him, Smiley, and Ralo had just rented. The creepy look it had, and the last murder made the 3 come up with a name for the house. They begin calling it (The House of Pain).

Blue reached inside his pants pocket retrieving his cell phone. And typing Janae's number in the contact and saving her name and sending a text as he pressed the send button.

Blue.

"B"   He sent, as a text came right back

Janae.

"J"   Her text read

Blue.

Safe?? He responded.

Janae.

Of course, thanks for everything. She replied.

Blue.

Anytime. He placed his phone back in his pocket.

  He hopped out the rental feeling like he had the winning lottery ticket in his pocket.

  "Yoooooo!" He shouted unlocking the backdoor to the House of Pain.

  Letting Ralo and Smiley know he was in the house. Since the New Years incident. They were held up in the house with a war-ready stash of guns. On the side of the front door was a Thompson submachine gun, better known as a Tommy gun. At the top of the stairs was a Russian AK47 and a Mac 90. And on top of that they each kept a glock on their waistlines. This was the new headquarters. Only rules was, must lock doors behind you, and no playing in the house. This was the House of Pain. So love making or women was a no no. These was the rules they got from Blocka and stood on. The house had only two sectionals and a blow-up mattress. And they parked the rentals in the backyard to avoid any attention to the spot.

  Upstairs on the second floor Ralo and Smiley sat smoking a blunt while in very deep conversations, feeling as though they were in their own world. Both sectionals were positioned in the far corner of the room. Every sound was echoed being it was barely anything inside the house. So

Blue footsteps was louder than normal getting Smiley and Ralo's attention once he made it up on the top step.

"Salamu Alaykum", Blue greeted the 2.

"Wa Alaykum As Salam", They responded in unison.

"Man, we need to get out this house and move around, I'm tired of being in here feeling like I'm in jail." Ralo exclaimed.

"We need to let things calm down first, I gotta go with my pops to this City Council shit. He is making me go", Blue said.

"Man, what kinda police ass shit is you on, is you going?" Smiley asked.

"It look like, I don't have a choice", Blue answered.

"Everybody got a choice in life", Smiley snapped, upset at the fact Blue was going to be around all these high-ranking officials of the city of Jacksonville. When he had just witnessed a murder. His paranoia was at a all-time high.

"Brah you trippin, I'm a team player my daddy showing me the way so we can be straight in the game."

"That's real, I hope these couple of weeks fly by. Because the faster we can open shop the faster I come up. My money starting to run low." Ralo spoke.

"Niggas been spending money on shit they can't even pronounce", Smiley chuckled while pointing at Ralo's Ferragamo slides.

Vrrrrrm! Vrrrrrm!

Blue phone began going off. He felt the vibration in his pocket and began to smile thinking of Janae calling him. The smile was quickly replaced by a frown when he seen "Angel" appear on the screen.

He scowled at the phone. Then pressed the accept button. "What's up? Alright I'ma be around there." Then hung up the phone hitting the end button.

Ever since the club. They kept things at a mutual understanding for the sake of his son. Also, he knew he couldn't just end things, without her being spiteful. And the 2 bricks of coke were still in her backyard buried under the doghouse. So therefore, his hands were tied up. "I'll be back I'm bout to walk around the corner to Angel's spot, one of yall come lock the door." Blue stated while grabbing his glock off the sectional placing it in his waistband.

Stepping out the house, he looked both ways making sure nobody seen him coming out of the yard as he crossed the street. A million things ran across his mind walking to Angel's house. She only stayed a block away on 14th and Canally in a white house on the corner. Ever since her mother passed away a year prior, she was with the house and stayed alone with Blue's son. And from time-to-time Kiki and Keisha came over to spend the night.

Walking down the street he heard from a distance, 2 Pac (So Many Tears).

"Back elementary I grieved on misery, grew up alone I grew up amongst a dying breed, in my mind I couldn't find a place to rest, until I got that thug life tatted on my chest, tell me can you feel me." Blasting through the speakers.

Bobbing his head to the beat. You can't look forward never turning around walking. Until he seen the red Benz G-Wagon truck passing by slowly. He reached under his shirt and grabbed the handle of the glock. He paused for a second readjusting the handgun. Seeing that this was the same truck in front of club 904. He began to stare intensely inside the tinted windows when he noticed none other than Caesar. He swiped his hand over his face then pinched the bridge of his nose as he blew out a breath of frustration. He wished he could have just handled the situation right now on the spot. But he wasn't equipped to handle the pressure. Especially doing something near his baby mama's house was a bad move altogether. But everything was becoming clearer with Caesar. He thought as he began to walk up the driveway to Angel's front door.

"Well, damn, nigga, what took you so long" Angel said stepping onto the front porch. "What?" Blue shot back. "Fuck you mean, what took me so long?"

"Aint that what I just said?"

Blue shook his head. "Aint nobody got time for this shit."

He turned around and tried to leave and Angel ran down the driveway and wrapped her arms around his waist. "Please don't go", she spoke in a soft voice. She squeezed him tightly placing her tongue against the back of his neck. "I was only playing with you", damn! "Why you gotta be so sensitive all the time?"

He stopped walking and flexed his muscles. He couldn't explain the feeling, but for some reason, Angel hugging him made him feel safe and secure. They made him feel wanted and needed something he had never experienced before.

He wiggled himself free and turned back around to face her. She was looking up at him with her bottom lip poked out like a big baby.

"What's up with you? What's wrong why you got me rushing over here and nothing aint wrong? And where Jr at?" Blue questioned her.

"I'on know." "I guess I just miss you, and he at Kiki sister's son birthday party." Angel confessed.

"Go in the house I'ma be in there," he said. Once seeing her enter the house. He walked around back to the doghouse and moved it slightly. Kicking the dirt up, once he felt the leather MCM bag he had buried with the cocaine inside of it. Satisfied, he placed the doghouse back in its secure place. And headed back towards the front of the house to go inside.

"I wanna take you to a place that's nice and quiet. Where there aint no one there to interrupt, baby- I just wanna take it nice and slow." Angel crooned along with Usher as the warm water from the shower spigot rained all over her well-defined curved body.

She needed to put on a good show so she could win Blue back over and stay in good grace. From seeing him in the mall to the club she knew he had something going on. She just couldn't figure it out. He was moving to creep these past few weeks. The only things he came by and did was drop money and clothes off to his son Blue Jr.

Entering the house Blue looked around the candle-lit living room and down the hallway at the candles trailed all the way to the bedroom. Walking down the hallway following the candles to the bedroom. He heard the sounds of one of his favorite songs by Ginuwine as sounds of Usher faded away.

"If your horny, let's do it, ride it, my pony, my saddle, waiting, come and jump on it." He started humming Ginuwine and smiling. This was one of the reasons he loved Angel so much. She brought out a different side of him. He never showed nobody except his best friend Chris who died in the Army. Over in Vietnam. This song brung back a lot of memories. He and Chris shared.

Dripping wet, Angel carefully removed her shower cap and draped it over the shower glass sliding door. She grabbed her towel from the towel rack and wrapped herself up.

The bedroom was steamy and hot, so foggy from Angel leaving the door open to the bathroom that was inside her bedroom. That she barely made it to see Blue lying on his back awaiting her on the bed.

Looking up into Blue's eyes, Angel slowly removed her towel and let it spill down to the floor. The burning glow from the candles had her entire body glowing like it was dipped in honey.

Winding her hips to the music, she placed her trigger finger inside her mouth and pulled it out glistening wet. Then she motioned for Blue to come closer. He licked his lips and nodded his head. Closing the space between them.

He slipped out of his clothes. While Angel was still winding her hips to the Ginuwine "My Pony" song.

Completely naked he stood before her with his manhood still on soft. Angel was used to this problem. Using no hands, she moved her face up and down all around his shaft. Still there was no erection. She kept going to work- slurping. And sopping, humming and moaning. When she seen that he still was extra soft. She slid her finger down Blues cheeks inside his loose butthole, and began moving it around quickly, causing him to get harder than steel. Looking up in his eyes, she mouthed the words, "I know how to get you right." Seeing his eyes rolling in the back of his head.

"Oh yeah? Blue moaned crying like a bitch.

Angel giggled lightly taking him outta his ecstatic moment. He opened his eyes embarrassed she had caught him having a moment. She was used to this side and constantly joked with Kiki who she told everything when she got mad. How he was a gangsta in the streets. But liked his rearend played in.

Viewing his embarrassed facial expression. Angel quickly removed her finger and pushed Blue back straddling now his erect manhood. Sliding down his shaft she added extra emphasis each time she sat down on it. Bringing her rose pedals to the top of his lower head squeezing her fuck muscles gripping every inch of him.

Her nails dug deep into his back, and she bit into his neck. Ooh shit! She fake cried extra loud trying to put on an Oscar performance.

Angel felt his body tense as she tried to re-grip his thick wand with her powerful gyrations pulling all the way out to the tip. Trying to go back down balls deep. When she slid back down feeling nothing inside her. Opening her eyes, looking between her legs, seeing his manhood had gone soft again.

"Really?!" She blurted out upset she almost made it to her orgasm. And he couldn't even stay hard.

"Don't start that shit," he expressed while putting back on his clothes.

"Don't start what" What? Huh! You can't even stay hard for fuckin five minutes!"

Angel was getting madder by the second watching him put his clothes back on. She blocked his path making it impossible for him to leave.

"Move out the way I got things to do people to see," Blue said as he tried to walk out the door Angel had blocked and only met her hands pushing him back.

"Nope! You aint going nowhere until you tell me where you are going."

"I'm going back to the spot with Ralo and Smiley," he said as she let him walk pass.

Before he left the house Angel stopped and looked at him one last time speaking her mind. "You leaving some wet good pussy to be with some niggas, Yeah, okay," Go play in each other's ass's that's what you like anyways."

Before she got another word out. Blue slapped her so hard, forcing her to the ground balling up in a fetal position.

"What?" "Say it again now!"

Angel looked at him in a daze. The blood leaking from her mouth was trickling down the left side of her cheek. It slid down her neck and began making its way down her left breast. Still woozy from the blow, she stirred around with her eye lids fluttering. She looked to her left, where Blue was standing in front of her mugging.

"Didn't I tell you I don't wanna hear you ever say that?" What happens in the bedroom stays in the bedroom." He said while removing 5-hundred-dollar bills and throwing them next to her.

Watching him leave out the front door, Angel picked up the 5 hundreds and begin to smile sinisterly showing bloody teeth. One way or another she would get the last laugh. She initially called him over to her house to get money anyways. So, she didn't mind taking a slap with some sex to get it. She thought while picking up her phone to call Kiki and tell her about the latest drama.

Chapter 5

Caesar rode through the city of Jacksonville, sitting safely behind the tint of his luxury truck as he took Highway 295 in a circle taking him across the Dames Point Bridge from the southside to the northside. All he could think of is the money he was losing by having to relocate his trap after G-Moneys murder. The last conversation the two of them had was inside Club 904. He replayed the events inside of V.I.P. He moved in silence and couldn't figure out how one of his was caught lacking. Twice within 30 days. First Rich lost the 2 keys of coke and 60,000 dollars. He never had the chance to fully recover from the first loss. Then G-Money lost his life. He didn't know which one he should worry about. Hector sending his hitmen, or the female robber who attempted to rob his trap and ended up killing G-Money. He'd already paid the bounty of $30,000 dollars for G-Money's F.M.B chain. So, he knew eventually how the streets worked somebody would say something.

Suddenly, he seen his phone screen light up looking down seeing he had a text message. Grabbing the phone he smiled and frowned, seeing he had 2 messages. One from Angel the other was from Hector.

He chose to read Angel's text first. Thinking about how talented she was with her mouth. The text simply read "Hey stranger." He decided to send her a text to go out with him tonight. Which she had to decline cause of her swollen busted lip. But she lied and told him she didn't have anything to wear. And asked him to stop by after he left wherever he was going. He accepted the invitation to her house.

Opening Hector's text message, Caesar's temperature begins rising. Reading the text message slowly. It read "Ashes to ashes, dust to dust." Viewing this his blood began to boil and his anxiety started to kick in. He begins searching the rearview mirror making sure he isn't being followed. He was in need for a drink and needed something to distract his mind off the hell he was going through on Earth.

Caesar pulled into the parking lot of the Silver Foxx Gentlemen's Club and rolled down his window. It was a known hangout spot in the city when the wife was on your azz at home, you came to the Foxx. When you wanted to politic with other bosses in the city, you come to the Foxx. When you wanted to get the latest gossip in the streets you came to the Foxx. Even if you wanted a new taste of pussy you came to the Foxx. It was a low-key spot-on Beaver Street. Where after 12am it turned into an anything goes spot, with pretty girls in all kinda provocative costumes barely covering their bare assets.

Parking in the express zone Caesar weighed his options on rather he should carry one of his desert eagles inside the club or leave it. He decided to leave it and placed it under his seat before exiting his red Benz G-Wagon.

Entering the club, he was escorted by a worker who had on short shorts showing off her plump butt cheeks. And a halter top showing off her 6 pack and belly piercing. She led him to a small room in the back of the club. That had a sign that read PRIVATE on the door.

Tonight, Caesar wanted to be alone, so he paid top dollar to get a private room where everything was brought to him. The private room came with a bottle of Remy Martin in a bucket of ice with a stripper pole and a comfortable sofa. Caesar rolled up a swisher sitting in the private room puffing inhaling the strong exotic weed smoke. When he heard a knock at the door.

Knock! Knock! Knock!

"Come in", Caesar said loudly over the music blasting through the speakers inside the private room.

A light skinned Cuban woman with a stripper outfit decorated in her Native Cuban Flag with a pair of stilettos stepped inside Caesar's private room. Soon as she entered the room she began to sashay to the beat, making her body move in any direction she wanted it to move in. She was 5'5 no more than 165 pounds. Her body looked surgically perfected. She had no fat around the waist or back. And below there was nothing but fat in the right areas. Her bottom looked like 2 basketballs and with every move she was bouncing them back and forth.

Caesar sat back taking in the image of the Cuban doll. He loved the fact that she did no talking just went str8 to work. After performing her strip tease going to the top of the pole and sliding down slowly. She untied her bikini like Cuban flag 2 piece. Showing her perfect breast and clean shaved camel toe and got on her knees and begin crawling towards him. He was so in a zone from the exotic weed and Remy Martin he was drinking straight out of its bottle. He thought he was seeing things as the Cuban doll got closer grabbing his pants and unzipping his zipper on his Gucci shorts going for his manhood. But he wasn't. This Cuban doll was who he thought she was. This was Hector's little sister Isabella, who often he would meet to get the bricks of coke with the Cuban Flag stamp on it. Apart of him told him to leave. Because he didn't believe in coincidences. But the lustful and revengeful side told him to finish the job and get his get back from the disrespect Hector showed him on the phone and through text messages. So he stayed and let the liquor and weed take its course and Isabella as well.

Isabella released his shaft out of his Gucci shorts. In one swift motion she deep throated his entire erection. "Umm!" She moaned on his dick. The vibrations from her vocal cords were driving him crazy. She focused on the head of his manhood using both hands to jerk his shaft. After 10 minutes of non-stop jerking and sucking Caesar began to explode. Isabella wasted no time slurping every drop swallowing it all. Slurping so loud it sounded like she was mopping up a bowl of spaghetti and Rague sauce.

Caesar rested his head back on the sofa like his nose was bleeding. Relaxing while Isabella put back on her 2 piece.

"Ju good Papi?" Isabella asked, making sure he didn't need any more of her services.

"Me good Mami," Caesar replied mocking her Spanish accent. Reaching in his pockets grabbing a handful of hundreds out of the wad that rested inside of his shorts. It was a tip for the extra work.

"Gracias", "I'll be back to bring Ju receipt for Ju private room." She said winking at him.

Isabella left the private room and went back to the ladies' dressing room. She disregarded the receipt to buy time. She didn't know if the man inside the private room knew who she was, but she knew who he was. She never forgot a face. She remembered vividly the times she dropped off cocaine for Hector to him. And just the hours before Hector had called her and told her to give those locations to Paco. Paco was coming into town to either receive Hectors money or take Caesars life. So, Isabella was well aware of the situation.

Making it to her locker inside the ladies' room to retrieve her cell phone she called Paco immediately.

"Primo, he's here inside private room #6." Isabella whispered inside the phone. The voice said nothing on the other end. The only thing heard on the other end of the phone was breathing. And the call was disconnected.

Seeing Caesar alone in the private room. Another well-known dancer by name of Dynasty entered the room and started to entertain him. She was working the pole like the 2 of them was magnetic. She climbed up the pole spinning around coming to the ground and begin to clutch the pole in between her ass-cheeks smothering the pole.

Watching the show Caesar pulled out the wad of 100's and begin to make it rain down on Dynasty as she put on a professional performance. Hearing the DJ call, last call for alcohol and last song. Dynasty begins to collect the floor full of 100's. And exit the private room.

Caesar stood up in the private room seeing double of everything and begin staggering out of its door. The club was emptying out and dancers were wrapping up their last sets. Checking his surroundings, his spirit told him something wasn't right. He begins to regret leaving his desert eagle inside the truck under the seat. The lights cut on inside the club illuminating the exit door. Caesar seeing his truck through the door, pressed the automatic start button on his alarm making the trucks twin turbo V-8 begin to make the truck sound like it was growling.

Everybody outside the club was observing the red luxury truck on Forgiato's. Unlocking its doors Caesar headed to the driver's side to enter the truck. When he seen what looked like a leprechaun holding a big ass gun. Sobering himself up from the liquor and weed. Then seeing it flash like a camera.

Boom! Boom!

One shot whistled past his ear and the other made contact with his chest pinning him to the driver's side backdoor. Hearing the shots made everybody scatter like roaches outside the club. Making Paco the Cuban hitman not being able to take another shot. This gave Caesar enough time to hop behind the wheel and hit the gas hard as he could.

Boom! Boom! Boom! Boom! Boom! Ting! Ting! Ting!

The gunfire could be heard as 3 bullets hit the frontside of the passenger bumper. Causing the truck to smoke. The stinging Caesar felt in his chest was nothing like the shot he felt when he got shot in the leg. So he believed his Teflon bullet proof vest served its purpose. He pulled out his phone and called the only person he knew he could call on with medical experience this time of morning, Janae.

"I'm on the way right now" Caesar said urgently.

"Okay", was all she replied in her soft voice.

Pulling up to Janae's townhouse on Collins Road. Caesar backed in the driveway. And exited the truck quickly staggering to the front door. The liquor was making everything move in slow motion.

Opening the door she stood there butt-naked forgetting to put on any clothes. Her mind was racing once she received the call from Caesar. She prayed and read Psalms 23 soon as she hung up with him. Now seeing his white Gucci shirt with a blood stain on it, made her begin to shake and cry quickly. She began to take Caesars' shirt off calming down once she seen the bullet proof vest. Releasing the straps on the side of the vest and pulling the sticky vest off Caesar.

Aaaaaagggggggghhhh! He clamped his teeth together desperately trying to fight the pain. The blood-soaked vest was sticking to the flesh wound Caesar had. A piece of the bullet was stuck inside his chest plate skin.

Uuuuuugggggggggrrrrrrr! He gritted his teeth and wiggled his toes. As Janae poured the peroxide on the wound. She moved like a registered nurse with the first aid kit and medical tweezers.

"On the count of 3 I'm going to pull it out", Janae said confidently counting aloud.

"One, Two, Three" …

Aaaaaagggggrrrrr! The numbness in his chest and collar bone was rigid and tender. She placed the tweezers inside the wound, and he begin to feel the blistering pain ravaged his body from the neck up, as she pulled the small piece of bullet fragment out.

Pssst! Caesar let out the breath he was holding in looking at the piece of bullet she was holding in between the tweezers. Silence filled the air while she patched the wound and gave him 2 Lortabs.

Janae was bending over picking up the wrappers to the patches and medical tools. She'd just finished using out of the first aid kit. When Caesar viewed the tattooed paw prints on her bare phat ass cheeks.

"Roof! Roof! Roof!" Caesar began barking jokingly like a dog staring at her backside. Waving his hands like paws.

"Ooohhh! Uunn! Uunn!" She expressed in embarrassment realizing this whole time she didn't have on any clothes. She rushed to put something on.

She came into the front room wrapping her Chanel bathrobe around her body, gently pushing her arms through the sleeve one at a time. Seeing Caesar sitting on the sofa dozing off with his bare back pressed against the suede sofa that sat in her front living room. The 2 Lortabs she'd gave him earlier were kicking in she could see. This was the perfect time to give him the news. With the funeral and everything else they hadn't had that much time alone lately.

She kissed his forehead waking him up. He opened his eyes and begin to smile. They weren't a couple but would become intimate from time to time. So, the affection was normal.

"I got something I want to tell you", she said looking him in his eyes. As he stared back awaiting to hear what she had to say.

"I'm Pregnant", She smiled saying it and kept rumbling on.

"If it's a boy I'm naming him after G-Money, isn't that cute" she said.

Caesar said nothing.

The silence felt like an eternity. The smile faded away and wrinkles creased her forehead. The energy of the moment was unbearable, and Janae burst into a bucket of tears while Caesar sat silently like it was nothing.

Janae got up grabbing the bulletproof vest and car keys, throwing them at Caesar. With the keys hitting him in the face. He jumped up grabbing both of Janae's wrists and pinning her to the wall.

"You really trippin right now, you man enough to fuck me and I'm woman enough to hold your drugs. But you not man enough to take responsibility of what comes out of me!" She yelled as tears ran down her face.

Caesar continued to hold her wrist against the wall. Trying to find the right words. He just couldn't. His life was in pieces right now. Every day something new was happening in his life for the worse. So, he thought before he spoke and hoped the next words he chose was the right ones.

"I told you I got you no matter what", "But, but, I'm just not ready for a child right now. Tomorrow is not promised to me. I feel death is around the corner and I don't wanna leave you to raise a child by yourself. Are you sure it's mine??"

The last comment came out his mouth. Caused Janae to go in a rage. Trying to break free from his manly grasp. When she seen she couldn't, it resulted to her kicking him below the belt. Sending him over as he felt the pain in his stomach from his aching balls.

"Get out!" "Get out my shit now! I hate you, if it wasn't for you my cousin would still be here." Janae said with so much malice in her voice.

The words she spoke hurt worser than the shot to the chest or the pain he felt in life. This was his ride or die saying he was the reason G-Money got killed. It was a thought he thought about but pushed it to the back of his mind. But hearing her say it made him reconsider the thought.

"I'ma leave, just take me to my other apartment."

"What's wrong with your truck?"

"It took some shots to the front and I'm not tryna be riding around like that. They gone be looking for my truck. Just drop me off I'ma be good.

She ran to her room, grabbed her keys off the nightstand and handed them to Caesar. She was to hurt to leave. All she wanted to do is lock herself in the house and plan her next move. This wasn't the reaction she was expecting. What she thought to be the happiest day of her life and family she dreamed of. Turned out to be a day she would never forget. Watching Caesar leave felt like somebody ripped her heart out of her chest.

Janae sat there on the living room floor weeping. Her hysteric cries could be heard down the street. Sniffling as snot ran down her nose and tears soaked her Chanel bathrobe. She buried her face in the cuff of her thighs breathing heavy.

Vrrrrm! Vrrrrm!

She heard her cell phone vibrating and jumped up running to it thinking Caesar had changed his mind. Grabbing the phone, picking it up. She became more upset seeing it wasn't him. She had a text from the contact that read "B".

She tossed her phone on the bed and fell on the bed crying at the fact that she was let down again.

Behind the wheel of Janae's Benz Caesar sat outside his Gateway Apartment. He only came here in case of emergencies and to stash money. The painkillers were weighing on his body as he fought to keep his eyes open. He closed his eyes and seen himself in a casket. Opening his eyes very quickly he breathed a sigh of relief seeing he was still in front of his apartment. Dozing back off this time he heard what sounded like an automatic assault rifle.

Whop! Whop! Whop! Whop! Whop!

Was it his time up? Or were the pain pills he took earlier playing tricks on his mind?

Chapter 6

(A Week Later)

It was a little past 3:30pm, when Janae pulled up in front of Regency Square Mall on Atlantic and Monument. She had spent the better part of her week shopping and buying things for her new bundle of joy, cruising around the city in Felicia's brand-new Maserati Coupe. Top down with her hair blowing.

Caesar stayed true to his word about keeping it real with her no matter what.

A few days ago, he blessed her with $15,000. And told her to look for a bigger car for her and the baby. While he used her Benz for the time being. He also agreed to give her G-Money's end of the money he used to profit every time they would re-up. He opened up shop again on the 13th Street. By using one of his old connects to score some bricks of coke. Until he could get the situation handled with Hector. And run his money back up.

So now that her money was right, and her living situation was good. She was now focused on doing right by her child. And being happy as a woman. She took 2 weeks of paid time off from Bank of America to get her thoughts together. And cope with the fact her and her child's father wasn't going to be a family. She always visioned in her mind her first child would be with a man she loved, and they would be a family. She wanted to be a wife and child's mother, not girlfriend and baby-momma. But the reaction Caesar gave her when revealing her pregnancy, spoke volumes. It was a harsh reality that hurt her that she couldn't change. But life went on. So, she was going on a date with the nice man that helped her at the Texaco gas station on Kings Road in front of Flag Street Apartments. That she knew only by "B". She enjoyed his convo and sweet text, feeling it was time to give him a chance. She agreed to go on a date tonight.

After her and Felicia checked their makeup in the sun-visor mirrors. Felicia put the car in park and killed the motor.

Janae was feeling good about her date tonight. So, after getting her something to wear today, her next destination was the Dominican's and Koreans, to get her a blow out for her long natural hair and her nails done.

Then after that, it was back to her townhouse on Collins Road to get ready for her date. Since Caesar was laying low using her car and his truck was still at her house. She decided to let "B" pick her up for tonight. The sun was shining, the wind was blowing, causing her long hair to flow with the breeze. She grabbed her Gucci tote from the backseat as her and Felicia climbed out the coupe and went inside Regency Mall.

Back at The House of Pain on the second floor, music could be heard of "JT Money's" real niggas run the yard. "I was just a nigga everyday out on the block, socks full of rocks, dodging them muthafuckin cops."

The trio of Ralo, Smiley, and Blue rapped the lyrics altogether. While Shaq poured brown Hennessy inside clear cups. And mixed them thoroughly with Coca-Cola, from the small, customized bar that was positioned on the floor in the right corner. Once finished, he passed everyone their cups and sat himself at the end of one of the sectionals to add himself in the rotation of the smoke session. They were having without him.

"Pass that shyt, yall got me round here bartending." Shaq joked.

Shaq was a cool laid back down for whatever type nigga. He was more of a get money robbing type. He would slang iron if he had to. But he really just wanted some money. And that's what brought him back around them. He seen them elevating. Then how they played the G-Money situation and how they were moving like every decision was a calculated step. Taking the blunt from Smiley he begins to puff inhaling the strong smoke.

"You know they switched spots", Shaq spoke as the smoke escaped his lungs coming out his mouth as he was speaking.

"Who you talking bout", Blue replied curiously.

"I seen Caesar and Rich them when I was coming down here in front of the house at the end of 13th and Division. Them boys spot doin numbers.

After downing his entire cup of Hennessy. Blue grabbed the remote off the sectional and pressed the pause button on the radio. The room went silent.

"Maaannnn!" Blue exclaimed. "We gotta kill this faggot pretty boy ass nigga Caesar. My money running low and sooner or later the ground gone eat the coke up. So we gotta make a move. And open up shop."

"Yeah, I'm damn near broke to. But I say this time we hit the head. You know if you hit the head the body dead." Ralo concurred.

"I'm down", Shaq continued. "It's gone be good cause once we shut that down, we can direct all that traffic right here up the street."

"Now that's gangsta!" Smiley smiled and hopped up from the sectional. It's about time we spank something! "Smiley grabbed the kutta. And begin waving it from side to side. Causing the rest to move anyway the assault rifle didn't. "Bang! Bang!"

"Bang! Bang!" Everybody replied, except for Blue.

Blue was getting deeper in the game and starting to see what his father meant, when he said, "Line people up to take the fall." If he never did anything he could never be caught. Remembering his father quoting the 48 Laws of Power get others to do the work for you. But always take the credit (Law #7) by Robert Greene. The picture was becoming more clearer, and he liked it. Sitting back smiling.

Ralo looked at him and smiled seeing he was smiling. "What's up nigga? What's on yo mind?"

"Nothing", Blue replied. "Just thinkin bout this chick I met last week. I'm bout to get ready to pull off. We going out to eat tonight."

"Yo name should be Trick Daddy Dolla, trickin ass nigga." Smiley said.

"That sounds bout right", Blue replied. As he headed to the bottle of Hen. And took a sip right out of the glass bottle. "I'ma be back a little later if yall can, see can yall do some homework on that spot they at."

"We on it", Shaq replied.

The sun was starting to set. When Caesar left the new trap house with a duffle bag full of money. Ever since the night he got shot and had those nightmares inside the car. He had been moving differently. No answers came up yet about none of the incidents from G-Money to the Hector story. He tried to call Hector to play him to the left. And tell him he had his money. To calm the flame down a little. Hector had too much money to go to war with. Only how he could win that war was to get big man himself, or not play by the rules. And the latter wasn't in his playbook. But his plans fell short when he tried to call and got a disconnected answering message. After taking in his surroundings then checking his rearview mirrors. He reached under the drivers' seat and pulled out his 50. Caliber all chrome desert eagles. He cocked back the hammer to both one at a time. Started the ignition and put the car in drive leaving the spot on 13th and Division.

Cruising down the street headed to drop the duffle bag off. He was bumping and bouncing his head to Jay-Z's (The Streets is Watching).

Kidnap niggas wanna steal ya, broke niggas don't want no cash, they just wanna kill ya, for the name, niggas don't know the rules, disrespecting the game, want you to blow cool, force ya hand, of course that man's plottin', smartin' up nigga, The Streets is Watchin'.

Jay-Z's lyrics was the ghetto gospel to a hustler. It was the story of his life right now. Different questions and scenarios came through his mind while he was driving up to the four ways stop sign on 13th and Canal. The traffic was busy and backed up. He sat six cars behind the car at the stop sign. Watching the cars wait on the next car to move according to who had the right of way. Once it was his turn he seen a white F-150 with dark tint had the right of way but didn't move. So, he let his foot off the gas a little to see if the truck was going to let him go. Seeing the truck inch up a little he stepped on the break. Giving the truck the right of way to turn. Seeing the truck wasn't moving he blew the horn of the Benz. And took the turn speeding off around the corner of Canal.

Beeeeeeepppppp!!!

Watching the small Benz bend the corner, Blue had an eerie feeling that washed over him. For some strange reason he had notion that he'd seen that Benz before. He searched his mind and didn't find anything, but yet and still, his intuition was telling him he knew that car from somewhere.

It was now dark outside. And Janae was exhausted from the shopping and pampering she had treated herself with today. After getting dropped off by Felicia. She took a quick shower making sure not to sweat out her blow out. She picked up her phone to make sure she didn't miss any calls or anything. Even though she had taken off from work. She still was on call 24/7 for the bank's other managers. Janae was one of the top 3 in her accounting class in college and numbers seemed to be her second language. And that's why the Bank of America regional director loved her and also Caesar. Because she always made sure the money was handled correctly.

Vrrrrrmmm! Hearing her phone vibrate, she looked down to see a text from "B". That read "On the way."

She began to blush. Getting dressed she put on a midthigh Christian Dior dress that was mainly white, except for the red rose pedals that was swirling around the sides of the dress. Her white and red, suede and leather pumps made by Dior, had her long shapely legs looking good enough to eat. And her apple shaped bottom sitting just right, as she stared herself in the mirror rubbing her non-showing pregnant belly. She accessorized herself with diamonds on her neck, wrist and earlobes that were shining so brightly. A white and red Gucci tote was draped over her left shoulder. Soon as she was done getting dressed. As if on que her cell phone rung and she answered and heard her ride was outside. Then hung up and begin to head for the door.

Blue cruised up the street to the nice set of townhouses that sat off Collins Road and Blanding Blvd. Reading the text with the address making sure to pull in front of the right house. He was dressed head to toe in nothing but Gucci. His all white, two-piece, linen Gucci suit was tailored to perfection, concealing the outline of his shoulder holster that was tucked underneath holding a Glock. With a single red rose sticking out the top lapel to his Gucci suit. Pulling in front of her townhouse. Blue was impressed of how neat the yard was kept and different floral arrangements surrounding the front of the house. He also noticed the silhouette of a truck with a car cover covering it that he didn't pay much attention to.

The front door of the townhouse swung open, and Janae appeared in the doorway. Blue shook his head in amazement. For some reason Janae was way prettier than he remembered. Just the short walk from the front down the driveway, she made it look like a runway. The diamonds she wore appeared to be shining like Blue lasers. They both smiled seeing they were matching with the colors white and red. And she smiled as he pulled the rose out of his lapel and handed it to her.

"You sure you not a model?" Blue complimented.

"No, I'm a accounting manager at Bank of America. Janae replied, cutting her eyes at Blue in a seductive way. "Very Funny."

Blue opened the truck door for Janae and closed it after she got in.

It was now going on 9pm as Blue drove down the street away from Janae's townhouse. Once he pulled up to the stop sign to exit the neighborhood, he seen a car creeping slowly. The Hennessy had him paranoid. He felt the same eerie feeling from earlier. Seeing the car, he looked in the rearview mirror until the tail-lights disappeared inside the subdivision of houses. He went to thinking somebody was watching. But who could it be? As far as he knew outside of his immediate circle nobody knew where he was going. Waiting and seeing the car didn't appear again he brushed the thought off and pulled into the ongoing traffic on Collins Road. He smiled as he seen Janae looking in the passenger side rearview mirror. "You okay?" He asked as he adjusted the radio volume and turned up the sounds of Monica's beautiful voice singing. Janae just nodded her head.

At 9:30pm, they pulled up to the Hibachi Restaurant, A Japanese upscale restaurant that cooked the food in front of you and served you as it finished cooking.

"I heard a lot about the spot from my coworker's." Janae mentioned.

"Yeah", this is the first location they've built in Jacksonville." Blue replied.

They exited the truck and entered the upscale restaurant, the first thing that grabbed their attention was the sound of the foreign instruments that played over the intercom and the distant aroma of Asian sauces that filled the air. They approached the staff booth where a Japanese woman with long hair led them to the grill. Where different couples were seated around the cooking grill making their orders of different sorts.

Blue ordered a steak with rice and vegetables, Janae ordered sushi and water.

Watching the chef prepare meals in front of them on the cooking grill. He was a professional in how he made different shapes and figures with the vegetable oil turning it to flame. Seeing the vegetable oil turn into a heart shaped flame the chef pointed at Blue and Janae.

"Marrie", "Marrie", he tried to pronounce married in his Asian native tongue.

"No", first date." Janae responded.

"Aahhh! I see, I see."

When the food was finished. They both enjoyed their meals. And made small talk about life and each other. But what stuck out the most was when Janae begins to get emotional talking about her cousin who'd just passed away. Seeing it was a sensitive topic, Blue didn't ask any questions. He just sat back and listened. One thing he did catch was her cousin was killed on New Years after leaving a night club. Acting off intuition he reached inside his Gucci linen top and tightened his grasp around the handle of the Glock making sure it was still in its correct place.

After enjoying their meals and talking for a couple hours. It was 11:07pm when Blue pulled back in front of Janae's townhouse. Immediately he noticed Janae's Benz was now parked in the driveway. He had to admit, she really had motion for herself. This was the type of woman he needed. She was independent and beautiful as well. Blue put the truck in park while trying to mentally prepare himself for a hug and possibly a kiss. But she seemed to be bothered about something. Janae's whole demeanor changed upon arriving in front the townhouse. She was rushing to find her belongings. Blue went around and tried to open the door and seen she was already out. Walking fast for the front door. Appalled by seeing this he said nothing. He just hopped back behind the driver seat, put the truck in drive and pulled off slowly. Analyzing everything that just happened within today and tonight.

Janae entered the house through the front door. As she stepped into the living room. She immediately noticed the large duffle bag and seen a trail of clothes on her hallway floor. She grabbed the duffle bag unzipped it and seen it was filled with rubber banded stacks of money. She shook her head at how Caesar thought. He could just come and go as he pleased, then drop money off and disappear. She made her way down the hallway and headed toward the bedroom door. She slipped inside the room, and the sight of him lying on her black and gold Versace bed set in nothing but his dark skin, his semi-erect manhood standing up slightly made her become wet instantly between her thick thighs. The light from the window of the moon was illuminating his chocolate skin. All she could do was shake her head. Damn, I love this man. She thought to herself as she admired his athletic build.

After taking off her Christian Dior dress. She climbed on top of the bed and placed soft kisses on his chest. She then slid the tip of her tongue along the length of his abs.

"Ummm!" He moaned in ecstasy, "Nae, whatchu doin?"

"Whatchu think?" She softly replied and then took his whole shaft inside her now drenched mouth. Until she felt it in the back of her throat.

Blue pulled off very upset and drove around the subdivision. He didn't know if he was feeling played about the way the date ended, or the suspicion of seeing the way she was acting afterwards. Giving in to curiosity he turned back on Janae's Street and parked 4 houses down.

The white F-150 pickup truck was parked alongside of the road. The headlights were turned off, but the engine was still running. Blue cautiously climbed out of the truck and crept up to Janae's driveway. Approaching the truck with the cover on it first, he removed it's cover slightly not to cause any alarm to go off. First viewing the Forgiato rim as he removed it some more and seen it was a red Benz G-Wagon with bullet holes in it. He gasped upon the revelation. Was this the same truck he remembered from the night at Club 904? He was trying to think back.

Kneeling down beside the Benz truck. Blue was stuck between a hard place and a rock. He didn't want to seem like a stalker. But he was already out the truck not the type to front his move. He begins to move inconspicuously in search for answers. The entire night replayed in his mind. As he reached inside his Gucci linen top and grabbed the Glock and cocked it making sure it was ready to fire. He spent the next minutes meticulously searching the premises. Until he came across the side window and could see through the crack in the blind's a woman's head going up and down on who he believed to be Caesar.

"Goddamn." Blue shook his head in disappointment. He turned around and jogged back to the truck he left running and pulled off with a devious grin. He loved when a plan came together. He thought as he left the sub-division.

   The following morning Caesar awoke and snuck out of Janae's queen size bed. He had no intention on staying tonight or no sexual intercourse. A drop off turned to him waking up to some head. He smiled glancing at her shapely body and backside with the paw prints. Apart of him was aching cause he knew Janae was a good woman and he would never be who she deserved. All he could do is be here for her as much as the streets would allow him to. He gave her forehead a kiss and made a mental note to make up for leaving her lying alone and not telling her he was leaving. He seen sticky pads with numbers written on the front of each and removed a small paper and wrote in pen I love you, promise to make things right. Leaving it on the pillow.

   Janae woke up at 11:27am she saw as she veered at the alarm clock on the side of her bed. She felt around the bed and felt Caesar was not there. Janae's mind began to turn, wondering did she make a mistake. She couldn't believe she ran out on a date, left her date hanging, and came to bed with Caesar and took his soul with her mouth. She thought, shaking her head at how vulnerable he made her feel and low. When she noticed the sticky note on the pillow. "I love you, promise to make things right." She exhaled deeply not knowing what she was feeling. She was in her feelings and hoped Caesar came back by. She wanted him there every night not just to drop money off.

Chapter 7

At Metro Diner on San Marco Blvd. The father and son sat and made small talk over one of the restaurant's most popular meals. Fried chicken and waffles.

Blocka was seated at the back corner of the restaurant making sure he had a visual of every occupant entering and exiting the building. His eyes quickly scanned the room before he opened his mouth to talk to Blue. As the clock struck high afternoon, a older looking man walked in. He was tall, slim, and had a ball cap on like Blocka with its brim covering his eyes. Blocka gently grabbed his brim pulling it down slightly. The man approached them and took a seat across the table from Blue, as he sat next to Blocka.

"This must be my nephew?" The older man asked in a whisper like tone.

"Yes, but why are you never on time? I been preaching the same shit to you for the last 40 years, and you still can't get right."

"That's yo problem you always preaching." The two elders begin to quarrel like they always did every time they spoke or come into contact.

"Son this is your no-good ass Uncle Doc."

Blue finally noticed the resemblance in the two brothers. And spoke, "Why I aint never seen or met him at any of the family reunions?"

"Muthafucka been on the run for 15 years duckin the Feds." Blocka spoke with a wave of disgust over his face.

91

His younger brother Doc as everybody called him, had been dodging the alphabet boys his whole life from D.E.A to F.B.I to ATF or any other letters. But he always stayed two steps ahead of them. And being he was back in Jacksonville from California. Where he had been hiding out for the last 15 years. When he called Blocka and said he was in town. He knew his brother was a crack cocaine expert. Who ran with the infamous freeway Ricky Ross. A dealer who made millions of dollars selling cocaine to Cali during its crack epidemic. Who earned his name freeway from the freeway his house was next to. He had a name for making money and distributing crack, which was cocaine cooked using different methods. California was supposed to be where crack cocaine was discovered first in the mid-80s. And when everything was going on Doc was in the mix. So Blocka took advantage of the opportunity and connected his son and his brother, having an epiphany his brother could teach his nephew something about crack cocaine.

"Enough of the bullshit, I set up this meeting so the two of you could meet and you can help your nephew out with getting him some." Blocka explained.

"My pleasure, neph." Doc said as he smirked and rubbed his hands together. "I'ma show you how to make a mil ticket with your wrist."

"Only thing is I got problems in the way." Blue stared down at the half of a waffle and chicken bones left on his plate.

"I thought that was handled", Blocka responded.

"Nawl, they just opened shop down the street from the house we are renting. That only made things worse. I got a plan and I think I know where the money at."

Blue mentioning the money got both of the old timer's attention, causing him to focus intensely on his every word.

"How did you find out this information?" Doc questioned as he stared intensely at his young nephew that reminded him of himself in a youth.

: Now that's information I can't share", Blue giggled to himself.

"Doc and Blocka both smiled at one another.

They both gave each other a look of approval. Knowing he had their bloodline running through his veins. He wasn't going to give them any more information. Because he caught on to his Uncle Doc's motive trying to get to much information. Either way too much information about another's business was never good no matter who you were.

"Just remember son keep your hands clean and be ready for the dinner tonight, at 9 o'clock. Now excuse me and your uncle we got some catching up to do." Blocka expressed as Blue got up and casually exited the place.

Blue felt his phone vibrating and quickly reached down into his Gucci linen pants he still had on from the night before. He pulled his phone out and saw he had a call from Ralo and pressed the answer button.

"Yoooo", he spoke into the receiver. "Aight I'm on my way right now I got some good news too." He said before ending the call.

He couldn't wait to get back to The House of Pain to give them the details on how just from meeting Janae at the gas station dropped Caesar right in his lap.

Smiling from ear-to-ear Blue jumped out the pickup truck and ran straight up the stairs. Causing everyone to look at him like he was crazy.

"What the fuck yo problem is?" Smiley spoke first.

"Who you tellin!"

"You won't believe what happened last night?" He paused to catch his breath. "Brah remember the bitch I told yall I met at the gas station? That's G-Money cousin and Caesar bitch!" He rambled off fast.

"Hold on, hold on, hold on, what the fuck you talking bout." Ralo asked as he studied his face making sure he was serious.

"Man, we went out to eat, she went to running her mouth and told me bout her cousin died on New Years after the club. And when I dropped her off, I seen a small Benz there and a truck with a cover on it. At first, I aint think nothing of it. But the bitch went to acting nervous and jumped out and ran to the house." He blabbered.

"What did you do?" Shaq interrupted.

"I pulled off and doubled back. I had to see what the hype was about. I go around to the window and see Caesar counting money on the bed." Blue lied making sure to add extra emphasis on counting money on the bed. He lied because he didn't wanna make himself feel or look bad. Caesar was on every female trail he was on and succeeding. So he left the part out about seeing Janae top Caesar down.

"So let me get this shit right, you on a date with G-Money and Caesar people?" Smiley questioned.

"Yeah, and I know fosho cause I seen his Benz truck."

"So, what we gone do" Ralo spoke up

"What you think we gone do?" Smiley replied. "Handle up!"

Silence filled the room. This was the opportunity they all waited on. A lot of things in life was about timing and position. Doing things at the right time and being in the right position at that time. It was no way they were going to let this chance pass by. This was a business move to go to the next level and get established in the dope game. The streets were always hiring, it was just up to the person rather they were going to go out and get it. And just the little taste they had of the lifestyle from the shopping sprees, to clubbing with already established dope boys, was an addiction that only jail, or the grave could get rid of. They were already in love with the almighty dollar bill. And the root to all evil in the dope game is the dollar bill.

"Tonight, I gotta go to this councilman dinner with my pops. If yall handle that situation. Everything else will fall in line. My uncle here from Cali and gone show us how to cook it up and get it hard." Blue said.

Everybody exchanged looks and nodded their heads in agreement. What was understood doesn't need to be explained.

They all loaded up inside the F-150 and headed towards Caesar's new spot on 13th Street and Division. Before even getting in front of the house they saw a bunch of dope fiends scattered amongst the sidewalk, some were leaving, and some were standing in line outside the small house. They had the house front door moving like the free lunch line.

"Look, look, look." There go the Benz right there. Blue pointed as him, Shaq, Ralo, and Smiley drove past the house. Nobody spoke the truck just was filled with silence. While they all watched the small Benz behind the trucks dark tint.

After viewing what they needed to view off of 13th Street. Blue steered the truck to I-95 to head to Janae's townhouse. He knew in order for the plan to work he would need to show the guys both spots. They had all agreed earlier the move would be made at Janae's house. They didn't want any unwanted attention from the police in the neighborhood with another murder. It wouldn't be good for business. On the way to Janae's house the plan was sat in stone to lay on him at the house on 13th and wait to make the final move at Janaes house or wherever he would stop.

Pulling up to Janaes townhouse the sky was cloudy and grey. Light rumbles of thunder could be heard as the strong gust of wind penetrated the truck's windows making a whistling noise. The wind had the car cover on the red Benz truck showing the right side of the truck giving everybody in the F-150 a visual of Caesars shot up truck.

Everybody made some type of celebrative sound in the truck. And applauded Blue for the good homework he had done on getting the location and whereabouts of Caesar. This move alone solidified his spot as the leader of the crew. It showed everybody not only did he have resources from his family. But he had the mind to organize and direct a group and it was showing from the progress they were making.

After leaving Janae's townhouse they made it back to Blocka's house. Each one of them felt good that in only a short amount of time they were headed to the top. That's how the streets was up today and down tomorrow.

Entering the house Blocka observed they each had a mischievous grin on their faces. His street cleverness and prior conversation from earlier in the day with his son, led him to believe the problem Blue forementioned was either handled or about to be handled. So, he invited the 4 of the young men inside his home office.

Stepping inside his office, Blocka removed his Jalabah Islamic garb and hung it over the chair. As the 4 followed him into his office. They seen he was playing chess against himself in the middle of the oakwood and marble desk. Looking around the office they noticed a fully stocked bookshelf. But Think and Grow Rich (by Napoleon Hill), Get Anyone to Do Anything (by David J. Lieberman), The Four Agreements (by Don Miguel Ruiz), The 48 Laws of Power by Robert Greene stuck out the most being they were on his desk.

"Have a seat young brothers", Blocka instructed them gesturing towards the 4 chairs that sat in front of his desk. He leaned over his glass and marble chess set analyzing the board before picking up his rook and moving his king 2 blocks over indicating he was castling to protect the king.

"I'm proud of how yall been moving." Blocka said, looking each of them square in the eyes. "But just remember getting money and murder is like oil and water it doesn't mix. Never will and never have."

They all nodded their head and understood the advice he gave them during a time like this. Either he seen the way they were moving, or he knew the plan to execute Caesar tonight.

Blocka fired up a Cohiba and took a deep pull. "Always think before you move and never start what you can't finish."

Ring! Ring! Ring! Ring!

"I need you brothers to excuse me while I take this call." He spoke as he picked up the phone and the four exited his office.

The four were discussing tonight's plans until the sun was starting to set and they heard the alarm clock in the front of Blue's father house calling the Adhan the Islamic call to prayer. They all looked at one another and began to remove their shoes and socks to prepare for their cleansing before making Maghrib the sunset prayer for Muslims. When they finished, they all embraced and shared the Islamic greeting of As-Salamu alaykum (may peace be upon you).

Before Shaq, Ralo, and Smiley left. Blocka shared words of wisdom. "I love you brothers for the sake of Allah, and I want the same for you as I do for myself. Be careful and always remember Allah protects the believers." The 3 left with their game faces on, leaving Blocka and Blue to get ready for the councilman dinner.

Chapter 8

"Gentleman are you comfortable?" The driver asked. "You gentleman are dressed real spiffy." He complimented Blocka and Blue they were dressed in matching black tuxedos, and both had Bossalinie hats that was slightly cocked to the right.

His eyes found Blocka's through the reflection of the rearview mirror. "Thanks Jeffery", Blocka responded. For tonight's occasion he decided to go through one of his long-time friends' escort services. And hired a driver to drop them off and pick them up tonight.

Taking his eyes off the driver he fired up a Cohiba Cigar and started puffing as his eyes were staring out the window taking in the streets of Jacksonville. These last couple months a lot of robberies and murder were taking place in the name of cocaine. And Blocka was starting to reconsider backing his son's decision on being in the drug game. But with this dinner and if it went well this could be a life-changing political connection. It was all on their mindset. This dinner was not only for top Councilman of the city of Jacksonville but also judges, state attorneys, and different high ranking police officials would be present. This was a who knows who and somebody gathering.

The driver opened the backdoor to the Lincoln town car the father and son were escorted in, as the 2 exited the backseat. They both adjusted their bowties and lowered their Bossalinie's as they walked towards the entrance of the player's championship in Ponte Vedra. Judging by the parking lot of Benz's, BMW's, Porche's, and fleet of foreign cars. This area of town had to be for the rich and famous. Removing their Bossalinie's before entering.

"Welcome gentleman. First and last name please." One said, scanning the clipboard.

The two men stood at the entrance of the golf club lobby in black suits and white shirts. Blues eyes went to the devices inside their ears and his gaze slid down to the 9mm that were visibly showing under the suit jackets.

"Raheem Robins" Blocka said. "Welcome", one of the men said. Blocka smiled and then proceeded into the spacious plush lobby that was used for tonight's events. As Blue followed.

Entering the dinner instantly Blue seen a familiar face. He could never forget. It was none other than Vanessa Young the news reporter for News4Jax the local news station. And also, the news reporter who covered the story of G-Moneys murder. Blue grabbed a champagne flute from the tray of a server walking by and downed it nervously and grabbed another flute. Taking in the scenery he watched how all the different men carried themselves and how their postures and aura's showed power. He was stuck in a trance. Then Blocka whispered something in his ear observing how nervous he was.

"Anything you ever wanted to be in life, you can be it tonight. This damn dinner was $5,000 per plate. These are the type of friends we need in high places." Blocka whispered leaving Blue to mingle amongst the elite of Jacksonville.

Blue found himself a table and took a seat as he anticipated the night's events. If all went as planned, he would leave here with more power than he came with.

Blocka sat at the table with Mayor Johnson's assistant and 2 Duval County judges. He led the conversation on how the City of Jacksonville needed more programs for the youth. And how he'd just started a non-profit organization that had a mission to lower the conviction rate of juveniles, and also open a center that would teach the youth vocational skills. Such as resume' building, mock interviews for jobs, landscaping, and carpentry. Just to name a few. His charisma and words of choice had the entire table wanting to back him in everything he was saying.

   "So, who do you work for?" Judge Angela Walden spoke first.

   "Excuse me." Blocka responded.

   "Well, this was an invite only dinner and without invite we're talking 5 grand just to be sitting where you are. Somebody sent you, was it Janet Reed." She explained speaking of the Democratic candidate for the Mayor of Jacksonville next election.

   This was a majority Republican crowd and anyone who wasn't, after tonight would either be one or one of its supporters. This dinner takes place annually. And every year everybody smiled in each other's faces to get what they needed done for their own political gain. Then continued the rest of the year like they didn't know one another. So, everyone knew if you were here, you were either connected in the higher society, or you were one of the elites. Half of the politicians, lawyers, judges, officials, either went to college together or had some type of under the table association.

   So, Judge Walden's statement held weight at this table.

"Actually, I'm here on my own behalf, I never was into politics. But by me retiring I'm trying to give back to the community. Also, I'm interested in becoming a Republican."

Blocka mentioning becoming a Republican got everyone's attention. They were always trying to recruit to further their cause. They believed politics was about classism not racism. Only color they seen was green, for money.

"Retiring?" And may I ask from what, Mr? We never got your name." Mayor Johnsons assistant Cherry Wilson concurred.

"The name is Mr. Raheem Robins, and I was a contractor. Also, I own a bunch of properties Blocka responded. He knew they would check his name and credentials. And everything would come back clean through his corporations and many LLC's he cleaned his money through. But they wouldn't get any further than the names, all his companies were based outta Delaware, New Mexico or Wyoming. Where business owners were kept private due to its laws in each state.

"I see", Cherry expressed in a tone of satisfaction.

"So how about we get the Republican form and Mayor ballot for the next election." Judge Chelsea Moody spoke for the first time going in for the kill. The three did this every year they didn't give two fucks about Blocka's occupation. They just needed him to come correctly on the legality of things. They knew money when they seen it. And not only was he looking like money with the thousand-dollar tux. But he smelled like it also with every movement he was making wearing the Dolce and Gabbana for men.

"That sounds fine, but the election isn't until November if I'm not mistaken." Blocka mentioned.

"Your absolutely correct, we just tend to keep our aces in the hole, the mayors our guy and we need to have all voices secure ahead of time." Judge Walden confessed.

They were trained for situations as such. The three took turns speaking, giving each other eye contact letting the other know to speak. This was politics at its finest. Everyone here was for a purpose or had a hidden objective. And so did they.

"Favor for a favor, I see." Blocka stated making eye contact with the 3 beautiful black women.

"Absolutely", with a donation to Mayor Johnsons Campaign it's not too many problems or places we can't reach. The mayor's assistant stated while motioning her eyes to the 2 judges indicating they were down as well.

Blocka said nothing as he reached inside his tuxedo and pulled out his checkbook. Then begin writing a check for $10,000 to the mayor's campaign. He knew this was the starting point he needed to get where he wanted to be. There was never something for nothing.

At the table adjacent to Blocka and the 3 powerful women. Sat Blue and a young man with the build of a athlete or someone in the service. He kept a close eye on his son watching him out the corner of his eyes. From the looks of things and his body language Blocka could tell he was nervous as hell. "Tighten up now" he said under his breath before the flute touched his lips.

Sitting at the table was Blue and Shawn Walden who was employed by the Jacksonville Sheriff's Office (JSO). Every year he would attend the event with his mother. So, they both had something in common they were led here by their parents not themselves. So, neither wanted to be here. Seeing he was alone from the rest of the event; how he would usually be every year before. He decided to join Blue at the table.

"Must be your first time here? Don't think I have ever seen you around. Shawn exclaimed.

"Not at all, this not my type of scene. I'm here on my father's behalf", Blue said.

"Sounds like the story of my life," Shawn exhaled a deep breath "Nice Tux."

"Thanks", You don't look so bad yourself. Blue complimented him on the cranberry Dolce suit he wore.

Shawn was no fool and knew the name of the game at these type events. His mother was Angela Walden. So, him and Blue was here pretty much for the same reasons to build political connections and gain anything useful they could.

So, Shawn got straight to the point. His criminology experience from working at the Duval Pre-trial Detention Facility/County Jail. And being a task force officer for the last year or so. He knew a street nigga when he seen one. He could also see the nervousness in Blue's eyes and his body movements. He stuck out like a lion at a petting zoo.

"Who you run with Henry Mann?" Shawn asked.

"What?" Blue screwed up his face. He couldn't believe a name like that was mentioned at this table. Henry Mann was a major boss player moving major weight in the streets. He was known in the city for supplying his hood and also keeping the people fed.

"Never heard of him", Blue shot back.

"Is that right", Shawn chuckled noticing how he had Blue in the hot seat. He was making him uncomfortable, and it was showing.

"Yeah", Blue shook his head up and down.

"You know I met your kind before, just not under these circumstances, so I'm impressed."

"And what's my kind?"

"You tryna find your way, but you don't know rather you wanna be a robber or a hustler." Shawn fired back.

Blue remained quiet he recognized the bald truth in Shawn statements. He just couldn't figure out how he read him so well.

"I been doing this for the past 6 years. I got 5 years working in the county jail and a year on the task force working the streets." Shawn explained to him.

The impact of Shawn's words of him being a officer of the law hit Blue like a ton of bricks. He couldn't believe he was holding a conversation with a pig. He stood on his feet and Shawn did the same.

He attempted to speak, but Shawn waved him off. "No need to speak, just remember people like you need people like me on your team."

As Blue turned to leave the table, Shawn stopped him in his tracks. "Learn to look at things as they are, not as your emotions points them."

(At F.M.B New Headquarters on 13th and Division)

Sitting at the table was Caesar, Rich, Ronnie and Demon. They all sat around the table counting up today's profit than rubber banded each stack of bills in 1 band a piece.

"Damn I wish Gizzle was here to see this shit." Rich mentioned as he knocked down a double shot of Gin. He was thinking bout G-Money who nickname was also Gizzle.

Ronnie was leaned forward, puffing on his kush filled dutch. As he counted the last stack of bills and placed them inside the duffle bag.

"Don't worry sooner or later it's gone come to the light. My Me-ma used to always say. What's in the dark will always come to the light. "Ronnie said waving his pistol from side to side that had its own flashlight attached.

"Man put that gun down, we focused on getting this money. Life is too short and on top of that I gotta baby on the way." Caesar gave the news to the crew he was having a baby on the slide.

A roar of laughter erupted inside the small living room. Everybody had caught his drift immediately.

"From Whom?" Rich asked.

"Janae", Caesar replied.

"Damn G-Money's cousin brah!" Rich snapped and picked up the Gin bottle and drunk straight from it. "Ummm", He groaned when the white liquor scorched his throat.

"I know, shit crazy cause it just started as business and one night shit got outta hand."

"Just respect her and don't do her wrong on the strength. You know that's like G-sister." Rich said seriously.

"I'm already knowing", Caesar fired right back feeling uncomfortable now. He knew he had to tell the crew sooner or later. "I'm bout to head out" He announced grabbing the duffle bag to drop it off to Janaes house than headed out the door.

Rain poured down and thunder could be heard echoing through the night's skies.

Shaq mumbled to the lyrics of Trick Daddy "Bout my money" under his breath, exhaling a thick cloud of the loud smoke. He was leaned back in the driver's seat of the F-150. Ralo sat quietly on the passenger side with Smiley in the backseat behind him. They were parked at the top of 13th Street, about 3 houses down from the spot Caesar was at.

"I'm saying though why we can't just run up in that muthafucka." Smiley suggested, so anxious he couldn't stop his leg from shaking. As he held the AK-47 in his arms like a newborn baby.

"Nawl, Smiley, It's a time and place for everything. We do something here that's gone defeat the plan. We can't shit where we sleep." Shaq voiced.

"Caesar in there, that's the car right there." Ralo pointed at the Benz.

"Look like him right there" Smiley stated seeing somebody running to the Benz tryna dodge the rain drops.

"Huhn." Shaq hit the backwood extra hard, then passed it to Ralo. Before he cranks the trucks ignition back up.

He looked down the street as he saw the coupe and seen Caesar sitting in the driver seat. "Yeah that's him right there." Shaq said, leaning back in the driver's seat, as the headlights passed by hoping he didn't see them.

Seeing the coupe turn on Kings Road and head towards downtown Jacksonville to I-95. They followed behind the Benz making sure to stay a couple cars behind.

Caesar reached down and checked his phone as he veered onto I-95 West ramp heading towards the westside of Jacksonville.

Once Shaq seen he was heading towards Janae's house. He sped past the Benz. He didn't want to be noticed following him. So, he decided to beat Caesar there. It was a gamble, but it was worth it. He accelerated as he felt the truck slide on the wet highway.

"What the fuck you doing?" Smiley panicked looking out the back window of the truck seeing they were leaving the Benz through the rain.

"Pass that blunt to him so he can shut up", Shaq responded. While Ralo stuck his left hand over the seat and passed the blunt clutching the Glock with his right.

The weather was a tad bit worse than it was on the northside. It was raining so bad that the road wasn't even visible out of the windshield. As Ralo, Shaq, and Smiley awaited Caesar to pull in front of Janae's townhouse. They were across the street parked. The Trick Daddy cd www.thug.com had ended and nothing but silence filled the truck and the sounds of burning trees could be heard as the 3 of them smoked backwood after backwood.

Patiently waiting across the street, the loud smoke burned their eyes. As they sat inside the truck hot boxing trying to breathe through the thick clouds of smoke. They all sat staring at the townhouse watching it's front window. They'd just seen the porch light cut on. And believed this was a indication Caesar was near.

By Allah, I gotta make this one count, Smiley thought to himself, slowly exhaling the smoke from his nose. He placed the backwood between his lips, then cracked his knuckles one at a time. This was all business, no feelings were involved. So Smiley was tryna put his mind in the right perspective to handle business.

Ralo looked down at the Benz noticing its headlights shining inside the trucks interior. "Yo that's the nigga right there. Damn we slippin!"

"You think he noticed?" Smiley asked his right hand was clutching the door handle his left hand was flexing into the grooves of the handle on the A-K.

"I don't know, I don't think so." Shaq replied, still looking at the small Benz. "If he tries to pull off I'ma box him in, yall hop out and handle up. Make it count."

"Say less", Smiley replied while nodding his head. He released the door handle now having it cracked slightly, hearing the rain drip through the top of the door.

"Be on point it's bout to go down." Shaq said excitedly as he seen the dome light inside the Benz cut on.

"I got him." Smiley stated with a heartless notion at the same time snatching back the lever on his AK-47 click! Clack!

Smiley popped out the rear passenger door and slipped out slowly. He motioned for Ralo to do the same. Crouches down low like a tiger, he tip-toed around the front of the truck and slowly made his way toward the back of the Benz. Ralo crisscrossed behind him, slowly making his way to the driver's side.

"Damn it's raining cats and dogs." Caesar thought as the rain drops poured down hard sounding like pebbles were dropping on the windshield. He reached down onto the passenger floorboard and grabbed the duffle bag, so worried about the money he failed to watch his surroundings. This one mistake would prove to be fatal.

Caesar had the duffle bag clutched in his right arm as he stuck one foot out at a time preparing to run to the porch of the townhouse. Soon as he stood straight up and turned around to make sure the car door was secured. He saw a dark figure through his peripheral vision and turned his head quickly. His eyes damn near popped out of his head when he saw Ralo creeping on the side of the car. "Nooooo!!" He shouted at the top of his lungs when the Glock barrel appeared in plain view.

He never got the chance to finish his last statement. Smiley was already squeezing the trigger.

Whop! Whop! Whop! Whop! Whop!

The recoil of the assault rifle was so powerful. Smiley missed the first 3 shots and the last 2 hit him in the right shoulder, causing him to spin around and land on his back.

Ralo approached Caesar who was now lying on his back as a gush of blood sprung from his shoulder looking like a small pipe had busted. The sight of so much blood causes his mind to go blank in a trance-like state. Until he seen Smiley come around the front of the Benz and snatched the duffle bag off of Caesars right arm. Aaaggghhhrrr! Caesar begins to panic upon viewing his last options in life and from the pain of the shoulder wound.

"What you waiting on?" Smiley asked Ralo seeing he was standing over Caesar holding his glock at his side.

Caesar trembled from the reality of seeing firsthand death was around the corner. His fate was sealed already, and there was nothing he could do to stop it. "Our father with John in heaven." Caesar begin to pray in a low audible tone that only him and his maker could hear. Before the ending to his life came.

Boom! Boom! Boom!

The 3 hot slugs from Ralos Glock ripped through Caesars' face and exploded out the back of his neck. The force from the blast turned him slightly on his side. As Smiley placed the kutta to the back of his head making sure the job was well done.

Whop! Whop!

Smiley and Ralo ran back to the truck and hopped back inside. Glancing up and down the block. The houses that were once pitch black was now lit up. The silhouettes of the people who lived inside were now standing at the windows. As they pulled off into the darkness of the night.

Judge Walden and Blocka were making small talk outside of the golf club under the car port awaiting their drivers to pull up. Blue and Shawn was exchanging looks. But never said a word the rest of the night. The dinner was long over and only the elite of the guest list remained inside. The Lincoln town car pulled up and Blocka's driver exited the car and opened the back door. Before they entered Shawn handed Blue a card, that read P.A.L standing for Police Athletic League. The card showed Shawn was a boxing trainer for the youth. Blue scowled him and snatched the card away as he entered the back of the town car. Blocka watched the entire scene play out. Before they left, he said his good byes to everyone who were now awaiting their cars to arrive. And got in the car as it pulled back off. The drizzle what started before turned into an unexpected storm.

The windshield wipers were going fast in an attempt to stop the rain from covering the windshield. But failed as the rain kept pouring. Blocka looked at Blue and seen he had a look of displeasure.

Blue shrugged "I just aint feeling that police officer", He was speaking of Shawn who was Judge Angela Walden's son.

Blocka chuckled you mean to tell me that boy was a police officer who gave you his card?"

"Yes sir", Blue smiled thinking his father was seeing things his way.

"I should slap the hell out of you right now!" Blocka snapped.

Blue looked down at his shoes hating to have disappointed his father.

"Son, You….. You" he stammered.

Blocka loosened his bowtie and struck the lighter to light his Cohiba cigar. He exhaled a cloud of smoke. Thinking before he spoke.

"Son listen, in this game of life it's like chess. It's not about who got the most pieces it's bout who got the strongest pieces. With those two pieces there we can take over the city."

"But in the game daddy it's rules I got to live by, and no snitching is one of them. If I'm doing business with a cop that's like snitching." Blue voiced.

"Rule number #1, look it aint no rules. Sacrifices gotta be made and you gotta do anything to win." Blocka explained.

"So, you saying I should work with police?" Blue asked.

"No, I'm not saying that I'm saying you should stay open minded and use him if need be. In that game you need people like him." Blocka answered.

Upon Blue hearing his father's words that sounded similar to Shawns he begins to think. He didn't have to work with him he could just use him for information. So, he kept the card and placed it inside of his wallet.

Chapter 9

(The Following Morning)

After offering the Muslim morning prayer of Fajr. Blocka and Blue were relaxing as they both were sipping Cuban coffee, and their eyes were glued to News4Jax Channel 4. News stations all over the city were covering the latest events of Jacksonville Florida. The breaking news headline flashed as Vanessa Young appeared on the tv screen and began speaking.

"It was just announced that 29-year-old black male Caesar Barner was found dead this morning in front of this townhouse. As you can see family and friends have gathered at the scene of what JSO is saying is a robbery gone bad. They are still investigating so we are waiting for more details. But I did get to speak with a neighbor who said they seen a white pickup fleeing the scene, after 2 people were seen running away shortly after gunshots were heard. If anybody have any details about the individuals who were in this truck, or about the truck you will remain anonymous if you call 1800-crime-stoppers."

"Look at this shit" Blocka said to himself.

"He drunk the last of his Cuban coffee, then sparked up a Cohiba cigar. After taking a long drag and releasing a cloud of smoke, he lounged in his chair and closed his eyes. He massaged his temple and thought about a day he would always remember.

Jan 25th, 1975

It was a typical night in Harlem. But not for Blocka, Sunny, and Supreme. They were 3 young bulls riding round in Sunny's momma van looking for ZeeLo. He was a neighborhood hustler who had Harlem locked down with the heroin he was getting from Italians. Blocka and his team had made it up in their minds it was time they start getting money. First, they had to get ZeeLo out the way, and that was their mission for tonight.

After making a right turn on a 116th and Lenox, the black minivan crept down the block at a calm 10 mph when they approached the corner of 117th Blocka spotted Zeelo. This skinny man was accompanied by white woman who was handing him money and quickly walked off. After Sunny eased the minivan to a halt, Blocka slid back the sliding door on the minivan as Blocka and Supreme hopped out.

"Yo Zee", Blocka called him by his nickname.

"Who dat" He called out as he squinted his eyes trying to make an attempt to see who was calling him.

Before he uttered another word. Blocka and Supreme both had .357's pointed at his face.

Looking past the guns seeing it was Blocka and Supreme. He begins to beg for his life.

Terrified he looked as he began to beg Blocka and Supreme.

"Man, please spare my life, what you want money? I can give you whatever you need, please, please." He begged.

"Nawl, when the reaper come it's yo time" Blocka said in a cold voice.

Boom! Boom! Boom! Boom!

Both of their 357's came to life as each bullet struck Zeelo in the head knocking off chunks like an ax would do a pumpkin.

After climbing back inside the minivan they left a lifeless body on the curve. From then on, they began to make money and took over Harlem. Until one day 2 officers showed up at Sunny's momma house and questioned her about the whereabouts of her van on January 25th. Of course, she said Sunny had the van. And Sunny became a nervous wreck. Seeing Sunny's actions under pressure led Blocka and Supreme to plan Sunny's demise.

They got Sunny on the rooftop of one of the tall project buildings and sent him sky diving. It hunted Blocka for years. But it saved him prison time. And he made it this far in the game where he could actually say he made it out. But he regretted killing his best friend.

From that day forward he made many other sacrifices his heart didn't agree with. But he always knew to trust his head and never his heart.

Back to the Present

"Daddy, you good?"

"Huh?" Blocka responded.

He looked up and saw his son standing in front of him. Blue was pointing toward the burning cigar stub that was between his thumb and index finger, almost burning him.

Blocka put out the cigar and wiped the ashes away from his bathrobe. "I must've blacked out for a minute." He returned his gaze to his son. He never wanted his son to be a gangsta or be a part of his criminal lifestyle. He sent him to nice schools, brought nice things and made all the sacrifices so he didn't have to be in the streets. But none of these things could overcome the Robins bloodline that ran through his veins. He was destined to be a gangsta.

"So, son what's next?"

"Everything is going according to plan", Blue answered while staring at the tv looking at Vanessa Young. He was amazed at the fact how small the world could actually be and how connected his world was. Here he was staring at the same woman on tv, that he was in the same room with last night.

"You need to call them brothers, and make sure they get rid of that truck." Blocka said.

"I been calling them all morning; all their phones are off. I hope they aint in jail. Blue said while pressing the call button on his cell phone. Still receiving an answering machine. He hung up looking at his daddy for answers.

Blocka leaned back in the chair. "That's the reason we moving the way we moving. We gotta have political pieces in the right political places, and that way we can always be two steps ahead of everybody."

Ding! Dong! Ding! Dong!

The doorbell could be heard through the spacious living room. Blue and his father made eye contact, as Blue rushed to go to the peep hole. He looked through it viewing it was Smiley, Ralo, and Shaq.

Opening the door to let them enter the house. He seen they were all dressed to impress. Smiley wore a button up Polo color shirt that was all white with the big green Lacoste Gator and white shorts with the matching all white Air Force Ones. Shaq had on a Jordan red, black and white Bulls jersey #23 with some Jordan gym shorts and the black and red 12's. Ralo had on a red Fendi sweater with the big double F in the middle and Fendi stitched at the bottom of the sweater in white with some red and white checkerboard pants and a pair of sheep skins dress shoes.

Blue sat in the doorway sizing the 3 up and down with his eyes. This wasn't the look he expected. They were fresh off a murder and looked as if they were ready for a fashion show. Reading his facial expression Smiley broke the silence.

"What, a cat got yo tongue", Smiley asked reaching into his pocket throwing Blue six bands.

"I aint know what yall had going on, yall seen the news?" Blue answered smirking as he counted the money.

"What news?" Smiley replied nonchalantly.

Peeping Smileys facial expression and the way Ralo and Shaq was acting and moving. Blue could tell they weren't up to speak on what happened last night. He knew Smiley didn't agree with his decision to go with his dad to the dinner. So, he assumed that was the issue. But seeing they were in a different rental, and nobody was dwelling on yesterday, he just went with the flow. The best secrets were kept untold anyways.

Later that day . . .

Caesar mothers house Ms. Judy was packed with family and friends from the neighborhood. Being true to the black culture, each of them arrived with some type of soul food pot, attempting to ease the pain of her losing her only son. In the front yard Ronnie, Demon, and Rich were chain smoking big blunts of weed and thinking who killed Caesar.

"I think it was Hector." Ronnie propounded.

"Hector?" Rich questioned.

"Who else would do him dirty like that? He said it was a Spanish dude who ran down on him at the Silver Foxx." Ronnie explained.

"It's just weird they got the drop at Janae's house, when nobody knows where she stayed at. Even I didn't know. Rich expressed.

Ronnie took a deep breath, and then wiped away the tear that fell from his right eye. "Janae told me before Caesar left this morning, he left a note saying he would be back, so somebody knew where he was headed at." Staring into Rich and Demon's eyes thinking one thing.

"Hell naw!" Rich interjected shaking his head from side to side. Everybody knows Janae is solid as they come. She wouldn't set him up even if she wasn't pregnant."

"You damn right but somebody know something."

Demon just sat there puffing on the blunt as his trigger finger started itching. He wasn't much for talking cause he was born with a speech impediment. So, he was all bark no bite.

Scurrrrrr!

The sound of tires screeching could be heard down 16th Street causing Ronnie, Rich, and Demon to point their desert eagles at the Maserati as it pulled in front of Ms. Judy's house. Until they noticed a distraught Janae. She was looking a mess as she quickly exited her homegirl Felicia's Maserati. Her day was a living hell after finding Caesar dead. She was forced to go to JSO's memorial building. Where she was interrogated like she was the killer. She just wanted to vent in peace. So, she came straight here where she knew everyone would be. Soon as she recognized Rich she ran into his arms, as he embraced her in a brotherly hug, and she wept on his broad left shoulder. She was hurt about Caesar's death but was in more pain at the fact. She was going to have to raise her unborn child by herself without a father. Just thinking of it made the cries more hysterical.

Ms. Judy called all family and friends inside to join in prayer. Throughout the small 3-bedroom house only thing could be heard is sniffing and silent cries.

"Lord, I know you will not put nothing on us that we can't handle, but this is going to be a tough one. I ask that you forgive our sin's as we forgive the ones who have sinned against us. And may those who committed these acts that brought us here today be punished and may your will be done in Jesus' name Aman." Ms. Judy concluded.

"Aman" everybody repeated in unison.

After everybody made prayer, they began to fix their plates of food and the immediate family made funeral arrangements for Caesar's funeral.

Back outside Janae, Felicia, Rich, Demon, and Ronnie all were now standing around Felicia's Maserati. The guys were back smoking blunts and the ladies held clear plastics cups drinking Remy Martin. Blasting through the speakers was Trick Daddy's Thug Holiday. The song was a perfect fit for the moment. Only thing Rich could think about is how in the matter of some weeks G-Money and Caesar could be dead. This whole year felt like he was in a dream. But he knew he wasn't. He needed answers and he needed them fast. Without a plug and Caesar dead tomorrow wasn't promised. Only thing he could smell, and taste was revenge. He had some big shoes to fulfill taking leadership of the crew. But first thing first he needed to find out how and why was Caesar caught slipping at Janae's house.

   Rich took another pull on his blunt. "I'ma ask you this one time and one time only." He said more in a accusing tone rather than asking. "How did whoever kill Caesar know where he was?"

   Janae shook her head in disbelief. "How the fuck am I supposed to know!!" So, the fuck is you sayin? Huh! Richard! "Janae snapped calling him by his government name."

   "All I'm sayin is, if you don't know, somebody got to know something", Rich shot back.

   Ronnie glanced at Rich and returned his gaze to Janae. "I'm tellin you she aint got nothing to do with it. But let me ask you this did you ever bring anybody to your spot?" Ronnie questioned Janae.

   That's when it hit Janae like a freight train going full speed. And the tears begin to fall, and her body begin to shake profusely. Suddenly she begins to vomit everything she ate. Down on both knees she begins to try to speak but no words came out. Felicia tried to console her. But she rejected swatting her hands away. Rich, Demon, and Ronnie picked her up placing her on the passenger side of the Maserati.

"Take your time don't rush to get it out." Ronnie wiped away the tears she was shedding.

"Okay, okay, okay, Janae pleaded in a whiny voice. I, I, met a man after G-Money's funeral at the Shells on Kings Road and we went on a date and he picked me up in a, "before she could finish her sentence, she broke down crying again.

Before anyone could stop him Rich lunged at Janae grabbing her by the throat and begin choking her. "You bitch, you bit." He barely got the words out as he tried to choke the life out of her. Ronnie and Demon both grabbed a hand a piece and restrained Rich the best they could. All Janae did was cried even more. She had everyone's attention awaiting her to release more details.

Finally, when Janae and Rich calmed down. She begins to speak again in a low voice. "I met him at the Texaco on Kings Road, he was in a white F-150 we went out to eat and he dropped me off. That's the only man ever came to my house besides Caesar and that's on my unborn."

"What's his name?" Demon said clear as day. Causing everyone to look at him. He wasn't a good speaker but spoke those words with perfection.

"B, is the only name he gave me, but I got his number." Janae said pulling out her phone.

"Call him, let's see if he pick up." Rich demanded.

Janae complied and placed the call on speaker phone. And was let down when they all heard the operator saying, "this number has been changed or disconnected." Beep! Beep!

Chapter 10

A Week Later . . .

It was around 12:30pm the day of Caesar's funeral, the weather outside of Holmes and Glover Funeral Home was a scorching 101 degrees. The heat from the sun and the dark clothing the funeral attendees were wearing was attracting the sun rays causing everybody to sweat.

A long line of cars was lined up and down Golfair Blvd, and inside everyone hand was an obituary for Caesar. At the head of the line was a Cadillac hearse which was waiting to be loaded with Caesar's silver-plated casket, and directly behind the hearse was the luxurious black Benz sprinter van for the immediate family.

Rich was standing behind the sprinter van consoling Janae. Ever since She revealed the information about her date with a mysterious man who she only knew by "B". She had been taking Caesar's death harder than the rest of the family and friends. She was even considering having an abortion. In her mind she did not want to relive the pain for the rest of her life seeing Caesar's child. Rich was wiping the tears away from Janae's face trying to keep her makeup and eyeliner intact. When someone walked up behind him and placed their hand on his shoulder. He looked at the feminine hand on his shoulder. He released Janae and spun around seeing the hand belonged to Angel.

"Rich, how you doin today?" Angel asked with a fraudulent concern sizing him up like she wanted to eat him. He extended his right hand.

"I'm doing good, I don't think we met before." Rich replied as he locked hands with Angel.

"Well, you prolly don't remember me, last time we seen each other was at Club 904 in the V.I.P. Caesar was special to me we had a lot of good times together." She said swirling her tongue around her lips.

Rich glanced over his shoulder at Janae hoping she didn't hear their conversation. But before he knew it. She was up in the Angels personal space grilling her.

"What was said?" Janae spat close enough Angel could smell the winter fresh bubble gum she was chewing.

"And who was you?" Angel shot back.

"His fiancé and child's mother." Janae said rubbing her stomach.

Girl ain't nobody bout to take care of you, I aint know people still fake pregnancies."

Before she can get another sentence out. WHAP! Janae struck her with her fist balled up connecting with her bottom lip, causing her busted lip to bleed instantly. Rich stepped in and grabbed an Angel taking her away from the other funeral goers who were now watching the show.

"Period!!" Janae snapped at Angel who was now in the air as Rich carried her away while she yelled and screamed all type of obscenities.

Once Rich was down the street where a majority of the cars parked, he placed Angel on her feet. "Look you need to come back around at a later time. This is supposed to be a time of peace. That back there was uncalled."

"What! You really gonna sit up here and play in my face like you ain't see her hit me." Angel's voice was full of rage.

"I don't got anything to do with that, that's who she says she is so she got rights. If you were who you say you were we would know you." Rich cracked his knuckles and gritted his teeth.

"You acting like you gonna do something to me, the fuck!" Angel snapped. Rich just shrugged his shoulders and calmly walked off leaving her alone and headed back towards the Funeral Home.

As the pallbearers exited the Funeral Home and began taking Caesar's casket to the hearse. Rich made it back just in time to the Benz Sprinter with the rest of the immediate family.

"Where's she at?" Janae asked soon as Rich sat down next to her in the spacious sprinter van.

Rich held up his left hand, stopping her mid-sentence. "It's a time and place for everything and now it's not the time."

The procession line of cars pulled up to the Restlawn graveyard on Edgewood and Moncrief. Upon Caesar's request he wanted his going away to be quick as possible. So, the family held his Funeral services at his gravesite.

Everybody stood around the grave where Caesar would spend the rest of his existence on earth. Watching as his casket was lowered into the ground. Cries and mourns were heard from his family and Ms. Judy. Rich, Ronnie and Demon stood erect with their trench coats and desert Eagles tucked. It all seemed like Deja vu all over again.

Everything just was good a couple months ago. Now it seemed this life had a curse on them. They shed tears behind the dark shades. But they understood the streets and knew it was 2 sides to every coin. Only thing was on their minds was to get back.

At the House of Pain . . . .

Blue was standing in front of the "House of Pain" waiting on his Uncle Doc to show up. Just like Blocka said he was late. He was supposed to be there at noon, but now it was going on 4:30 PM. It had been a long week seemed like. The police were adamant about finding the truck involved in Caesar's murder and put out a $5000 reward. Which made the trio of Smiley, Ralo, and Blue lay low. Word was buzzing around the neighborhood that nobody was supplying the free basers and snorters which was driving some to rehab and some to drinking beer. Before word spread it to outsiders outside the neighborhood. Blue had to react. And that's what brought him to meeting up with his Uncle Doc who was never on time.

Suddenly, a Yellow Cab pulled up at the corner and blue waved it down how he'd seen Blocka do it in New York. And to his surprise it worked. When the cab pulled in front of the "House of Pain". He' seen his uncle in the back seat.

"Unc!" Blue called out excited.

"What's shakin nephew", Doc called out as he exited the cab with a black book bag."

"Not much we've been waiting on you since 12 somethin."

"Well, I'm here that's all that matters. I'on got all day let's get to the business." Doc fast talked Blue.

Back in the house, in the kitchen Doc opened the book bag and begin to pull out different size jars. It was like he had a jar for every size extra small, small, medium, large, and extra-large. Afterwards he pulled out a small yellow box of arm and hammer baking soda and a digital scale.

"Where's the snow?" Doc asked.

"Huh?" Blue, Smiley, and Ralo questioned looking at him loss of the lingo of another nickname for cocaine often used by pimps.

"The goddamn cocaine man! Yall muthafuckas actin weird." Doc said skeptically peeking out the kitchen blinds. No matter where he went it was a habit of his. And it's how he survived on the run for so long.

The 3 both shifted in place until Smiley took the initiative to open the oven and pulled out the kilo of cocaine. Which he tried to hand to Doc like it was nothing major.

Upon viewing Smiley with a kilo of coke. Sweat beads instantly appeared on Doc's forehead. He had dealt with different amounts of cocaine over his years. But it wasn't an everyday thing to be passing around 1008 grams. Blue noticed how nervous he was and decided to speak since he was the one who actually knew him of some sort.

"You good Unc? You need some water?"

"Ugh, ugh, yeah I just need time to make sure I'm not tripping." Doc stuttered as he sat down at the kitchen table watching Smiley still holding the brick.

Smiley tossed it on the kitchen table causing Doc to jump up like he was running from the white square wrapped in plastic with the Cuban Flag stamp on the front side.

They all burst into laughter except Doc. He was looking at them crazy. He couldn't wrap his mind around how these young dudes were throwing around a life sentence like it was nothing. 36 ounces, 1008 grams, 1 kilogram of coke however you wanted to name it would get you a long time in the feds, Doc thought.

"Yall got a hammer or something?" Doc asked.

"Naw, Unc, what you need a hammer for?" Blue questioned back.

Doc exhaled frustratedly. He disliked showing somebody something and be asked questions. He saw a glock on the counter and pointed at it for Ralo to hand it to him. Ralo was looking crazy until he snapped. "Gimme the damn gun!" Ralo complied looking nervous thinking the worse.

Once he retrieved the Glock, he ejected the clip first and removed the bullets from the chamber then reinserted the clip. He removed the compressed kilo of cocaine that was shaped like a large brick and began to use the Glock as it was a hammer and breakdown the white square. The fumes instantly arose in the air. Seeing their first kilo being bust down made the three smile like a fat kid at the candy store.

After Doc broke the coke into small chunks, he began to weigh it in different amounts placing it on the digital scale and separating it in small piles.

"Turn the stove on medium." Doc stated to no one in particular. Grabbing the largest jar he brought with him known as the thousand jar. And went to the sink and added barely enough hot water to fill up the bottom of the jar, before he poured a little bit out. Placing the jar on the stove until he seen the water boiling, he then added the baking soda which quickly dissolved. Once he did this, he added the cocaine and watched as it mixed with the baking soda turning into liquid form. Seeing this Blue, Smiley and Ralo crowded around the stove in amazement as they watched the crack cocaine being cooked for the first time. They began to stare intensely inside the jar, before he removed it off the stove and took the jar to the sink. Turning on the cold water he placed his index and middle finger under the water faucet and started splashing cold water inside the jar. This made the liquid instantly start to stick to the bottom. Seeing it sank to the bottom he poured the excess water off the mixture of cocaine and baking soda. And place the jar on the counter to let it lock up and form into the cookie shaped circle he was looking for.

Blue, Smiley, and Ralo watched astonishingly how he had just performed. He made it look like he was on the Martha Stewart show. The kitchen was looking like a chef was prepping for a meal. Only difference was this wasn't food this was coke. And they were getting ready to feed the streets.

After each of them took turns cooking the new recipe they'd been taught. Doc also showed them how to recook the cookies if they didn't form correctly. It was like a culinary arts class.

Once they were finished cooking the kitchen was looking like a bakery with all the different sized crack cocaine cookies awaiting to dry. They each gave Doc a $1000 apiece for the new knowledge they had learned. Seeing it would make them more than they imagined, it was a well worth it investment. The four parted ways leaving the

House of Pain to get ready for what they all had been waiting for.

Leaving the funeral, arriving back at her townhouse Janae felt the pain from losing Caesar all over again. Felicia had let her borrow her Maserati since the police seized Janae's Benz and Caesar's truck. She sat behind the steering wheel letting her eyes cry waterfalls. All she could think of is the last moments in their last argument. She regretted the things she said and wished she could take them back. She shook her head back and forth telling herself this could not be true. She forced herself outside of the car and made it inside the house. Today was one of the worst days of her life. She felt like giving up, but her bundle of joy was all she had left of Caesar. She took two aspirins and poured a glass of Moscato. She opened her laptop and opened the Google browser and typed in names that start with a B in the Kings Road area in Jacksonville Florida. A list of thousands of names, pictures, and addresses appeared on the Dell laptop. Feeling the pain pills kicking in and the feeling of revenge alone was enough to bring her to an orgasm. As she sat scrolling with the sinister smile on her face. One way or another, she cried so somebody else had to cry was how she was feeling, and it was stuck in her mind forever.

Chapter 11

In the kitchen at the House of Pain. Ralo, Blue, and Smiley sat at the kitchen table with a razor blade and dinner plate with a circle shaped cookie of crack. That they each were cutting off different sizes of rocks to be sold. The first Ralo was going to give samples out to let the customers know what they were buying.

It was around 7:30 AM in the morning when Ralo pulled up to Tom's Store that sat on the corner of 12th and Palafox. A group of store customers awaited the store owner's arrival to get there early morning cigarettes, scratch offs, groceries, and beer. Ralo hopped out the black suburban with its dark tint with a bag full of crack. The crowd froze seeing all the different shaped butter colored crack rocks. Ralo smiled a smile of power. Looking at the lustful gaze in each of their eyes, made him feel like he was on top of the world. He reached inside the small zip lock bag and grabbed a handful. Then began passing rocks out like candy at a Halloween party.

"Damn this shit thick" One of the people in the group told Ralo looking at how thick the rocks were.

"Yeah I know." He said arrogantly." Shop open at the two-story greenhouse over on 13th Street. "This on me next time bring your money it's plenty more where that came from."

Just by word-of-mouth customers quickly came knocking at the door with fists full of money. It was only 8 something in the morning and a bunch of cracked things could be seen walking up the street trying to find the new crack spot in the hood. It wasn't hard to find from the people they've been seen walking up and leaving with smiles. In the last 30 to 45 minutes, they had stopped counting The Dirty money at 5000 and begin putting it in a black trash bag. They each sat back relishing the feeling of being paid with ease. This is how it felt to be a boss. Each of them felt a rush from the instant success they seen in just a couple of months.

  Right up the street Rich and Demon sat in front of the house on 13th and division and watched the House of Pain which was between 13th and McMillan and 13th and Palafox. So they can see all the heavy traffic. But once they start to see familiar faces who were usual customers of theirs. Caused them to pay attention. And with every second they paid attention the more vex they became. It looked as if they were losing the stronghold they once had over the neighborhood. With Caesar dead they had no connection to Hector. So therefore, this caused their customers to roam freely. By Blue, Smiley, and Ralo opening up shop at a time like this was a chess move. Business is all about supply and demand. You have to be able to give people what they need when they need it. Right now, Rich couldn't cause they didn't have any coke. The feud with Hector made it hard for business. They had been locked in with Hector for the past 24 months and expected the connection to grow stronger. In deep thought and still watching the House of Pain. Rich called out to old man Odis. Since the incident with him and G-Money getting shot he was back to normal.

  "Odis!!" Rich called out the car window at Odis who was cleaning the yard.

  "Talk to me?" Old man Odis answered.

"Huh, take this dub and see what they got going on down there." Rich instructed old man Odis handing him a twenty-dollar bill and pointed in the House of Pain direction. He was frustrated and couldn't take not knowing what was going on any longer.

Old man Odis made the short walk with pride. He had been detoxing off crack since Caesar died. And loyalty lied with Rich so he never planned on buying anything. Until they got back in business. But Rich telling him to go was like an invitation to paradise. It was shown at every step he took towards his destination.

When making it to the front of the House of Pain. He felt his body going through changes. He believed it to be a rush from no one he was about to get high. Making it up to the front door he began to tap lightly, hearing whoever was behind the door was very close.

Smiley hearing the door got up and opened the door. When he seeing it was an old man Otis his heart sank to the floor. This was the same man who got shot with G money. He wondered if he could recognize him now. The entire scene replayed in his mind. Shaking the thoughts, he spoke quickly.

"What you need old times?" Smiley stated trying to feel the old man out.

But Odis didn't say a word, he just handed him a twenty. Smiley shut the door quickly and let Ralo and Blue know what was happening.

"You won't believe who at the door?!" Smiley pointed.

"Who?" Blue and Ralo asked, not wanting to guess.

"The man who got shot with G-Money?" Silence filled the room as they each thought the worse.

"Man, just serve and give him a little extra. He wouldn't be here buying no dope if he knew anything." Blue reasoned with Smiley.

"You right, I'm trippin on some noid shit." Smiley begins walking to the kitchen grabbing more rocks than a twenty could buy. Making it to the front he opened the door and gave him the rocks.

"All this for twenty? Old man Odis asked surprisingly looking at all the thick crack rocks.

Walking back to the house Rich and Demon were awaiting at. Old man Odis palms begin to sweat in anticipation of the high he was waiting to feel from the crack.

Arriving back at the house with Rich and Demon. Soon as he stepped through the door, they rushed to see what he held in his now open palm.

"What the fuck is that?" Rich asked, also surprised. Seeing how big and how many rocks were given for twenty dollars.

"This is crack cocaine." Old man Odis said as he wiped the sweat off the top of his forehead. "You mind if I try?"

"Go ahead." Rich instructed.

Old man Odis pulled his crack pipe from his right sock and begin to pack the small hole full of crack. Satisfied with the amount he begins to light the end of the pipe and exhale the deadly toxic smoke. "Pssst!" He made a noise feeling the high he missed and chased for the last 2 years. That he thought he would never feel again. Everything he felt was just like Caesars dope.

"Ayeeee! Yo, you alright?" Rich asked old man Odis.

"Yeah, I'm, Ugh . . ." Old man Odis was at a loss for words. Once he came back to his senses and the extreme high settled down a little, he begins to speak.

"I been smokin this dope for a minute now." He paused, looking Rich in his eyes. "It's like Caesar rised from the grave and cooked it himself. This the same shit."

Rich knew Odis wouldn't lie. But he didn't know what to think of what he'd just heard. So he told him to go get the top customers and gave Odis a hundred dollars this time to go back and get more crack. And just like that the first time he returned with more crack than a $100 can buy.

Odis, Rita, and Cut sat around packing their crack pipes. As Rich waited for the opinion of the other two. Rita sparked her lighter first and took a big pull from the pipe. She was a expert smoking crack and known customer to Caesar's product. Cut fired up his lighter and repeated the same process. Him, Odis, and Rita all exchanged shameful looks. They didn't want to be the bearer of bad news. But the dope tasted the same and was cooked better.

Rich had a stern look and was gesturing his hands for somebody to say something. Odis decided to speak first.

"It's not exactly the same."

"What does exactly the same mean? Nothing is exactly the same. But you know what we got and what these other niggas got. So, what is it?" Rich snapped.

Odis, Rita, and Cut shook their heads yes. The coke Caesar was getting from Hector was pure as it gets. It had built its own brand in the city named Cuba for the Cuban flag stamped on the front of each brick. Hector only dealt with Caesar in the city. So, Rich knew nobody else had the same coke. The connection with Hector was cut about a month ago. So where did this coke come from, he wondered.

After he dismissed everybody out the house but Demon. He begin to walk back and forth thinking of a night he could never forget.

A couple months ago . . . .

"Why the only time you can come see me is at night?" Gold digging ass Kiesha asked in a husky voice. She was on her knees talking to Rich's dick and him at the same time.

"I'on know, you gotta give me a reason to keep coming back." Rich gamed her.

Gold digging ass Kiesha wasted no time as she kneeled before him. She spat on his dick and begin to stroke him with both hands. She put the tip inside her mouth than brought him to the back of her throat and gagged on it.

"Just like that." Rich said in a lustful undertone.

Stroking him with both hands and slurping like she was eating a cup of Ramen noodles, she looked him in the eyes, and blew him a kiss. "Gimme that nut" Kiesha demanded. Looking down at her caused his balls to tighten and the head of his dick to tingle. Feeling the cum about to shoot from his pistol. He pulled out her wet mouth and aimed for face. A thick stream of cum shot from the depths of his balls and right into her right eye and rolled down her right cheek.

"Rich daaammmitt!!" Kiesha panicked running to the restroom to rinse the cum out of her eyelid.

Rich was smiling listening to her moan as she rinsed his seeds from her eyelid. Until he heard the car alarm begin to blare on his 96 Chevy Impala.

Beep! Beep! Beep! Beep! The car alarm begins to scream. Either somebody touched his car or was inside it.

Rich pulled up his boxer briefs and grabbed his gun from his shorts pocket and ran to the front door of the 2-bedroom apartment in Flag Street Apartments.

Rich was now standing in the doorway, looking stupid, with his mouth wide open. Three men were kneeled on the side of his car with a MCM duffle bag he was supposed to drop off to the spot to meet Caesar. Tears welled in his eyes and goosebumps covered his entire body. He wanted to scream and beg them to leave it. But he knew that wasn't an option. So, he aimed and squeezed.

Boca! Boca! Boca! He let off the 3 unsuccessful shots.

This caused the 3 men to run ducking below the cars. He ran to try to corner them off. But he never seen them again.

Boca! Boca! Boca! Boca! He let off 4 more shots in desperation towards the direction they ran in.

Back to the present . . . .

Rich was walking back and forth as the night replayed in his mind. A lot of times alone he would fight himself for not being more responsible and just dropping the two bricks and $60,000 off like Caesar said. He always questioned himself if things would've been different if he made the right move. And right now, he had to get to the bottom of it.

   Demon jumped behind the wheel of Rich's 96 Chevy Impala while Rich settled for the passenger seat. As he brought the ignition to life and steered the Chevy to the House of Pain. They both had murder on their minds.

   Before they pulled up in front of the house, they seen Blue and Ralo posted in the front yard. The speed limit was 35 mph, but Demon was going every bit of 15 mph. He was trying to savor every moment as he and Rich stared the 2 down.

   Viewing the car moving slowly past them. Ralo and Blue paused their conversations and began to become alert.

   Once they passed by, they both ran into the house and grabbed a gun a piece preparing for whatever was to come next. Realizing they were not on point outside. They placed a Glock on their hips. Watching as more people came than expected.

   The first day of them opening up the House of Pain, was a dream come true. Basers spread the word quick. And customers came from all the surrounding neighborhoods. From PYC, Myrtle Avenue and even Moncrief. Money was coming in to fast to keep count. So they started stuffing black Glad trash bags with the dirty money.

This was the life that they dreamed of. And it came to them. With their dreams turning into reality. It was the beginning and only to get better.

Chapter 12

Back at the "House of Pain" it was Blue, Smiley and Ralo sitting at the table counting stacks of money. Besides two smokers fighting over the last crack rock everything was going well. The first seven days they had made $80,000 and still had a whole brick.

After the first week they noticed how everyone was amazed at how much crack they were getting for the low prices. So they adjusted the amount to the correct sizes. Only thing they did differently is they didn't sale nothing for less than $10 dollars. This made the money easy to add up evenly, and also easy to count.

"Where Chevy and Val at?" Ralo asked.

"They should be on their way" Blue answered.

Ever since they seen Rich and Demon didn't re-act how they expected them to. Blue decided to add more muscle to the team. So he reached out to Chevy and Val. They were a dynamic duo killing and laying everything down. Only flaw they had was an addiction to cocaine. But their work in the streets overshadowed their habit. And Blue, seeing another way to manipulate he jumped at the opportunity to recruit the two.

A knock was heard at the door, as Ralo made his way and opened it.

"Chevy and Val, what's up with yall boyz?" Ralo asked nervously. Everybody knew about Chevy and Val's gangsta, so both of them was on eggshells around the two except for Smiley. He was ready to go body for body with any nigga.

"What the fuck you niggas want?" Val asked, sniffing hard as his nose attempted to run.

"You niggas tryna get money or be in them dirty ass Flag Street's the rest of your life?" Blue asked taking control of the situation.

"Who the nigga is and what yall paying?" Val snapped back at Blue not feeling his energy.

"If I had a problem, I would go handle it and pay myself." Smiley spat back looking Val in the eyes feeling as his gangsta was being tested.

"Man, yall check this out." Blue waved the two over to the table where they were counting different faces of money and handed Chevy and Val a stack of bills a piece.

They both accepted the bills but kept a close eye on Smiley. They both knew he wasn't to be underestimated.

"We called yall over here cause we eating and we wanna make sure everybody eat." Blue slick talked tryna make it sound gangsta. But in reality, he knew if he didn't feed the wolves, they would get hungry and eventually eat him. So, he needed to divert their hunger to his opponents and not him.

Chevy hadn't uttered a word the whole time he just watched the situation unfold.

"We down, but we aint with all this hustlin shit. We like to get ours the ski mask way or off the muscle." Val said as him and Chevy exited the House of Pain looking over their shoulders.

When the door closed behind Val and Chevy, Blue begins to count the money again. Smiley and Ralo sat back down and continued doing the same thing. Life was going well, and the way things was set up it was only to get greater later.

"It's something about them crazy muthafuckas." Ralo said counting money at the same time.

"Them niggas loose cannons."

"An empty wagon makes the most noise, aint taking nothing from they gangsta but Chevy the one we gotta worry about. The quiet ones be the most dangerous." Smiley commented with a sinister smile.

The three of them continued to count the profit. And was amazed how much money they made in such a short time. Blue sat there thinking about Janae. Ever since everything transpired between the two sides. She often came up in his thoughts. Now that he was on the top and up he wanted a Bosslady to spend and spoil the riches he accumulated on her.

The chatter and laughter were common between the employees of Bank of America located on Edgewood Avenue. But today wasn't a common day for Janae. She wanted to quit and just lay in bed and cry her heart out. Time was moving slower than usual, as she watched the digital clock moving at a snail's pace. She wanted this Friday to be over with. Although she was emotionally scarred on the inside, her demeanor and facial expression was that of a businesswoman. Her all black and white pin stripe Versace pantsuit was a perfect fit, and her long natural hair was pulled back neatly in a bun. Her hands were shaking inside the banks vault while she placed crispy bills of 20's, 50's, and 100-dollar bills inside the three money counters that were placed in front of her on the desk.

Beep!

Beep!

Beep!

The money counters made the noise indicating it had completed the task of counting the bills in $10,000 increments. Janae removed each stack of the bills and placed the Bank of America band with $10,000 printed on the front around each stack. Repeating the process with less energy than before. She heard the door open to the safety deposit room leading to the vault open. And noticed it was the new Police officer on duty at the bank.

His eyes quickly scanned the room, and his eyes got big as saucers at the thousands of dollars Janae was busy counting. His mischievousness was written all over his face as he spotted Janae.

"Is everything okay back here ma'am?" Officer Monclair stated.

"Yes, I'm good, how's the job coming along?" Janae reached down into the bag of money and removed another large stack of bills. He had a look of deceit in his eyes.

"All is well, just doing my rounds." Officer Monclair casually exited the back of the bank's most discreet room.

Almost instantly, Janae felt relief upon feeling the tension in her shoulders begin to melt away. She didn't know why but she had a creepy feeling about this police officer. As the bank's manager she'd never been robbed, or nothing ever happened at her branch. And she didn't plan on letting nothing happen. So, she always went with her intuition.

Janae waited a few minutes, and then went to the door to check to see if he had left. Seeing he was gone she locked the door and pulled out her laptop. Since the funeral services of Caesar, she had been searching for a picture or anything that could link her to the "B" person she had met. Something in her gut was telling her he had something to do with Caesars death. She heard her phone vibrating and reached down into her Gucci bag that sat next to her. She retrieved her phone and saw she had gotten a text from Rich.

Rich

Block party this weekend for Caesar and G-Money (BYOB)

Before responding she retrieved another 20 vibrations and saw Rich had texted her in a group chat. Which she quickly blocked and texted him individually. She disliked having her phone number inside group chats.

Janae

BYOB??

Rich

Bring your own bottle.

Janae

Where's the party at?!

Rich

On 13th and Canal in the back of Flag Street Apartments

Janae's smile turned into a frown. At first receiving the text message she couldn't wait to celebrate and relieve some of the stress the weight of the world had on her shoulders. But seeing the party was in the same neighborhood she had met "B" and G-Money was killed in. The adrenaline rush she was getting was overwhelming.

Oh my God! What am I going through, Janae thought taking a few deep breaths. She closed her eyes feeling the anxiety inside her and her temperature began to rise. She sensed her armpits begin to sweat. As she stood up quickly to go to the bathroom to gather some composure. She stood in the mirror for a few minutes and began to run her make up pad over her face to smooth out any blemishes. She stared at herself in the mirror. And mouthed the words "You Are Strong." Rubbing her barely showing baby bump.

After sending the text messages about G-Money and Caesar's block party. Rich sat inside the black-on-black Porche Cayenne truck. For the party he decided to put up the Chevy and brought out the foreign. Rich thought to himself. Neva let em see you sweat, it's do or die. These niggas acting like I can't get my own money. I know Caesar paved the way. But I'm bout to take over.

Now that Rich had just got a new plug on some keys. He felt more confident and was ready to open shop again. It's been going on 8 weeks and no answers come up on the bricks missing or about G-Money or Caesar's death. He had a strange notion that the coke was theirs that old man

Odis purchased from the House of Pain. But he was from the streets and knew you couldn't go to war if your money wasn't right. So now Rich had money on his mind, and his mind on his money. With the block party being tomorrow Rich was getting ready to make some calls to the DJ and catering service for the block party. Rich was looking out the Porche window. What caught his eye was a girl walking down 13th street wearing some tight short shorts. He wanted to call her over to the truck but didn't when he noticed it was the girl who Janae punched at the funeral home. Shaking his head, he said "small world." As he watched her leaving the corner store in the back of Flag Street Apartments.

  Angel added more twist in her walk as she noticed the black Porche with its dark tint sitting in front of the laundromat and corner store. While she was walking back to her house on 14th Street.

Chapter 13

Bright and early Saturday morning the aroma of cocaine being cooked could be smelled through the House of pain. As Blue, Ralo and Smiley took turns practicing the recipe with the last brick.

This time they cooked 21 grams circle shaped cookies which left 7 grams of powder cocaine on each ounce. The crack game was a trending addiction. But one wasn't anything without the other they learned this from the last work of cocaine they cooked. So, this time they left room for every type of customers to crack smokers, cocaine snorters, and a new train was starting called smoking dirties. Mixing cocaine powder with weed.

It was early and the sun beamed down on Ralo as he stepped outside in the front yard. Observing no one he had made the $25,000 off these streets he held inside his Dickie shorts. Six people had just jumped out a truck and begin placing flyers on the light poles on each corner. And went to the next four way and repeated the same task all the way down the 1-mile stretch. When he seen they were out of his eyesight. He jogged to the nearest light pole and removed a flyer. Surprisingly the flyer was for a party that was being held tonight.

Ralo made his way back to the house, where Smiley and Blue were expeditiously with the flyer in hand.

"Check this fly shit out!" Ralo said excitedly as he made his way to the kitchen waving around the flyer.

"What's that?" Blue and Smiley said in unison.

Smiley grabbed it and began to read it. "Rest in Peace party for Caesar and G-Money. Food and drinks free. Music by DJ Chilli and Bigga Rankin. Location: West 13th Street.

"West 13th Street!" Blue repeated more shocked than anything.

Silence filled the small kitchen. They all were thinking about how the block party was being held in front of the House of Pain. Being it sat in the middle of 13th street. They didn't know rather to take offense or was this an invite.

Blue spoke first "I'm going." He simply said.

"Man, you wild as fuck, I knew you was gone go. Fuck it I'm down." Ralo agreed with him as they both turned their heads towards Smiley waiting for an answer.

"I'm tryna stack mines and buy me some wheels" Smiley finally spoke.

"Yeah, you right I'ma hit Mr. Boomerang up and let him know we gone pull up." Blue reasoned.

Mr. Boomerang was a known hustler who went legit, then he had started his own car dealership. He bought cars off the auction lots for cheap. Then sold them as a buy here pay here cars. You could put anything down and make payments until you're finished buying the car in full. Whatever you needed he had it from the old schools, new schools, to the exotic cars. They each had finished counting the profit off the first brick, which added up to $80,000. They each had made their first 25 grand a piece and put 5 thousand up to buy more artillery. Now that they had earned the money it was time to look the part as the hustlers they had become.

First, they went to Curley's Jewelry off of Norwood Blvd across the street from Gateway Mall. It was a small local jewelry store that welcomed all the dope boys and urban community. Everybody who was somebody knew about Curley's Jewelry. He sold majority gold chains, bracelets, and different brands of watches.

Entering the jewelry store, the bell could be heard alerting the Jeweler he had customers. "Welcome." A man who looked as if he had Cuban or Arabian decent appeared behind the counter. With all the chains he had around his neck he looked like he was tryna impersonate Mr. T.

"Hi, I'm Curly. How can I help you young men?"

The three sat there staring at all different Cuban links and Franko's around his neck. With his complexion and how much gold he had on he was looking like an Egyptian, with the gold on his neck, fingers, wrist, and ear lobes glistening.

"Damn! You stuntin hard!" Blue complimented.

"Thanks." Curly replied now smiling showing off his 10 golds to the top and 10 golds to the bottom.

The three of them walked around the small store looking at all the different gold jewelry smiling like a kid in a toy store on Christmas. Seeing they were dressed in regular street wear; Curly wasn't taking them seriously.

"We don't do any window shopping." Curly interrupted their moment. But his comment got all of their attention immediately. They all begin to grin and reached inside their pants pockets and dropped $25,000 a piece on top of the jewelry glass cases.

Once Curly seen they were holdin' major paper. He moved to the front door and secured it. Turning around inviting them to the back of the store.

When they entered the backroom, it was like they entered another world. The backroom was set up like a playhouse. The spacious room held a floor safe, bar, brown oakwood desk, and a waterbed. In the far corner was two naked Cubana's sleeping peacefully with their naked bodies interlocked like crabs. Curly begins clapping his hands stirring the two beautiful women out of their sleep. When they awoke and seen Blue, Smiley, and Ralo holding the stacks of money they arose and began to get out of the bed quickly.

"Com Esta's Papi." The first one greeted the 3 in Spanish. While the other one giggled.

"This is Isabella and her cousin Angelina." Curly introduced the Cuban women.

"I see you know how to work hard play hard." Ralo commented. Taking in the scenery of the backroom, while sizing the two defined curvaceous women up with his eyes.

"I try to my friend, get these guys something to drink." Curly instructed.

Curly covered the numbers on the keypad of the safe. And quickly entered the code. "Click click!" The locks could be heard opening on the floor safe. Curly went to pulling out different velour covered neck manikins and treys filled with bracelets, rings, chains and watches.

Isabella and Angelina returned to the 3 with flutes of crystal champagne. And handed them to Blue, Smiley, and Ralo. They were enjoying the five-star treatment.

"I can get use to this type of shit." Smiley boasted sipping champagne.

"Why don't you come see me at the Silver Foxx." Isabella advertised her services as Angelina slapped her basketball shaped bottom.

Curly set up the custom-made jewel's and motioned for them to come over to the oakwood desk. Upon them viewing all the different custom chains, watches, and bracelets. They instantly fell in love.

Blue grabbed a Cuban link chain with a cursive B that was bust down with small vvl's in the chain and B. Ralo and Smiley both reached for the "Anhk" Egyptian cross with vvl's and rubies flooded all throughout the cross. But Smiley held it and picked it up before Ralo could grasp it. So, Ralo settled for a lion piece with two big flawless stones inside the eyes.

Once they tried the chains on and were impressed with the image they now had with the custom jewelry. They each went to pick something for the wrist. Each grabbed solid gold Cuban bracelets to match their Cuban necklaces. Smiley picked out the Cosmography Daytona Rolex all gold steel plated. Blue grabbed the gold King Midas Rolex and fell in love instantly with its deep cut masterpiece. Ralo went plain with the Patek Philipe Golden Ellipse with its gold trim around the face and black leather band. Now that their neck and wrists were drippin with gold. They each picked up a gold bulky super bowl looking ring a piece and placed it on their pinky's.

Satisfied with his services Blue, Smiley, and Ralo gave each other victory handshakes at their success and their new image. They felt a sense of pride overcoming them while they were holding the money and wearing the gold.

"The world is yours" They shouted in unison. The popular mantra off the movie Scarface. It was the times where a key of cocaine was the Hood American Dream. And all black young street niggas watched that movie and got motivation, seeing how Tony Montana came up overnight gave every young hustler hope. And a fetish for the luxury the lifestyle brung.

Curly eased his 9mm Baretta from under his desk and placed it in the small of his back. After all, this was business not pleasure. He handled his business first pleasure later. Isabella was a cocaine supplier named Hector sister out of Miami, he met from doing custom Cuban link pieces. Her and her cousin was at his store to pick up Hector's jewels. And he ended up enjoying some free time. But now he was back in business mode.

"Yall ready to cash out?" Curly now spoke in his street demeanor.

"Yeah, what the ticket is?" Blue asked, counting the money proudly.

"I'll give you guys a package deal, just give me twenty-five.

"Twenty, twenty, five, five? What?" Blue stuttered not wanting to believe it really was twenty-five thousand.

"Twenty-five thousand, it cost to be a boss." Everything you all are wearing is pure gold melted fresh off the block. It's all original custom-made pieces.

Not wanting to be embarrassed Ralo spoke up. "Well, what's the difference between these and those out there on display." Ralo caressed the chains on his neck and pointed for extra emphasis in the front of the store.

Sensing the tension Curly removed the Baretta from his back and placed it on his lap, pulling the hammer back. As the four men exchanged looks and the women looked on puzzled.

"You ever heard of Blood Diamonds?" Smiley asked Curly.

Curly raised his eyebrows at the question. Because he had just read an article at how the diamond district was booming off the content of Africa. Where they were making Africans dig through muddy water for the diamonds and pay them little or nothing. And often times kill them for the diamonds. Which coined the term, Blood Diamonds.

Hearing this Curly became alert and wondered where Smiley was going with the statement he made. His palms began to get sweaty as he clutched the handle of the handgun. Until he seen Smiley produce something out of his hoodie.

"This what I mean." Smiley said holding the 30-inch chain that was smothered in Bugette diamonds with the F.M.B charm that was also flooded in flawless stones glistening off the room lights.

Nothing but heavy breathing could be heard inside the room. As everybody stared at the chain. This chain was identical to Caesars. But was the chain G-Money worn when he died. Hell of chatter began in Spanish between the two beautiful women while they sat back watching as spectators.

"It's amazing," was all Curly could come up with. Staring at the masterpiece Smiley was holding. "Can I see it?" He asked pulling out his colonoscope to view the clarity of the diamonds.

Smiley turned his attention to the two Cubanas speaking Spanish. He didn't speak it fluently, but he caught drift of the conversation. Isabella was telling her cousin Angelina they had to leave, and she knew who chain that was.

Upon hearing this smiley was on Isabella like a female lioness on her prey. He wrapped his hands around her neck so tightly her sun-tanned face began to turn purple. Ralo and Blue were at a loss of words as Curly began to snap now brandishing his 9 millimeter pointing it at everybody.

"Not here!!" He snapped.

Smiley paid no attention to nobody; he was instilling fear inside of Isabella before he got the answers he needed. But he had to make sure he took her as closest to the white light of death you possibly could.

Finally, when he released her, she began to gag and gasped for air as if she had just finished drowning. Smiling seeing her gain her composure began to question her immediately.

"What do you know and how do you know him?" Smiley demanded answers.

"I just know him as Caesar, and I worked as a mule between him and my brother Hector. But once he crossed my brother on 2 kilos of coke and $60,000, he went missing and the next thing you know we heard he died." Isabella told barely the truth not knowing if these were Caesar's friends or not.

Smiley pulled his Glock from his waistband pointed it at Isabella giving her a look of death. But Isabella held her head high giving him a good shot if he decided to shoot her displaying her gangsta. "So y'all still fuckin with these niggas?"

"The best disloyal person is a dead disloyal person." She spat venomously spitting on the ground showing disrespect for the dead.

Smiley smiled evil smile. "And dead man tells no tales", then he lowered the gun and turn back to Curly like nothing ever happened.

Seeing the fiasco was over, Curly continued doing business. He wanted this business to be over with quickly as possible. His place of business almost turned into a murder scene.

"How about I give you 3 two more chains apiece and one ring apiece." They all shook their heads in agreement. They knew the chain was probably worth more with all the diamonds. After they shook hands on the deal, Smiley stepped to Isabella in exchange numbers. He respected her gangsta. And after all, "an enemy of my enemy, is a friend of mines." So mutual understanding was built.

After leaving Curly's, they made their way to Mr. Boomerang's car dealership on Cassat Blvd. Soon as they arrived, they noticed three luxury cars were being rolled off a tractor trailer. They each exchanged satisfactory glances.

"I gotta get that blue Benz." Blue called out excitedly.

"I'm getting that green Jag you know I'm fuckin' with the home team." Ralo said comparing the Jaguar car with the Jacksonville Jaguars football team.

"Look at that "Lexus." Smiley spoke in a tone of amazement.

Few seconds later, the three emerged from the rental they drove in and approached Mr. Boomerang anxiously. He was shocked to see the three. But even more shocked to see them jeweled up how they were. Once Upon a time Mr. Boomerang had the hood sewed up. And each one of them used to work for him before he turns legit. So, he was familiar with them, just not in this new light and image.

"What's shakin young bloods?" Mr. Boomerang asked.

"These!" The three called out in amazement pointing at the luxury cars. He looked at the young bloods proudly and with admiration.

"Youngbloods you sure y'all don't want to get one of them Acura's or Honda's?"

"Acura or Honda?" Blue interrupts with anger.

"Sometimes you gotta stay down until you come up, don't chase the image, cause one thing about these streets they don't love nobody. We all die or go to jail, it's always gonna be somebody to replace you. You gotta worry about bond money and lawyers. All this shit depreciate value once drove or worn." He dropped priceless game on the three. Pointing at the cars and jewelry.

"Man, we young niggas we live for today fuck tomorrow." Ralo spat.

Shaking his head, he led the way to his office to get his assistant to do the paperwork and make the sales final. He was an old timer and learned the hard way, stunting got the feds attention and cliques brought conspiracies.

Leaving the car dealership only thing could be heard was screeching tires. They were back-to-back driving like NASCAR drivers in the Daytona 500. Now it was time to get something to wear as they headed back to Designer Factory. They planned on making this a night the streets were never to forget.

Chapter 14

The entire Grand Park area was lit, particularly the flag St. apartments and 13th St. On this hot summer day, the smell of charcoal and BBQ filled the air. Music could be heard from a loudspeaker as DJ Chilli and Bigga Rankin took turns on the turntables in the middle of the apartments. This was a block party to remember.

During the time of Caesar, he made sure the hood was fed and everybody had a spot at the table. And although he and G-Money were gone. Rich did everything he could to bring the spirit of them back. And let the people of the neighborhood know F.M.B still ran shit.

"One Time for The Fast Money Boys!!" DJ Chilli could be heard through the loudspeakers.

Rich, Demon, and Ronnie were standing atop the Porche truck. Each wore F.M.B chains and held bottles of Moet in the air as the summer sun rays beamed off the Bugette diamonds in their necklaces.

Everybody crowded around the Porche truck like the 3 were rappers or politicians of the hood. They enjoyed the spotlight while nobody paid attention to who was sitting behind the 5 percent tint inside the truck. A beautiful Janae sat reclined in the A-C of the truck as the twin turbo V-6 motor silently ran. Taking in the scenery she finally gained composure and stepped out the truck. She looked exotic with her long natural hair pulled back into a ponytail and big hoop earrings on. She had a slim frame, but her stomach was showing the baby bump she tried to hide in her sundress. As she sashayed to the music Bigga Rankin was mixing of Reggae and R&B. With every movement her backside was performing like it had a mind of its own. The thin material of the sundress was barely concealing the plumpness of her backside.

Smiley played the cut and sat on the hood of his Lexus watching the party from afar. He wasn't inside the crowd, but he was close enough to see what was going on. He watched as Blue, Ralo, Chevy and Val enjoyed the attention. People weren't used to seeing them in this new image.

Everybody's attention was focused on Rich, Demon, and Ronnie. Nobody paid attention to who stepped out the Porche truck, but Blue did. He immediately recognized Janae from her exotic features. It was like he remembered his eyes had become lost in her beauty. Taking in the entire scene. He seen she was posted with Rich and his crew. His mind went to racing replaying the events. When it dawned on him that Janae was on the other side of the field. Them being a couple was impossible. So, Blue kept a close eye on her watching her every move. He already put inside his mind if he seen her alone, he would shoot his shot. For some reason his pride wouldn't let him accept defeat.

Once the sun faded and the day turned into night-time. The food was gone, and all the kids were in the house when the streetlights cut on. DJ Chilli and Bigga Rankin had left with the turntables and speakers. So, the one block party had turned into several parties. Each set of nice cars with rims had its doors open with its stereo system blasting each person's music of choice, with Blue's entourage and Rich's having the largest crowd. They both were the center of attention.

Blue sat back bobbin' his head to the beat watching Janae from a distance. It was like he was in a world of his own. He wanted to get her to look in his direction just so he could show off the excessive jewels he had on and the "B" that shined around his neck. But his staring was only met by Rich. If the looks Rich gave him could kill he would've been dead. The only reason why Rich didn't press play cause of the people around. And he could see Ralo, Chevy, and Val were all clutching.

Across the street Angel and gold-digging azz Kiesha was observing everything.

"This bitch got some nerve; I tell you that" Angel said with much attitude.

"And who the fuck Rich thinks this bitch is the queen."

Gold digging azz Kiesha and Angel were both upset about Janae's presence. But when Angel noticed Janae was the same woman from Caesars funeral. She couldn't let the black eye Janae had given her slide. Angel took off full speed across the street and like a thief in the night. Stole a lick as she connected with Janae's jaw. "Bitch"!! She yelled. Dropping Janae and sat on top of her. Punching her while gold digging azz Kiesha assisted with kicks to Janae's ribs.

Viewing the commotion of the two women fighting. Blue ran immediately with Chevy, Val, and Ralo close behind. Fist balled jogging full speed to assist Janae, when Blue finally reached the fight Rich pulled Angel from Janae. Soon as Janae opened her eyes when she felt the licks stop coming. It was like she had seen the boogeyman himself as she gave Blue a menacing look. This was the man she had been searching for, for months. And to solidify her thoughts this was him; he had the nerve to have on a shiny bright "B" on the Cuban link. Blue reached out his hand to help her up off the ground. Janae grabbed it as she smiled a sweet devious smile. Once she was on her feet, she begin to swing on him. She snatched Blue's chain off his neck and punched him in the face with the right hand. He grabbed his chain and backhanded Janae with so much force, she flew into a parked car and shattered the driver side window causing the car alarm to blare loudly.

Everybody who were trying to control Angel and gold-digging azz Kiesha now were headed to Janae's rescue. Rich, Ronnie and Demon came off the hip no questions asked. Val, Ralo, and Chevy did the same. Both crews were face to face with each other at gunpoint. The silence was deadly as they all stared in each other's eyes and down each other's barrels.

"Kiiiillll Hiiimmm!" Janae yelled. What sounded like it came from the soul. This was a beautiful nightmare, and she didn't want to wake up. Seeing nothing was happening she reached for the gun in an attempt to grab it and shoot the man she only knew as "B". In the split second she reached for the gun, was all it took for the Angel of Death to take a soul. And return to heaven or hell with it.

"Boom! Boom! Boom! Boom! A rapid succession of shots could be heard. The shots from a automatic gun was loud. Ronnie barely made it as a bullet whistled by his ear as he tackled Janae to the ground.

Blue was stuck with his eyes closed thinking his life was over. Until he felt Ralo tuggin' at his shirt then opened his eyes and seen a pool of blood with Janae on top. He was confused cause he knew nobody had shot who he was with. So, he wanted to stay to make sure Janae would be okay.

Scccuuurrr!!! The blue Benz pulled up.

Get! In! Get in! Val screamed as sirens and the police lights were seen on the next street. Blue complied but this wasn't the way he wanted to see things between him and Janae to end. The Benz pulled off as nothing could be smelled but gun smoke and burning rubber through the summer night.

Chapter 15

"Jacksonville Sheriff's Office." The white detective said sternly knocking on Blocka's door at 6 in the morning.

Blocka was already awake watching the news as reporters talked about a homicide that had occurred in Flag Street Apartments last night. Shaking his head in disappointment. He knew the knock at his door and the homicide on tv were going to be connected somehow. He fired up his Cuban cigar and went to the door to see who was banging.

"Good morning officers" he asked through the crack of the door. Blowing a cloud of smoke in the two homicide detectives' faces.

"Good morning, sir, we are with the Jacksonville Sheriff's Office. I'm Detective Robinson and this is Detective Greene. We need to have a word with your son about a homicide that happened yesterday."

"Is he being questioned as a witness or a suspect?" Blocka asked.

"At this time, this is a ongoing investigation. So, we don't wish to give any details."

"Well, he doesn't wish to do any talking without his lawyer present" Blocka attempted to close the door. But was stopped by Detective Greene's boot.

"Sir you can try this my way or the highway. It will only take a couple calls and we'll have a Judge sign a warrant and come in and get him. And anything extra we find we'll charge you."

Blocka thought about it. He knew it wasn't supposed to be nothing inside the house. But he didn't want to chance it with his son's lifestyle.

"I'ma wake him up, give me 5 minutes." Blocka stated as he closed the door.

Stepping into Blue's room, Blocka walked in soon as he was sticking his right leg out of the window. "Uh uh. We don't run from our problems. They aint got nothing if they did, they wouldn't be asking you to come out. You aint seen nothing you aint hear nothing" Blocka coached his son.

Blue walked outside the house to speak with the two homicide detectives.

"Hello Raheem Robins. I'm Detective Robinson, this is my partner. We need to ask you about the Murder of Bobby Newman A.K.A Demon we were told you all got into a fight last night."

"I aint seen nothing I aint heard nothing." Blue said nonchalantly.

"Well, how you get this?" Detective Greene said, grabbing his face turning it to the side so both of the detectives could see the fresh bruise that he had received from Janae the night before.

"I fell in the shower." Blue answered.

"Uuum Uuum." Blocka cleared his throat and handed them a business card to his lawyer.

"Detain him Robinson! He lawyered up." Detective Greene commanded his partner.

"You have the right to remain silent anything you say or do will be used against you in the court of law. You have the right to an attorney if you cannot afford an attorney one will be appointed to you" Detective Robinson read Blue his Miranda rights while he handcuffed him behind his back.

In the back of the police car was uncomfortable, as he was led to the Memorial Building to be questioned. JSO often used the memorial building as a scare tactic to make some people confess, or snitch being it was across the street from Duval County Jail. Better known as PTDF (Pre-trial Detention Facility).

Once he entered the Memorial Building, he was taken to a small room where his attorney Tom Files was awaiting him.

"Hey, Mr. Robins, how's it going?" He asked, extending his right hand as they released the cuffs off Blue. The detectives left the two alone. Look I know you don't know what's going on, and neither do I. But apparently you have a woman saying you slapped her, so that gives them probable cause to detain you. About the murder, witnesses are saying a bunch of you guys were pointing guns at each other, and shots were fired. Now this guy is dead." Tom pushed the Times Union Newspaper in front of him which displayed a prom picture of Bobby Newman A.K.A Demon.

The stillness in the room gave Blue the chills as he thought about his whole future. Basically, his lawyer had just told him he was going to jail. He had forgotten all about him slapping Janae. But he did say something about one person dying. So, he felt a slight relief that Janae wasn't dead. "Am I being charged with Murder?" Blue questioned.

"Not at this moment, but if you don't have any information on who was the shooter. Her word is going to be credible, because she is saying you also shot the guy who practically died in her arms. So, if you can't give them any names, you're probably going to get charged."

Blue took a deep breath and thought long and hard about who could have been the shooter. Basically, he was about to take the fall for something he really didn't do.

"Show me my cell!" Was the only response his lawyer got from Blue.

Being processed into Duval County Jail was like entering a different world. You were stripped of all your personal belongings except your shoes and given a green uniform if you were a male, grey if you were a female with Department of Corrections Jacksonville Sheriff's Office Inmate stamped on the left side over the heart. People screaming and crying hysterically could be heard on the 1st floor, while the inmates waited to be fingerprinted and assigned to a floor. Depending on the seriousness of your charges was where you were housed. The jail's most dangerous inmates were housed on the 5th and 6th floor.

After being fingerprinted and booked for murder and simple battery. He took the elevator to the 5th floor. As he gave the officer his face sheet, they pointed to the first dorm on the right. Standing in front of the dorm it looked like a world inside another world. Some dudes were working out, some were shooting dice, playing poker, playing spades, or walking circles around the dorm.

Once entering his dorm 5 west three. He began to see so many familiar faces. Some guys he hadn't seen in months, some he hadn't seen in years. I guess it's true what they say. When you stop seeing somebody out there on them streets. Either they dead or in jail. Blue thought to himself as he made it to his cell with his plastic mat and bedroll.

Observing his cell his stomach begins to toss and turn at the thought of him spending the rest of his life in the 8 X 10 cell. The cell had 2 single bunks, one which was unoccupied. The other was occupied by a old man with glasses and a big head. His nose was inside the book "The Art of War by Sun Tzu." Never taking his concentration off the book he begins to speak.

"This cell aint big enough for 2 people" he said.

"Well, somebody gotta go and it aint gone be me." Blue responded dropping his mat ready for whatever.

In one swift motion the old man got off the bunk and pulled a jail made weapon known as a shank out. "You sure bout that." he asked, staring Blue deeply in his eyes.

"Only thing I fear is Allah. So, if you gone put me to sleep handle up. If not I'ma go to sleep on my own. Today has been a long day I don't got time for this extra shit." Blue cracked his knuckles not backing down.

Hearing him refer to the creator in Arabic as Allah changed the old man's mind. He was Muslim and knew it was unlawful to spill another Muslim blood without reason. "Alhamdulilah, Salamu Alaykum brother. I'm Jihad."

Blue took a long pause before returning the universal greeting of Islam. "Wa alaykum as salam." He grinned happy to be amongst a brother in faith of his. As he made his bed and dozed off.

"Chow time! Chow time!" The officer announced over the intercom indicating it was time to eat lunch.

Blue woke up to the smell of chicken patties, with inmates screaming out different deals trading and bartering canteen for state food. He noticed there were more people inside the dorm then before as he watched everybody line up and receive their lunch treys.

Leaving outside his cell, he checked his surroundings and didn't see anything out of the ordinary. He received his trey then returned to the room not wanting to be friendly or socialize.

Once he returned to his cell, he seen brother Jihad was still laying in the same position this time reading "Bobby Fischer teaches chess."

"You not gone eat Ahki?" Blue asked.

"I eat to live, I only eat once a day, and sometimes once every two days." Brother Jihad explained.

"How long you been down?"" "I been down 17 calendars I started with a day and night."

Huh? What you mean a day and night? Blue questioned with a confused look on his face.

"That's what we call life without parole in the feds. I'm back on a 5k motion." Brother Jihad said as he sat the book down.

"Okay." Blue shrugged his shoulders not being familiar with the legal terms.

The next day he went to first appearance court, and he was given a million-dollar bond. Feeling depressed he went back to his cell and went to sleep. The murder charge was weighing down on him. Here he was sitting in a cell eating 3 meals a day, wearing used boxers and socks. Just the thoughts alone made him go into a deep state of depression.

After coming back from court, he stayed inside his cell for the next 3 weeks. He wasn't eating or talking.

"Mail call! Mail call!" Raheem Robins this is your last day to receive your mail, if you do not get it today it will be returned to the sender." The mail lady officer screamed. She had been calling his name for the past 3 weeks to receive his mail.

It was 6:30 am majority of the other inmates had been up since breakfast. Blue was falling victim to the saying: Sleep late and you lose weight. He was doing what they called dead time. Hearing his name, he woke up and went to the flap to get his mail.

"Mr. Robins let me see your arm band with your name so I can verify you are who these belong to." The mail lady said.

Blue retrieved the 3 envelopes and 5 money slips and made it back to his bunk. Once he laid down, he tossed the envelopes and papers on the floor. Jihad being the observant type of person he is got up and read the addresses and money slips.

"Ahki!" Jihad called out. Not being the one to repeat himself he grabbed the blanket and pulled it off of Blue.

"What type of time you on!" Blue asked confused.

"I'm tired of you sitting in here acting like you dead. You haven't been showering, eating, or taking care yourself. You got people that love you. Those money slips say somebody sent you over a thousand dollars.

"So, what the fuck you care!" Blue yelled.

"You right me as a person I don't give a damn. But me as a Muslim it's my obligation to want for my brother what I want for myself."

"And what you want for me?" Blue asked expressing the aggravation in his voice.

"I don't want you to become me. Because rather you believe it or not. I was you once upon a time. I spent my time sleeping, gambling, and jacking off to these officer women. When I was supposed to be studying my case and going to the law library." Jihad spoke from the heart.

"That's what we pay lawyers for." Blue shrugged his shoulders arrogantly.

Jihad begins to laugh like he had just heard a joke from Kevin Hart. And shook his head at how lost Blue was to the system.

"Lawyers are not magician's; you know that right?"

"I know they help us get our freedom and defend the criminals" Blue answered.

"Between the judges, prosecutors, and lawyers they are the biggest criminals in the courtroom. One hand washes the other, both hands wash the face. The Feds gotta 97% conviction rate and 98% of the cases in the state do not make it to trial. That mean a lot of lawyers are coping pleas." Jihad stated.

"So, I don't need a lawyer?" Blue wondered.

"I'm not saying you don't need a lawyer. That's just like me saying you don't need a mechanic to fix your car. But if you don't have knowledge about something, a person can tell you anything. So, you must do your research about your own case."

Blue sat there taking in the words he was speaking, and it all made sense. He only knew what his lawyer told him. But if he studied his own case, he would be able to know for himself. I need to get to the law library. Blue thought to himself.

As if Jihad read his mind, he pulled out a clear trash bag full of books and begin handing Blue different books. The first book he handed him was the "Black Law Dictionary", then the "Florida Rules and Regulations." "You sleep in the law library." Jihad said. Then handed him 500 pages of different cases and case laws about murder.

Chapter 16

The humid night felt like the sun was still out. Everybody in the city was on the way to the Silver Foxx Gentlemen's Club. The line was wrapped around the corner with men and women from all sides of Jacksonville. The men were trying to put their game down and skip the club. But all the women's eyes were fixed on the ballers pulling up, hopping out, and skipping the waiting line. Just like any other night, you had anybody that was somebody in attendance. After everybody grind hard in the streets, they played harder in the strip club.

Smiley pulled up in the parking lot in his new car turning everybody's head in his direction. He knew he had the spotlight as he sat behind the steering wheel and watched everyone stare through the fishbowl windows of the small sedan. He placed his left hand on the steering wheel flexing his Cuban bracelet, Rolex, and Super Bowl looking pinky ring.

When finally, one of the clubs parking lot workers approached the Lexus seeing an opportunity for a tip. Smiley stepped out the car sharper than a razor. He gave the worker a $100 bill to make sure his car was parked out front of the club and the express zone.

He began approaching the club feeling the intense stares from the people awaiting in the long line. Saying it was more men than women. He turned on his heels and went back to the glove box to grab his Glock. Taking a deep breath, he tucked the Glock in the front and checked his reflection on the Lexus candy paint, to make sure it wasn't showing. As he made his way back towards the club. He heard his name being called, followed by light giggles.

Turning in the direction of the noise. He sees it was none other than Angel and gold-digging ass Keisha. He shook his head and poked his chest out drawing attention to the Cuban link with the Egyptian cross (Ankh) charm.

"Zamn Zaddy." Kiesha gave Smiley a seductive look.

"Can we chat with you for tonight?" Angel asked.

"We can keep another secret." Keisha said stepping closer letting Smiley smell her floral perfume and get a better visual of her 5'2 bricked up frame, that she managed to squeeze inside the one-piece bodysuit.

"Exactly you know I be lonely, I aint stepped out since Blue went to jail." Angel pleaded trying to get Smiley to let them hang with him for tonight.

Smiley sat there contemplating. He knew gold digging ass Keisha and Angel had a reputation for starting shit. But looking at how good they were looking, and their one-piece body suits made by Prada. He accepted the offer to let them chill with him for tonight. "Aight, but don't be on no extra shit."

Smiley walked past the long line of people waiting, with Keisha and Angel not far behind. They were loving the attention as they passed the numerous of women with mean mugs. Nobody wanted to wait in line. But only a few were willing to pay extra not to wait. And that's why the bouncers only let 5 to 10 people in every 10 to 15 minutes. Running the club like this separated the classes.

"I need a V.I.P for three, keep the change." Smiley said pointing at Angel and Keisha. After handing the bouncer $400 bills.

The bouncer left the three inside the club without searching. He then got them to the V.I.P section of the club. The music was pumping loud in the bass had the entire building vibrating every time the beat dropped. Once at their tables, buckets of ice and Hennessy bottles awaited.

After settling in, Smiley gave the attractive worker $100 dollar bills. He needed to get some ones to show the strippers some love. He wasn't the party type, but with everything going on and going wrong, he needed to relax a little. His main goal was to blend in with the bosses. Well, everyone was not focused and partying, Smiley was plotting, planning, and strategizing. He thought about everything he had learned in such a short time. Blocka had given them the game clear as day. He just left out all the losses and droughts. Ever since Blue went to jail and the news hit the streets about Demon getting killed. It was like the streets turned their backs on them. Their once loyal customers went back to copping from Rich and Ronnie. This caused the shortage in the cash flow. Blue being locked up for murder wasn't calling home. And Blocka was pursuing his nonprofit organization talking to troubled kids. So, the guidance wasn't as strong as before. Smiley stared out in the crowd and thought about how he would go from nobody knowing his name to a street legend who everybody would know very soon.

"Here you go sexy face." The attractive worker said handing Smiley a thousand ones.

"Appreciate that." He smiled, grabbing the money with his free hand. He downed half the bottle of Hennessy with the other one.

"Bitch! Who did the body?!" Keisha asked aloud to nobody in particular as she pointed to the center stage. Smiley's eyes shot in the direction of the stage where Keisha was pointing. And just like she said, it was a woman shaped as she was crafted by God's hands personally. The well-defined Latino woman was shaking her body like a saltshaker.

"Look at this bitch." He said to himself not believing this was Isabella. The girl he remembered from Curly's. I thought she said she worked at Amnesia", he thought to himself. Smiley watched her from afar. She had control of the crowd making her ass cheeks clap like hands in Sunday's service. Admiring her 5'5 coke bottle shape and bubbled ass. Smiley smiled and begin making his way to the center stage through the crowd. Smiley could not stop looking at how she was now twerking hanging on the side of the stage. Each cheek was jumping and rolling like tidal waves. Her golden accessories and see-through two-piece left little to the imagination.

"Thirsty ass nigga got all this pussy right here and he'd rather fuck with a white girl." Keisha stated viewing Smiley creep up behind Isabella. She didn't even notice him until she felt the stacks of ones raining on her backside.

Isabella began to put on a show for whomever was showing love with the shower of cash. Turning around, when she seen Smiley, she felt the euphoric and became wet instantly.

"Hey Papi, Ju wanna get a private room. Isabella invited Smiley to the private room in the back. She spoke over the loud music.

"I'm good, I just came to show some love. You know I respect the naked hustle." Smiley declined looking at the bigger picture. Ever since he found out who Isabella was, he had much bigger plans than just sex. What the average man seen as pleasure between her legs. He seen as an opportunity in a gateway to become rich. He knew the longer he waited, the more valuable he will be in her eyes. "I'ma be texting you soon. We might be able to do some business."

Smiley made his way back to the V.I.P section, which overlooked the center stage of the club. Him and Isabella's eyes were locked on each other the entire night. It was something about the eyes of Smiley. With the eyes being the windows to the soul. But his eyes said what the lips would never reveal.

Keisha sat back with a look of disgust seeing the chemistry between Smiley and Isabella. She couldn't take it anymore, so she made her move. Enclose the space between them, distracting his attention.

"Sit back and relax. Let me treat you like the king you are Daddy." She whispered in his ear, while grabbing his shoulders and began massaging softly. Feeling the delicate touch of Keisha, he sat back and enjoyed the moment. He had been so busy putting in work that he never really sat back to enjoy intimate moments like this. Keisha caught Angel staring jealously and gave her the eye to intervene.

Angel wasted no time and popped the cork on bottle after bottle of Patron. She even pulled out something to smoke. By the time the DJ called the last song, Smiley was too under the influence to drive, he could barely walk.

You should grab the keys out of Smiley's pocket and go to find the car. After pulling it in front of the club the trio got into the Lexus and got lost into the night.

Vrrrrmmm! Vrrrrmmm! Vrrrrmmm!

(The Next Morning)

The vibration from Smiley's phone startled him. He had gotten so drunk last night, he only remembered bits and pieces of the night before. He looked around the room and realized he was at the Hyatt of Regency. His head spinning and phone vibrating brought him back to reality. Grabbing his phone out of his pants pocket. He sees it was a 1-800 number appeared on the screen. It was 8:15 AM, he knew nobody had his number but the circle. So, he went with his first mind and answered it.

Smiley pressed the answer button and placed the phone on speaker.

"You have a collect call from an inmate at the Duval County Jail, Blue." If you wish to accept the charges press 0 zero to block future calls press 4. If you wish to decline press 8 or hang up the call." The operator said.

Beep! Smiley pressed 0 zero immediately.

Hearing the loud different voices echoing through the phone speaker caused whomever to move in the California king size bed.

"What they do?" Smiley called out excitedly to the phone.

"All is well, I miss yall boys. What you got going on?" Blue asked.

"Man, I'm tryna figure out myself." Smiley responded and pulled the comforter back. When he seen who it was, he lost his breath.

The silence on the phone and inside the room spoke volumes. Here it was Smiley was on the phone with Blue, while staring at the nakedness of Angel and Kiesha sprawled across the bed.

"What's going on?" Angel asked in a raspy voice barely conscious. The cool breeze from the air awoke her.

"Who that is brah?" Blue interrupted the moment.

"Where you at? Who you with?" He began to ask question after question.

Smiley knew he couldn't say where he was or who he was with. Instead, he told partially the truth. "I'm at the Hyatt with Kiesha." He shook Kiesha until she woke up. And gave her a look of horror. "Say hey to Blue."

"Hey Blue."

"What's up." He said dryly.

Kiesha catching the mood, begin to try to smooth the situation out. "Why you haven't been calling my friend? She been worried sick about you, and Lil Blue misses you."

"I been tryna walk this time down. I been studying the law and just found out they got 45 days to formally charge me. As of right now my lawyer saying it's a 90% chance, I'll be home in a couple weeks."

"Damn! That's what's up we need you out this bitch. Everything fucked up right now. We underground for the time being." Smiley said speaking in code letting him know things aren't what they was when he left. And that they were moving under the radar.

"What's up with our bestfriends? Blue shot back speaking in code asking about their enemies.

"They doing real good. That's the problem they doing too good." Smiley began to chuckle.

Hearing this was like receiving a blow to the ribs for Blue. Everything they had built was now being torn down. Inside his mind he had lost time and money. In the streets things moved so fast, if you weren't on point things that took weeks, months, or years to build, were destroyed in days or hours sometimes.

"Well, I aint gone talk too much on these phones. You know these crackheads listening." Blue said.

"That's fasho, hold ya head brother. Smiley responded, ending the call.

Smiley sat there with his head inside his palms on the bed. Every time he turned around and seen Angel and Kiesha laid out on the California king size bed. His heart begins to skip a beat. He didn't remember last night but the soreness in his body told a different story.

Ralo was in a deep sleep at the House of Pain. The shortage in traffic had him sleeping comfortably. Actually, he was sleeping a little too comfortably.

Outside the House of Pain were 2 masked gunmen armed with baby choppas. The AK-47's and ski masks concealing their identities had them looking like Isis. Only thing could be heard is a train horn as it traveled on the railroad tracks in the back of the neighborhood.

"Knock, knock, knock!"

A knock could be heard on the door echoing through the House of Pain. Hearing the knock this time louder, Ralo turned over. Looking at the clock it showed 8:27 am Ralo closed his eyes. Whoever it was would have to come back later, he thought to himself. That was one of the greatest decisions he ever made. The next thing he heard would change his life forever.

Boom! A loud crash could be heard as the door swung open. Whop! Whop! Whop! Whop! The sound of gunshots from an assault rifle could be heard throughout the house.

Ralo jumped up and ran to the closet grabbing the AK-47 that never left the House of Pain. His heart was beating at a thousand miles a minute as silence filled the house and the gunshots ceased.

Footsteps could be heard on the old wooden floors in the 2-story house. Downstairs of the house they were searching and flipping things Ralo heard. Ralo grabbed the AK-47 and laid down at the top of the steps. He was laying down on his stomach, with the kutta aimed downstairs like an American sniper. One eye closed, one eye opened, he had his open eye focused on the sights of the front of the barrel of the assault rifle. The footsteps were getting closer and closer.

Finally, when one of the mask gunmen attempted to climb the stairs, Ralo squeezed the trigger of the kutta Whop! Whop! Whop! He let off 3 rounds with the first 2 whistling right past the first shooter's ear. And the third shot struck the wall making a hole the size of a hand. Viewing they were not alone the 2 shooters abandoned their mission. But they left with a stash of guns and the remainder of the drug stash that was in the oven of the stove in the kitchen.

Police sirens could be heard nearby. Ralo jumped up grabbing much as he could running around the house. Hearing the siren's getting closer he made a quick exit. Soon as he pulled out the yard, he seen police cars fire and rescue. Only half of the neighbors on the streets were now awake outside their homes.

Chapter 17

(Back at Duval County Jail)

Ever since Blue had reached out to the streets his time was going by slowly. All he did everyday all day was think. The last phone call he made to Smiley had his mind everywhere. If he did beat this murder charge, he didn't know what was next. Everything he took his time building was destroyed in a matter of days.

Sitting in a daze staring at the pages instead of reading the book. Blue was in deep thought, when Jihad entered the cell.

"What's on yo mind Ahki?" Jihad questioned him.

"Just tryna think of my next move. Like I'm reading this book and trying to find the difference in what they did and what I'm doing." Blue spoke analyzing the book about the Five Mafia Families of New York.

"Shyt, that's easy to see. You don't know how to sacrifice. This game is just like chess. Every move has to be calculated." Jihad explained.

"When you say life is like chess. How can you compare a boardgame to life."

"Because everybody in life plays their position just like the board. And on a greater scale every move has an equal or greater reaction. From the pawns to the kings." Jihad said while pulling out the plastic chess set.

"What you wanna tighten up old man?" Blue challenged Jihad.

Those couple of sentences were making him look at the game differently, and it showed with his control of the board. Always be calculated he thought to himself. "Checkmate." Blue called out. He pushed his queen up and didn't see Jihad's rook. Jihad took Blue's queen with his rook.

"You got to have protection." Jihad broke out into a fit of laughter as he replaced Blue's queen with his rook. "And pointed" to his queen directly in front of his king. "Checkmate" Jihad called out.

Blue sat there puzzled at how Jihad had just stolen the game from him.

"Look Ahki." Jihad said pointing at the board. Where he had placed his rook back on the board. So, he and Blue could analyze the game. It's all about the sacrifice. I sacrificed my pawn for your queen. You were paying so much attention to checkmating me that you didn't realize it was a trap. This is how it works in life. At times sacrifices gotta be made at the right time in order to win. He explained.

"So, explain this to me. What do you think the mafia was doing that made them last for so long? Blue asked.

"They bended the rules they didn't break them."

"The mafia was the most stand-up guys to ever walk the face of the earth. They believed in Omerta. The code of silence." Blue explained holding the book up about the 5 Mafia Families.

"That's true, they killed one another if they told on each other. But when it came to others, they gave information.

They worked hand and glove with the police to take down the competition. They mastered the game of life. They figured out what a lot of people just can't seem to understand."

"What's that?" Blue questioned, anticipating the answer.

"They did anything they had to do to win." Jihad answered.

Everything Jihad had just told Blue was the same his father was trying to teach him. They both were trying to teach him to be swift. They both knew from experiences in the streets. That at certain times it was about who could think the best, or who made the sacrifice first.

But none of that sat right with Blue. He was as thorough as it gets. And he stood on the street principal no snitching. Even doing business with the police is a form of snitching. He thought to himself.

"I don't agree with that. Blue spoke again.

"It really doesn't matter what you agree with. This shit been going on before you were born. And you not going to be the one to change it. If you don't remember nothing else I tell you inside this cell, you make sure you remember. Sometimes you got to cut a couple of your own fingers off to save your hand." Jihad said as he looked Blue in the eyes and exited the room to walk the track inside the dorm.

One side of Blue was telling him Jihad was right. But being he was knee deep in the streets. He figured it was all about doing wrong and not getting caught. He had a cops and robbers mindset. Jihad was trying to teach him to be a thinker. And was using chess as a learning method. Only time would tell rather or not if he would adhere to the teachings Jihad was trying to give him, or would he live the same way.

The next couple days Blue had made his mind up. He was determined to be a winner. Being in the county jail showed him a different side of the game. He was surrounded around nothing but losers. Either they lost everything they had, or they were on the verge of losing their freedom for a long time. And losing wasn't an option. Even if he had to cheat. He made his mind up. By any means he would be a winner.

Blue was laying down reading The Four Agreements by Don Miguel Ruiz when he suddenly heard his name being called over the intercom in the dorm for visitation. He wondered who it could be coming to see him today. He didn't like visitation cause he knew once the visitor left he would want to leave with them. But it was a while since he had outside contact with the world. Jihad was teaching him about how to do time and beat his case. And simply put, told him the more he talked on the phone he let the government learn more about him and his moves.

Entering the visitation room where steel stools and the phones sat on each side of the bullet proof glass. Blue noticed Blocka dressed in a Islamic garb known as a Jalabah and wearing a Kufi. While everyone on the opposite side of the glass were standing up socializing. Blocka sat in the corner patiently waiting.

Blue picked up the phone and greeted his father. "Salamu alaykum."

"Wa alaykum as salam wa rahmutuallah. How's the brother holding up?" Blocka spoke while observing his son. And to his surprise he seen the eyes of a tiger. The eyes that showed humbleness but fierce as well.

"Surely all praises are due to Allah. I just been building my mind and studying the law." Blue said.

Upon hearing Blue speak of studying the law brought a smile brighter than the sun at noon to Blocka's face. He knew his son was now becoming more calculated.

"I'm proud of you son and I pray to Allah this isn't jail talk. You gotta keep the same mindset you have in here when you get out. I talked to the lawyer and the state doesn't have enough evidence to charge you with the murder. So, you'll get time served for the battery."

Blue excitedly jumped up and down until he noticed Blocka's facial expression was still serious.

"It's time out for the playing. You got snakes in your grass that you got to get out. I set a meeting up with some important people for when you get out. You ready for this city to be yours?" Blocka finished.

"What do you mean father?"

"You bout to turn into an Ace of Spade. This city is about to be yours. You gone be the strongest one in Jacksonville." Blocka aforementioned.

Mesmerized by his fathers' words Blue sat there in deep thought.

"I'm not going to stay that long. I just wanted to come tell you about the meeting I set up. And give you the good news face to face. But let me ask you a question before I leave." Blocka said as he was getting up and placed his palm on the glass. "If you could be any piece on the chess board which one, would you be?"

"None of them." Blue shot back quickly.

Surprised, Blocka looked Blue in the eyes and asked. "Why?"

"Because if I'm a piece on the board that means somebody controls me. I rather be the hand that controls the pieces. So, if I ever was to lose a game. I can always have a chance to spin the board and start over. But I do like the thought of becoming an Ace of Spade. Out of 52 cards kings, jacks, and queens I'm the strongest." Blue finished.

"That's my boy. Just remember what I told you son. Make this a learning experience. And keep the same mindset you have now when you get out." Blocka said before turning around and leaving the visitation room.

Blue was all alone in his small jail cell, laying on the bunk staring up at the ceiling. He was thinking about what his father had told him a couple hours ago about the meeting and him getting out.

Outside looking in, it appeared as though everything was heaven sent. But Blue was smarter than that. He knew everything in life was an illusion. Nothing was what it appeared to be. After all, the ocean was supposed to be blue. But if you went to grab a cup of water from the ocean it was clear.

And always, and I repeat son, always keep an Ace in the Hole or get out before it's too late. Blue could hear Blocka's voice in the back of his mind.

The statement was made to him when he told his father he wanted to be in the drug game. Blue let the words sink in and repeated them. This was something he planned to apply to his everyday life, especially knowing how intelligent and manipulative his father could be at times. So, he knew it was more to the story than what his father told him earlier. But all that mattered was he was getting out and getting a second chance at life.

A week had passed by and today was supposed to be the day Blue was to be released. His lawyer had waived his court appearance. So now he was waiting for the release papers to hit the jail and he was going home. He felt as he was being reborn again in a sense. One part of him was disappointed he was leaving Jihad behind. He laid on his bunk and analyzed his whole life. And he vowed to himself that losing wasn't an option.

"Salamu alaykum brother." Jihad entered the cell interrupting Blue's thoughts.

"Wa alaykum as salam, how did the attorney visit go?" Blue asked.

"It went well the United States is taking back the life sentence and giving me 25 years with my 18 years credit. I'm thankful!" Jihad expressed with much enthusiasm.

"Masha Allah, it is as Allah has willed." Blue responded.

But down in his heart he felt an aching pain for Jihad. Here he was happy about 25 years. And he was stressing about the months he had spent in the county jail. This was a lesson for him in all aspects. "Different levels, different devils." He thought to himself.

Noticing Blue thinking his facial expression change. Jihad knew he was thinking about his situation. "Don't feel bad about my situation. I'ma be good long as Allah keep breath in my body. You need to worry about you and remember everything you learned from this experience. You need to read that quote I got written on that wall. Jihad said pointing at a piece of paper stuck on the wall above the desk.

Blue walked over to the steel desk attached to the wall inside the cell. And noticed it was a quote (By Sun Tzu) from the book (The Art of War). It read "The skillful leader subdues the enemy's troops without any fighting." As soon as he finished reading the quote. The officer came over the intercom.

"Robins! Robins! Pack it up! Your heading home!"

Blue grabbed the quote off the wall, embraced Jihad and only left the cell with his bedroll and mat. His heart was racing, and stomach was turning. This was the day he long waited for.

Chapter 18

(The following Day)

Blue was finally home, relaxed, settled and enjoying his second day of freedom.

The humid, Florida weather was a breezy 80 degrees. He promised his father he would take the meeting he'd set up before he began to run the streets again.

He was sitting on the back porch heartbroken. Yesterday his father drove him past the (House of Pain) and seen the bullet riddled house. Viewing the house in that shape left him furious. He knew F.M.B and the rest of them were behind this. Word around the neighborhood was that Rich was back on top. He had reopened shop and was now servin weight and bust down work. Blue shook his head as he stared at the quote he'd taken from the cell as a memory of Jihad. "The skillful leader subdues the enemy's troops without any fighting." (By Sun Tzu) as he pondered over this quote. He imagined how the meeting was to take place today at 5pm. Blue decided to not contact the rest of his crew until he came back with a solid plan. Only time would tell what the future would behold.

It was 4:00 pm sharp, patiently waiting Blocka and Blue was sitting behind the tinted windows of the black Lincoln town car. Time meant everything to Blocka. And that's why he was leaving an hour early. As usual Jeffery the driver was chauffeuring today's trip. The father and son who were dressed in matching all white linen dress suits, both wore a pair of white Havana Joes.

The A/C was on full blast as the Lincoln town car veered onto I-95 South ramp heading towards Queens Harbor.

Queens Harbor was a gated community located on Beach Blvd. It was known for some of the biggest houses in Jacksonville and also its famous residents. Majority either Jacksonville Jaguars Football players stayed there or very rich/important people.

In the backseat, Blocka was puffing a Cohiba Cigar. A small mountain of big face hundreds was piled up in the middle of Blue and Blocka inside a Ziploc bag. The money had a funny stench to it. Blue sat back in amazement watching his father peel apart the sticky money. The bills were money that Blocka pulled out one of his many stashes. He separated the money into two stacks that he placed rubber bands on each. He gave Blue one and he kept one.

We must be going to see the connect. Blue thought as he smelled the money and then placed his top lip over his nostrils.

"Fix ya face boy, that money probably older than you." Blocka bragged.

"Yeah right! Stop cappin daddy." Blue responded.

"Always remember son, it aint bout how much money you make, it's about how much money you save." Blocka dropped priceless jewels.

The driver finally made it to the gated community's front tall booth. Where he was greeted by a fat overweight white guard with a thin mustache.

"Welcome to Queens Harbor are you a resident or a visitor?" The security guard asked.

"Visitor." Jeffrey the driver responded.

"And whom would that be for?"

"The Judges Chamber." Blocka interrupted from the backseat.

"Okay I see. You gentleman are going to go straight ahead. And it's going to be the only house sitting inside the culdesac. Welcome to Queens Harbor." The guard finished as he hit the button to open the gate to let them inside the gated community.

At first glance, the gated community looked as if it was located in Calabasas California broadcasting imported palm trees, green pastures, and in every driveway sat a luxurious vehicle over the $200,000 price range. This was something only seen out of the movies.

On the end of the street, sat what looked like a smaller model of the White House with its large pillars. And river view backyard of the ST. Johns River. Different gardeners, maids, and butlers could be seen standing along the property. They were the ones who maintained the beauty of 25,000 square foot mansion.

A butler waived the driver down alongside the mansion. As the town car crept down the cobblestone driveway that led to the back of the mansion. To a spacious backyard with a patio.

Upon the town car stopping, the butler opened the back car door then greeted the father and son. And led them to the patio of the mansion. From the patio you could see half of downtown Jacksonville. And the St. Johns River as the beautiful sun was changing colors in the summer sky.

Blocka and Blue found two lazy-boy chairs. The view was amazing, they both thought as they sat down. In front of them sat a small table with Cohiba Cigars and small pre-rolled joints in white rolling papers.

As if on que, they both turned their heads to face each other. Just like Blue knew his father loved Cohiba Cuban Cigars. Blocka knew Blue had a strong likeness for weed. So, they both immediately felt comfortable.

The two were sitting in the Lazy Boy chairs on the patio looking at the beautiful body of water that stretched across the backyard. It was a little before 5 pm and the yellowish sun was moving close to setting.

"This is a test to see if you are ready for the next level" Blocka beginned speaking in his baritone voice. Taking small puffs of his burning cigar. "An old timer once told me, if you can't beat em, join em. In this game you gotta know when to hold them and when to fold them."

Just as Blocka was finishing his sentence. Blue noticed a man and woman who he'd never expected to see enter the patio. "Gentlemen I see you all are making yourselves comfortable." Judge Angela Waldon spoke eyeing the pre-rolled joints and Cuban cigars the father and son were enjoying.

"Of course, I didn't expect these types of things to be here. Blocka said holding his half-burnt cigar.

"Well, we have staff members that are Cuban and Jamaican. So, we keep things of those nature lying around."

Blue didn't say a word. As he sat looking Shawn Waldon square in the eyes. It was all starting to make sense. From the meeting to his quick release. He suddenly felt the impact of his father's words down on him. And a smile appeared on his face.

Blocka looked to the left of his son. And seen his body language was more confident. As Blue got up and moved towards Shawn Waldon and extended his right hand.

Few months prior, Blue and Blocka attended the councilman dinner and met the mother and son. Angela and Shawn Waldon who are pre-eminent figures in Jacksonville's Judicial System. Angela has been a judge for the past 20 years with connections from the state attorneys to the mayor's office. So, when Blocka made the call for a favor. It was nothing to get things handled with Blue's case. But every favor came with a debt or favor. Sometimes equal, sometimes greater.

"Alright, I'm sure you two gentlemen had a long ride over. How about we relax a little and then discuss business?" Judge Waldon asked.

"Why not", Blocka replied looking at Blue who shrugged his shoulders.

Not long after, a dark-skinned chef who looked as if she had a Caribbean accent entered the patio with a food cart. One part was filled with plates of curry chicken and rice with vegetables. While the other had different bottles of wine.

About an hour later, the four sat across from each other. The parents sat side by side. And so did the sons. Everyone of their eyes were glued to the chessboard as Blue and Blocka played an intense game of chess. Over the last hour they each held individual conversations. To Blocka's surprise Blue held his own weight. Making some plans he and only Shawn knew. He was hoping his son made the wise choice. And from the looks of things as the meeting concluded. Blue and Shawn embraced like they had known each other for years.

Chapter 19

It was a quarter past one when Blue pulled up on the corner of 13th and Canal. Looking up the block, it was just like everyone had told him. Rich was back at it; anyone could tell from the line of cars lined up on the curve. Some cars were basic that pulled up. But the majority were fixed up Chevys. Indicating these were prolly dope boys. A Florida thing was to buy old school Chevys and bring them back to a new state, but better. So, the loud music, shiny rims, primed down bumpers, and the sound of racing and boat motors could be heard from afar.

"It's two ways to skin a cat." Blue sighed shaking his head while picking up his cell phone. He dialed a number and waited for the person on the other end to answer. When they did, he begin to speak. "Everything in motion, I'm just waiting on yall to pull the trigger." Blue expressed with malice in his voice and hung up the phone.

(A Month Ago)

Rich was enjoying the life he was living at the moment. I guess it was true what they said, with every adversity was an opportunity. And he had found it. It was not too long ago him and his most trusted Ronnie. Also, who people knew as Jack were at Ruth Chris Steakhouse out South in Ponte Vedra. The upscale restaurant sat aside above a lake with a spring gushing in the middle.

They awaited the waitress to bring their steaks. They were both enjoying the Florida summer weather. As they sat outside on the balcony of the steakhouse. Summer's sun was beaming and making the Bugette diamonds give the other occupants a show. Rich and Ronnie held their chests high as their F.M.B pendants danced in the summer sunlight. Viewing they were gaining attention. They both went to motioning their wrist's around as they spoke, knowing the diamonds was cutting up inside the face of the Bezels they each had on. It felt good to be outside the hood and getting attention from the rich white folks. But one person's attention would pay way more than others.

  On the other side of the balcony sat Amani. She also was paying attention to the spectacle behind her Chanel shades. She looked on in anticipation hoping these were ballers forreal and not wanna-be's. She was the daughter of a beautiful Queen Pin named Maliah. And moved to Jacksonville with a unlimited flow of cocaine supply from the Midwest. She introduced herself to Rich and Ronnie. And to find out they were the type of guys she was looking for.

  It took some politicking and networking, but by the end of their first meeting, they all agreed to a deal that would allow Rich and Ronnie to step outside Caesars shadow. At the beginning of each month, Amani agreed to front them 20 keys on consignment for 18,5 the extra $500 was for the front. At the time bricks were going for $20,000 apiece. In Rich eyes it was all about the money. Caesar, G-Money and Demon were dead. It was up to him to keep the team strong, and that's exactly the type of time he was on. Especially since Hector was no longer supplying them. He had to put his faith in this new plug. And hopefully the trap gods would answer.

(Back to the Present)

It didn't take long for things to pick up. Just like Amani said she dropped the load of 20 keys on Rich the beginning of the month. To cement his spot in the hood and get a little get back, he sent some hitta's to the House of Pain. He expected them to come back with a soul or two. But instead, they came back with a quarter key of soft and a stash of guns. He let them keep the drugs he wanted the guns. In Rich's eyes, he gained power with the guns. In two ways, he disarmed them and armed himself more. Only thing stuck out was a black trash bag with a Glock and AK-47 inside that had a strong odor of bleach. Money brought more problems. And to Rich that meant buying more choppas. He was getting ready for war. Not in a million years would he let G-Money and Caesar (rest) without avenging their deaths. Retaliation was a must rather now or later.

"Minus the bullshit, life's great." Rich said as he had finished serving the last person.

He was sitting in the kitchen watching Ronnie count stacks of money they received this morning. Every morning they had a long line of cars waiting to get served weight. And this day was no different.

"You went and checked on the kids?" Ronnie asked Rich.

"Nawl, I'm bout to now." Rich answered as he made his way to the backroom.

Entering the room, he flicked the light switch and there they were. Every time he got in the presence of them, he became nervous. He had to pick one up to face reality. He picked one up and cradled the small white square. It was too good to be true. He thought to himself as he looked at the other 9 white squares. Being in the presence of 10 bricks gave him a sense of nervousness and a surge of power. It was just like good times when Caesar was alive, only this time he didn't have to worry about no competition. Blue was in jail and Ralo and Smiley were missing in action. At least that's what he thought.

A team of drug task force officers led by Officer Shawn Waldon traveled from downtown to 13th street in unmarked cars in hopes of a drug bust. They received a tip that a drug house on 13th and Division had drugs, guns, and a lot of activity.

Minutes later the team made its move.

Scurrrrr! Tires screeching could be heard. Then masked men with tactical gear, bullet proof vests, and shirts that read police could be seen jumping out running to the front door.

Officers burst through the front door of the house.

"Police!" Don't move! "JSO!" a series of exclamations were yelled. As they swept through the house, footsteps pounding from room to room. It wasn't no chance for Rich and Ronnie to go nowhere.

Upon hearing the door come crashing down Ronnie tried to hide in the kitchen closet. But it was useless. They were everywhere and also surrounded outside of the house. He was quickly found and handcuffed. On the other hand, Rich hearing the loud commotion made a move to get out the window. But was quickly tackled and handcuffed and escorted to the back of one of the unmarked cars.

It didn't take long for the officers to find anything. They immediately found the 10 bricks of cocaine, different caliber handguns, $15,000 in cash, also AK-47 and the

Glock in the black trash bags. This was enough to put both of them in the feds for a lifetime.

"Great job Waldon", Lieutenant Carter stated.

The news crew, everybody and they momma came down to see, what the city was talking about. This was being televised as the city's biggest drug bust this year. And all the credit and praise were given to Officer Waldon and his task force. If it wasn't for his extra duty and extensive police work none of this would be possible.

(The Next Day)

It was early and the roads were barely visible from the fog. The sun was just starting to rise creating a yellowish-reddish glow in the sky. Officer Waldon was awaiting at Metropolitan Park. Not soon after he seen a black pickup truck pull up and came who he was awaiting for.

"Dawg, that was sweet yesterday! You got the entire police force happy. Next month I'm getting a promotion to handpick my own squad. This is going to be big." Officer Waldon went on boasting.

"How the fuck them being happy gone help me. Huh?" Blue questioned with a mean mug on his face.

"Calm down. I got something for you. I told you; you got me I got you."

"Oh yeah? What's that?" Blue begins to smile.

"I got a friend of mines who works at the Bank of America on Edgewood. He's the bank officer and knows a couple bankers who makes very large deposits. It's one guy who makes a $100,000 dollar cash deposit every other day. This is big stuff, you hear me. Don't mess this up!"

"Listen here, don't question my ability. If we gone be on the same team. Trust must be number one. One hand washes the other and both hands washes the face." Blue explained.

Shaking his head up and down in agreement Officer Waldon unlocked his trunk and gave Blue a cardboard box. "Take this and be careful how you use these, we don't need the feds in our business. One call and this is done. I'll see you very soon." He said as he pulled off.

A 100 grand didn't sound too bad for Blue. Everybody had motion but it was slow motion. How you came in the game you were supposed to go out like that, but just harder. And that was what he had planned. It was time to have a meeting with the crew.

(Later that Day) In Flag Street Apartments

Ever since Blue had gone to jail a couple months back, Smiley, Ralo, Val, and Chevy was shaking down anybody in the city with money. Their motive was simple – Get the Money! Anybody refused they let their guns do the bargaining. When they came through shit wasn't up for debate. Word had spread quickly they were hungry and on a rampage. Killing was a sport to them. They were all certified killers and numb to the feelings of sorrow and remorse. And to make things worse they picked up the habit of smoking Boonk's also known as smoking dirty's. This was when you added coke with your weed. This high was 10 times more intense than snorting coke. So, it wasn't no telling what they would do at any moment.

Blue parked and hopped out in Flag Street Apartments. He had got word earlier that the guys were sitting low in an apartment on the 3rd floor.

Deciding not to knock he twisted the doorknob and to his surprise it was open. He pushed the door open and stepped into the small hallway leading to the living room. He saw a thick woman with a voluptuous bottom laying on her stomach on the couch. In the next room, he heard the sounds of 2Pac's Hail Mary and could smell the sweetness of the aroma of the mixture of cocaine and weed.

After locking the door and scanning the room, he followed the smell of smoke and the baseline of one of Dr. Dre's hardest beats he approached the bedroom door and pushed it wide open. As the lyrics of 2Pac filled the room and everybody sang in unison.

"I aint no killer but don't push me, revenge is like the sweetest joy next to getting pussy." 2Pac lyrics was like a prophet. His 2 bars had so much power in this room at this moment.

When Blue entered the room, he saw that the room was sat up like a living room just with tables. It was 2 couches and two tables. One small table and one big table. Chevy and Val were sitting on the couch in front of the small table. While Smiley and Ralo sat at the big table counting money separating it in 4 piles. In the corner sat a small tv playing Menace to Society but nobody was watching it. They all noticed Blue's presence. But each chose to remain silent.

Blue was taking in the scenery and was thinking of a master plan. Anybody else would've been scared in a room full of killers. But not him, he was one of them as well. He was just as more vicious and smarter. Cause he knew how to analyze. It's a difference between a player and a coach. A player is in the game and plays his position. But a coach plays every position in his mind. And also analyzes the game and knows what position needs to be played by which player.

"What they do?" Blue addressed the room.

"You see it, getting to this paper." Smiley countered focusing on counting the remaining of the bills.

"Salamu alaykum Ralo."

"A lot has changed since you been gone. We love God but we aint on that Muslim shit. We gone drink liquor and eat swine my brother." Ralo tried to imitate Brother Shareef off Menace to Society.

This caused the room to lighten up. Everybody enjoyed a nice laugh off the comment.

"How's it feel to be back?" Val asked.

"Feels like I was born again. That jail shit is for the birds."

"You heard bout Rich and nem?" Ralo asked.

"Nawl, what the word is?" Blue acted as if he knew nothing.

"Shid word is they got caught with 10 bricks, guns, and the murder weapons that killed Caesar." Smiley finished.

"How the fuck?"

"Well, somebody paid us a unexpected visit at House of Pain. And decided to take everything inside. They kept the guns, I guess. "Ralo said smiling.

"Damn!" Was the only word Blue could muster. That was two birds with one stone. But on the flip side of things, he knew Rich would put 2 and 2 together and figure out the guns came from them. And that would solve the puzzle to who was behind it all. It didn't matter cause they were long gone.

"Enough of the small talk, I got something I wanna show yall." Blue said as he headed for the door with the 4 in tow.

Making it to the truck he opened the door and removed the cardboard box. What he was about to show them was going to change all of their lives.

Waiting in anticipation, Smiley, Val, Ralo, and Chevy waited as the clouds turned grey and thunder could be heard clapping in the skies.

Finally, Blue begins to pull-out bullet-proof vests with police engraved and stitched on the front. He had six in total. And also had six ski masks' with JSO stitched in front of each.

Smiley was the first to grab a vest and feel the heaviness of the steel plated vest.

"Man, that's a life sentence you got in that box right there. Val frowned.

"This the key to the streets. This power I got in this box right here. Niggas aint gone have no choice but to lay down if they see us coming."

"Oooohhhh!!" They all made some sound of being surprised by Blue's way of thinking.

"You a fucking evil genius." Ralo complimented.

Back upstairs, Blue told them he had a connect on some sweet licks. But the first one was only going to be him, Smiley, and Ralo. After the lick they needed to find a plug. Smiley reassured him he had regular contact with Isabella Hectors sister. And was confident he could get them served some bricks. Only obstacle was they would have to go to Miami to get the product.

Now Blue was waiting for the call and was to make sure everything was ready. Ralo was to get the stolen car, Smiley was to bring the guns, and Blue was to make sure everything went as smoothly as possible. And the only way he could do that was to make sure his new connect had 100 percent accurate information.

Chapter 20

It was 8:45 AM when the foreigner pulled up to the Bank of America. This was his ritual every two days. He had a string of convenience stores he would pick up money from. Afterwards he would make the deposit of 50 to 100,000.

Ralo pulled up on the corner of DOE Avenue and Imaginary St. Looking to the right in the banks parking lot, it was just as the text message said: black station wagon parked in the back entrance of the bank. Ralo made the right turn and quickly made another right in the banks parking lot. Noticing the police cruiser leaving the bank through the same entrance. Ralo begins to speak to Blue and Smiley who were laying down in the backseat. "Coast clear, I'm pulling around back and he'll be on the left side."

Blue and Smiley both smiled, gripping their kuttas nervously. They both grabbed their kuttas pulled the lever back and bolted out of the back seat of the car.

"Freeze! Don't Move!" They both screamed.

Caught off guard like a deer in a set of headlights. The foreigner was caught by surprise, as he lifted his head from reading the Florida Times Union newspaper. He couldn't react the passenger window and driver side were shattered, sending tiny pieces of glass everywhere.

"Where is the money?"

"What money?"

Not being the one for playing games. Smiley quickly hit the foreigner with the butt of the kutta. But reluctantly, he still showed no weakness.

While Smiley watched the foreigner who was now leaking from his top, Blue searched the car. And he came up with nothing.

"Hurry up! We don't got all day." Ralo said in an anxious voice.

"Pop the trunk! Pop the trunk!" Smiley commanded Blue quickly.

Blue complied and soon as the trunk popped. Smiley ran to search it desperate for time. The split seconds was all the foreigner needed to reach under the dashboard for his nickel plated 357.

Rising from the back seat blue had an eerie feeling. And seeing the foreigner holding the 357 in smiley's direction answered why. Blue quickly swung the cutter in his direction and squeezed a shot into his already leaking top. Whop!!

Instantly his brains with blood spilled on the windshield. The loud sound of the rifle echoed. Hearing this the rest of the surrounding bank goers began to flee. Blue froze.

Finding the black book bag under the spare tire smiley quickly headed to the front of the car and grabbed blue. His body had gone into a state of shock. "Let's go!"

Back in the car, smiley unzip the black book bag and seen it was filled with cash money. From the looks of the amount of money they were back to where they started. On Top...

(Back at the Flag Street Apartments)

The room was filled with silence while smiley unloaded the stacks of rubber banded bills. From the looks of the sizes of each stack the amount looked to be well over 100 bands.

They each took turns grabbing the stacks of money and begin counting. As time lapsed, they became frustrated viewing majority of the bills were 1's, 5's, and 10s.

After one hour of counting, they came up with the ticket of $50,000. Ralo and Smiley were impressed. On the other hand, Blue was heated.

In the back of Blues mind, he knew the risk wasn't worth the reward. 50,000 ain't enough to buy all us lawyers and damn sho can't bond us out on murder charges. He thought to himself.

"Put that shit up, I'm bout to step out and make a call." Blue stated before leaving the apartment.

Blue decided to call Officer Waldon. He was mad about the amount of the robbery. From his understanding he had plans on making 100 bands, 50 was a far cry from 100.

The phone stopped ringing in his ear and the only thing he heard was the beating of his heart. He was starting to feel like he failed the mission. And was uncertain rather Waldon would still deal with him.

It was a hard pill to swallow, but in Blues mine if he did lose his political connection. He knew he could make his the ski mask way or off the muscle. And at that moment he decided to double cross Waldon. What started out as thinking out of emotion and calling him to tell him the lick was $50,000 short, he would tell him they only hit the lick for 10,000. The element of surprise was on his side, and without it he was feeling weak. Smiley had Isabella on his line. So he had the connect to Hector. And the amount of weight he was pushing gave them the ability to flood the entire city.

Blue was staying two steps ahead. So, the next plan was to go to Miami and meet the plug.

And deep thought, blue noticed his phone was vibrating and lighting up. When he looked at the screen, he viewed it was Waldon. He answered the phone not knowing what was next to come.

"Yoooo",

"Don't fucking yo me! What was that back there? Is news reporters in every media buzzing over the incident." Waldon expressed.

"Yeah I know, things got outta hand. And on top of that it was only 10,000. Blue responded not trying to go into any detail over the phone.

"Well, I hope that 10,000 was well worth it. Because that connection is now dead. Nobody wants blood on their money. You understand?"

"I understand, but." Blue tried to explain but was cut off.

"But nothing! This is the big leagues. The type of syndicate we're dealing with is federal. In order to stay ahead we must move in silence. You need to get out of town and lay low for a while until all this blows over." Waldon finished and hung up not giving Blue a chance to respond.

The things Waldon expressed to Blue made sense. But he was from the streets. And over the years trained his mind and his trigger finger, to shoot first and ask questions later. All that mattered to him was they were 50,000 richer. Now it was time to solidify his spot in the dope game. It was time to take a trip to M.I. Yayo better known as Miami.

Back at Bank of America, Janae was distressed. It seemed everywhere she turned violence haunted her life. First it was G-Money, Caesar, Demon, and now it was Jafari. Jafari was one of the bank's valued customers. She knew him pacifically from his large deposits. He had been coming to the bank for years. And nothing ever went down like what happened today. She sat in her office reviewing the original video of the robbery. Something didn't sit right with her. It seemed like the robbers knew exactly when to come. The robbery happened effortlessly. The timing was perfect. As soon as the officer in charge of the bank exited the parking lot is when the robbery took place. Taking her time Janae zoomed in on the shooter and her intuition told her she knew who this man was. It was like she could see through the ski mask. At the time her mind just wasn't putting a face to the man behind the mask. She felt her growing baby tossing and turning inside her womb. Rubbing her belly as she often did. She began to smile, soon after she heard a knock on her office door. Quickly hiding the video off of her computer monitor. She invited whoever was knocking. The bank was closed for today. So, it had to be one of the banks employees.

The door swung open, and it was the banks police officer Monclair.

"Is everything okay in here?" Monclair asked with a slight grin. A strong stillness embraced the air as Janae stared in the eyes of the officer Monclair. Something about his eyes held a look of evilness that sent chills running down Janae's spine.

"Are you okay?" He asked waving his right hand to get Janae's attention.

"Umm, Umm, Yes. I'm okay." Janae responded when she came back to reality. "Today has just been a long day."

"I agree." He smiled and left Janae speechless.

Soon as Janae's office door shut. She sighed a sign of relief. She was trying to train her mind to stop overthinking. But she would never forget a proverb from her Nanna. "Always go with your first mind. That be your ancestors speaking to you." Her grandmother was always telling her some type of African proverb from the teachings of (IFA). She opened her drawer to her desk and pulled out a necklace her nanna gave to her to protect her and also communicate with the ancestors. "Show me light in the darkness." She said aloud to the spiritual force of the universe. Then place the chain around her neck. Ever since Caesar and the rest had died. Janae had been making sacrifices to her ancestors and becoming more in tuned with the consciousness of nature. To her the battle was spiritual not physical. She believed what was in the dark would come to the light eventually.

Before leaving to go to Miami. Smiley got in touch with Isabella and set up a meeting with the plug Hector. She convinced him her brother would let them grab 15 keys for $15,000 apiece. And would see could she get him to front whatever they would buy. Smiley plan was coming together. He had waited all these months for this opportunity. He thought thinking about the night at the

Silver Foxx. The night was a night he would never forget. Not only did he run into the plug sister. He also ran into Angel and her friend. Rumors were now circulating that him and Angel had something going on and he knew if he heard them, Blue heard them as well. He made a notion in his mind to stay far away from her.

Blue placed the two duffel bags inside the trunk of one of the rentals. The duffel bags were supposed to contain a quarter million dollars. In the other car following behind Blue, Smiley, and Ralo were Chevy and Val. Shaq had just had a child and was in the streets still but just not how he once was.

They made the six-hour drive, from Jacksonville at the top of the gun shaped state, to Miami the bottom. They all were hoping this deal was official. And Smiley did his homework and didn't get them robbed. This was the biggest deal they ever made. So, they needed everything to be on point.

Exactly, six hours and 3 minutes. They got off I-95 to exit onto the Turnpike to get to South Beach. Once they arrived Smiley called Isabella who gave him the address to a boat dock off of Collins Ave.

When they arrived, they were at a loss for words. The scene looked as it came off the set of a movie. Parked along the side of the street were numerous foreign cars. Majority of the cars were Porsche 911's and Ferraris. On top of the cars sat attractive women topless with suntanned skin. The guys all looked Cuban, and each had chunks of gold Cuban links around their necks and Rolexes on their wrists. It wasn't hard to see all these Cubans were no older than twenty. They were getting paid off the cocaine trade in America.

"It's a shame how these muthafuckas leave their country and come over here and get a piece of the American pie before we do." Ralo voiced while observing the scenery.

"Shid, it's out here we just gotta get on our grind and get it." After tonight we're gonna run the town." Blue manifested.

"That's the boat dock right there." Smiley pointed.

Upon viewing the boat dock, they were even more impressed. Each dock anchored at least a 50-foot yacht or better. But what stuck out was the 50-footer with the words "Blonco Chica" which meant white girl on the side of the yacht and bold letters. Flying high was the Cuba flag up top the captain's cabinet.

Smiley made the call and down came a beautiful Isabella. And just like he remembered her. She was fine as a bottle of wine in her sun dress, that left little too the imagination.

"K Ola Papi, welcome to Dade County." Isabella began speaking, noticing Ralo and Blue with the duffel bags filled with money. She was instantly turned on and had to control herself. Nothing turned her on like a bag of money. "Follow me." She announced leading her way onto the spacious yacht.

When the four made it to the top deck of the yacht. Isabella LED them to a dining table that was sat for five. On the table was a dead shark that looked to be about 6 feet long. The side of the shark had a large slash on its skin. They stepped back observing to make sure they were good.

"I'll be back. I'm going to get me Amano. He's waiting to meet Ju. I told him a lot about Ju." Isabella giggled as she disappeared on the spacious yacht.

"Man, what this some kind of joke!" Smiley snapped.

"I'on know, I'm glad this son of Bitch is dead." Blue said While touching the sharks' large teeth in its open mouth.

"Just get this shit over with. And get going." Ralo blurted.

It wasn't everyday people had 6-foot sharks laying around. This dude Hector was on some other shit. He was different, and it was showing. The smell of a fine Cuban cigar could be smelled. Before they seen who was smoking the handmade cigar.

"Hello my friends." Hector caught the three men off guard. Hector was a pale Cuban dressed in silk. He wore his long black hair in a ponytail. Only thing he had on was rosary beads. He wasn't the flashy type. The yacht was his first purchase in the U.S. He saved every dime he made and sent any extra to take care of his family in Cuba.

"I've heard a lot about Ju all." He motioned his eyes to the three, sizing them up and down.

"Likewise, but we came to do business. And what's with this shark?" Blue pointed eyeing the shark.

"This here my friend, was my pet. I fed her a lot of people. And now Ju see she has gotten too big, and now I must eat her. Ju see?" Hector patted the shark with the sinister grin.

The fact Hector was standing in front of them talking about feeding a shark humans like it was normal, made them want to reevaluate their plans. This Cuban was crazier than they expected. But they were crazy as well. And he had what they needed, and it was vice versa, even exchange.

"Junior! Are you behaving?" Isabella came from the front of the yacht. Son-Ing her brother.

"Yes, Mi Amor." Hector responded.

The three just sat there and looked on. They weren't sure if they made the right decision or not.

"Policia?" Hector questioned Isabella with raised eyebrows.

"No Papi!" Isabella answered.

"My sister must like one of Ju all. What's inside Ju bags?"

Blue unzipped one of the black duffel bags. And showed the stacks of money with $100 bill on each side.

Viewing this Hector's eyes began to glow. He was already loving this new clientele his sister brought to him. Usually, he fronted then received money on the back end. On this occasion they were cashing out and asking to get fronted whatever they bought. He liked the business smart of these young street niggas. He thought to himself.

"Come over here." He motioned for the three to gather around the shark. "This is a business partnership never to be broken." Hector began speaking as he stuck his arm up to his elbow inside the shark. In one motion the hollowness of the shark shrunk, as he began to pull packages of cocaine out of the dead fish. Immediately Blue, Smiley, and Ralo started to notice the sparkles showing off the cocaine. In all, Hector pulled out 30 white squares of fish scale cocaine. The sight of all the white made them believe their eyes were playing tricks on them.

"Each of these keys you can put one key on top. So, this is 60 keys you're looking at." Hector bragged of the purity of the coke.

"Once we count the money, I got a surprise for Ju all. Before you leave I wanna show Ju around South Beach." Isabella said seductively to the three. Then winked at Smiley.

Blue and Ralo handed over the bags full of cash. One to Hector the other to Isabella. They both unzipped the duffel bags and began dumping the money on the ship's waxed wooden floors. Isabella bent over giving them a show, through the sun dress she didn't have on any panties.

Blue, Ralo, and Smiley gave each other a look of doubt. The inevitable was to happen sooner or later.

Not long afterwards, Hector made a grunt of displeasure.

"What the fuck is this?" Ju piece of shit." Hector spat venomously.

Before him or Isabella could react about the money being majority small bills. That were faced with $100 bills. To make them from outer appearances look like stacks of hundreds. They were startled by the sound of footsteps.

Smiley and Ralo smiled at the sounds of a small stampede nearing. When a masked gunman appeared from each side of the ship.

"Everybody let me see your hands and lay face down on the ground." One of the masked gunmen with a vest that read POLICE on the front demanded waving a assault rifle.

Everybody complied except Ralo, Blue and Smiley. Hector noticing it was police officers. Tried to bribe them by offering them money and cars. Only response he got; was they didn't come for his money they came for his life. Isabella noticed the three others had begun grabbing the money and keys. And attempted to spit at them. Smiley weaved the glob of spit. And removed a handgun and jammed it inside Isabella's mouth chipping her teeth. As he was about to pull the trigger. He heard Blues voice.

"Fuck that, stay focus." Blue coached Smiley snapping him out of his rampage.

Once they were finished bagging up the 30 bricks and the money. They left the masked gunman, Hector, and Isabella behind. They came to Miami as thousandnaire's and left millionaires. The legacy of Blue, Smiley, and Ralo had begun. And only was to get better. As they made it down I-95 in the fast lane.

Chapter 21

After returning to the city. Blue, Smiley, and Ralo name was hot as fish grease throughout the streets of Jacksonville Florida. The white powdery substance brought money, power, and respect. Everybody knew you could go to Grand Park in Flag Street Apartments to get served. You could go buy jugs or jugglers. Which was double up crack rocks. Whatever you spent you can make double. Snow and cocaine, cooking cocaine, and recently they just started selling weight. After all, with this new operation they had with Blues political connection. They will never go broke again.

Since going from rags to riches, they each were flexing their wealth. Blue dropped a 2 door 68 Chevy on Dayton Rims and dipped it in candy apple red paint. The inside was guttered red and had six 12's for the music. Smiley dropped a four door Lexus with chameleon paint that turned colors every time the sun rays shined on the paint. He just put the gold rims on the feet. Ralo dropped a 73 Chevy all white top with candy blue hand rims.

Each of their cars were parked outside of one of the buildings in a single line. Music could be heard blasting from Blues 68 Chevy. They were watching the customers place their money inside a can and received the product. Tonight, was a slow night. But money was still being made. They were using the system Blocka showed them in New York. And just like it worked up there. It proven to birth the same results with them. They had two shifts from 7:00 AM to 7:00 PM and 7:00 PM to 7:00 AM. They only came by the spot at night. They were schooled on how the drug task were moving. And were told they were less likely to do a drug bust at night. So they only made their presence known at night.

"Damn where this nigga at?" Ralo asked Blue.

"I hope he don't think about trying no slick shit." Smiley voiced clutching the M-16.

"Only thing beat the cross is the double cross." Blue spoke while picking his teeth with the toothpick. He was waiting on a boss player named Slick out of Uptown. The historical part of Jacksonville around the eastside. Slick had run into Blue at club "After II." And asked for a quote on some birds. Another slang for keys. Blue assured him the birds could take one and still swim. Letting him know that one brick could be turned into two bricks and still be cooked for crack. He said the ticket was 22. And if he brought more the price would only get lower. Slick loved what he heard and agreed to buy two. Blue told him to pull up in the projects after sundown with 40 bands.

As they were leaning against their cars. Blue was telling Ralo and Smiley how he had 10 women pregnant at one time. Since he became rich, all he did was party. You only got one life to live so he was living it up. It seemed like every other night he was waking up with a different woman in his bed. And with 10 women pregnant the fruits of his labor were eventually going to show. He was just thinking of a way to bring all his babymommas to meet each other. When he noticed a black Chevy 4 door pull in the projects. He stopped talking and got into the game. He played hard but he also grinded harder and smarter. And that's what was keeping him atop his game.

Viewing the Chevy flash its headlights. Blue waved his hand while Ralo and Smiley stayed on point. They treated every deal the same. One did business while others made sure everything else was kosher. One false move and it could get ugly.

The Chevy slowed to a stop and down came the passenger window. There was Slick showing a gold tooth smile.

"What they do?" Slick shouted.

"Aint shit. You still wanted the two?" Blue asked.

"Yes Sir. I got the 40 right here. Each rubber band a stack."

"I'ma Step out on faith with you this time." Blue took the money and placed it on the front seat of his 68 Chevy. And walked to the building and made a strange noise. One of the workers had popped out the window upstairs.

"I need that." Blue demanded. And out came a black trash bag with the two bricks. Blue checked and made sure it was all there. Then walked to Slicks car handing him the trash bag through his car window.

Slick pulled out of flag street apartments and made a left onto Kings Road. He was headed towards downtown back to his stomping grounds. When he approached the first red light. He opened the black trash bag and was satisfied with the 2 bricks image.

Slick was looking in the review when he noticed a Nissan Altima following him. He immediately thought that Blue had put the Jack boys on his trail. He wasn't threatened at all. He reached under his seat and grabbed the fully automatic Mac-11. As he moved closer to downtown.

Game day Jaguars traffic had all the streets backed up. People could be seen wearing Jacksonville Jaguars jerseys and some tailgating on the side of the streets. The Altima was now on the passenger side of slick. Slick was so focused on the Altima. That he was blind to the fact, that a marked patrol car was now behind him.

As Slick pulled on the side street trying to avoid the game day traffic. The patrol car flashed its lights in an attempt to pull him over.

Noticing the flashing lights behind him, Slick tucked the Mac-11. And placed the black trash bag under the passenger seat. Watching in the rearview mirror. He seen the officer approaching the car.

"License and registration please?" The officer in uniform asked Slick.

A moment later, the Nissan Altima pulled up. Slick could see the officer in uniform go to the driver side of the Altima and began to speak. Shortly after, the officer came back to Slick and asked him to step out. Once he stepped out the officer placed him in handcuffs and put him in the back of the patrol car. After he was placed in the back seat, the patrol car began to pull off. "Officer, may I ask what's going on?" Slick questioned.

He received no response. The officer kept driving until he arrived at a parking garage in the middle of downtown. He picked up his cell phone and placed a call.

"I'm here." Was the only thing the officer uttered.

Slick wasn't worried about nothing. He knew the law and from this situation alone. He knew his vehicle could not be searched without his consent or search warrant. (Fruit of the poisonous treat doctrine.) He thought as he smiled to himself.

Slick was in a relaxed state of mind he was starting to doze off. Until he heard a light tapping on the window. Awakened, slick rose his head and began to panic. He was looking through the slits of a ski mask and a set of brown eyes.

"What, what, what's going on?" Slick stuttered.

The masked man opened the back door to the patrol car. Slick scooted to the other side of the back seat. He looked like a little kid trying to avoid the boogeyman.

Leaning against the driver side door of the back seat. Slick was sweating bullets. The other back door was opened. And he fell back first to the hard concrete.

On the ground, he was trying to crawl and get away. But it was useless he was handcuffed. He was like a harmless mouse inside a tank with a rattlesnake.

The masked man placed his 357 to Slick's head before speaking. "You making this harder than it could be. If you wanna make it back to those Pretty Little girls. You better chill before I knock the meat out your taco."

Hearing the masked man mention his kids Slick froze.

"Uncuff him." He commanded the officer in uniform.

Once Slick was uncuff, he turned around and seen the man in the mask was holding the black trash bag. His heart began to race. He knew what the two bricks and gun he was facing a boatload of time. All he could do was put his head down.

"Pick your head up, it's not over with. For 80 grand you can get the dope back minus the gun."

"I don't got that type of money laying around." Slick said in a voice full of sorrow.

"What you got for me then?"

"I can tell you where the dope came from."

"How about this, I'm gonna give you 24 hours to scrape up 25 grand. If you don't reach out to me by then. Next time I see you I'm gonna take something you can't get back."

"What's that?" Slick asked.

"Your life. Now go get my money." The masked man told Slick and threw him his car keys.

Back In flag St. Apartments, Chevy and Val had joined the rest. From the looks of things, they were doing good for themselves. They both were covered in Cuban links and Rolexes.

"Damn, where you niggas been at?" Ralo asked.

"Oh, we did a little shopping on South Beach." Val bragged.

"You niggas went and laid them Cubans down?" Smiley asked.

Val and Chevy both broke out into a fit of laughter. Robbing was their game. They got a kick out of making a man submit to a higher power. The gun!

"What happened with ole girl and her brother." Blue was wondering did they finish the job with Isabella and Hector. The last thing they needed was any loose ends.

"Let's just say they shark food now." Chevy spoke.

"That's good, check this out." Blue called them over to the 68 Chevy and handed them 10 bands apiece. Money was rolling in fast and easy. And what niggas they were serving who wasn't from around their way or down with them. They were fair game and being fed to the wolves. After they grabbed bricks, they were pulled over and the bricks were confiscated. Then given back to Blue. A lot of times the same bricks were sold to the same person twice. The second time they would ask for a front. And they would get fronted just with interest. Only time money would get spent was to buy the bricks back half price from Waldon and his task force.

The solid principal Blue stood on, was loyalty to his team. If you were a part of the chosen few. Your trap house was protected. If your name or your spot came across the drug task force's desk. You were given a heads up and sometimes a date of the drug bust. But that also came with a hefty fee.

After months of setting up shop. Blue, Ralo, and Smiley bought houses in the Paxton area. Real estate was low, and the area had a mixed community. Outside of them selling weight. They each maintained separate drug houses. These drug houses had workers that made from $1500 to $2500 weekly depending on the numbers the drug spot did. Every piece of work was accounted for and never too much money and dope were in the same spot at one time.

Word was spreading around the city that the feds were in town. A lot of people were making major money off cocaine. And majority of those people were black. But like they say, "more money, more problems." The money came with a lot of bloodshed. It was nothing for somebody to have 10 or 20 bands on them on a regular day. Every profile hustler birthed a dedicated Jack boy. This made the citizens of Jacksonville Florida complain that the Sheriff's Office wasn't doing their jobs. The numbers of homicides, robberies, and drug deals gone bad. Were at an all-time high. Rumors were also circulating about drugs turning up missing from the Sheriff's Office evidence room.

The city of Jacksonville was living up to its infamous nickname. "The Bang Em, Where We Hang Em." Which derived from being spray painted at the old courthouse, by its racist white citizens. Jacksonville is indeed a city where it's a lot of havoc, violence, and gun banging. Where also the court system is leaving its citizens to hang a long time in prison. For those who feel like they don't respect the laws that be.

Around this time, blue was not any different. He was 28 years old and on top of his game. Anything he wanted he got it one way or another. Just like his father told him, the city was his. The streets were talking a lot. But he didn't think they knew what they were talking about. It was time he showed who was the boss of bosses. With a team full of killers and the police on his payroll. He felt as if him and his team were unstoppable. They had the entire map to the underworld. If they didn't know about it. The police knew about it. And eventually they would tell Blue. True indeed he was an Ace of Spade.

Chapter 22

I always feel like, somebody watching me, I'm paranoid I can't sleep I'm in the dope game. Steady thinking that these niggas out to get me man. (Master P) Always feeling like somebody watching me.

The music from Master P was blasting through the speakers of the Chevy Corvette. The Corvette was all red and supercharged. The motor could be heard roaring, as Smiley dipped in and out of traffic on Normandy Blvd. Seeing the stretch was clear he stumped on the gas increasing the speed to 200 mph.

It was a little past 10:30 PM when Ralo, Smiley, and Blue pulled up to Herlong Airport. It was a small private airport used for private jets and also flying lessons. They were expected so they were granted access immediately.

"Over there." Blue pointed at the green camouflage wrapped helicopter. Its blades were already chopping through the night's air. And its spotlight was shining onto the ground.

Blue began to smile at the reaction of Smiley and Ralo. They had shocked expressions on each of their faces. They thought they were going to a party, not for a helicopter ride.

They each hopped out the vet covering their ears and jumped in the back of the helicopter. They each placed a headset on their heads over their ears.

"Take us to Club 904." Blue spoke through the mic of one of the headsets to the pilot.

The pilot lifted the helicopter off of its landing pad. And began to stare it in the direction of Club 904. The three felt like they were on top of the world. The view from the sky of the city was matching perfect with their personas. Kingpin status was the mood of this moment. They each had a name in the streets, trash bags full of money, plenty whips, and jewelry to show. It wasn't a soul in the game that wasn't familiar with the names Blue, Smiley, and Ralo. And if they didn't know, after tonight they would know.

Outside Club 904, the people were waiting for the doors to open. The waiting line at the door was wrapped around the corner. The music was bumping, and all the groupies were eyeing the Ballers pulling up stuntin in their whips. Big rims, loud pipes, and wet paint. That was the attention seekers of tonight's occasion. Everybody who was somebody was coming tonight. The cities DJ's DJ Chilli and Bigga Rankin were going live over the local radio stations 92.7 and 93.3 the beat jams. So, whoever wasn't in attendance would hear about it.

Suddenly, a sweeping gust of warm air shot throughout the streets, as everybody below looked up in the sky. A camo wrapped helicopter was hovering above the partygoers.

At first glance, everybody thought the helicopter was a ghetto bird, one that belonged to JSO. But when they noticed 100 and $50 bills falling out the open door. The crowd went bonkers and began to chase the money in every direction.

Ralo, Smiley, and Blue went to work, throwing money in every direction. The paper rained down like a snowstorm, causing the crowd to look like they were Easter egg hunting. People were heading in every direction. From the helicopter they can hear the crowd screaming for joy.

Inside the helicopter, everything seemed to be going in slow motion. To see people going crazy below made them feel like the kings of the city. And at that time, they were. Nothing was moving without their knowledge. But it was time to show everybody who was running the city.

After they each had thrown 10 bands of piece, a total of 30 bands. The helicopter pilot began to put on a show. He was hovering over the crowd as the club began to open its doors. He placed the headlight on the two big bouncers, while the helicopter was slowly landing.

Finally, when the helicopter landed, all eyes were on them. Blue stepped out first in mixed matched designers. He had on a Prada hat, Louis Vuitton T-shirt. Ferragamo pants, with Jimmy Choo super loafers. On his left hand he sported a name ring that said Blue in solid gold encrusted in diamonds. On his neck were three solid gold Cuban links and his left wrist was a gold Rolex. Ralo stepped out dipped in Hermes from top to his ankle. He even had the designers belt with the big H. On his neck he had on two solid gold Cuban links, a solid gold pinky ring with a 5-karat diamond in the middle. And a Cartier bracelet and watch set. Smiley stepped out looking like the Saint Laurent Don. On his shirt read YSL big and he also rocked the pants and loafers to match. Around his neck also he had two Cuban links made out of solid gold. He decided to have a light night. So, he spared his fingers and wrist from the attention for tonight's party.

Blue, Smiley, and Ralo were dressed like Mob Bosses. Everything was designer and sat in place like it was tailored. They each walked right past the bouncers like they owned the place. With each stride you could see people whispering. They looked like money. The people in the club assumed they were rappers out of Miami. Until DJ Bigga Rankin and DJ Chilli noticed the crowd make a way for the three as they headed to V.I.P.

"One time for my niggas Blue and Smiley!! I see you Ralo shining like a light pole!!" DJ Chilli announced.

Soon as the words blasted throughout the club the spotlight above was placed on the three. Blue and smiley was caught in the moment. But Ralo not blinded by the limelight. Began to notice something he never seen before. In the far corner of the club. He seen two white men with what looked like movie cameras snapping pictures. Feeling goosebumps arise on his skin. He grabbed Blue and Smiley by the arms.

"Let's leave, I don't feel right about tonight. Remember what happened the last time we were at this club." Ralo warned.

"Man, a nigga play crazy in this bitch tonight, I'll put so much money on their head, you'll be able to wrap them up like a mummy." Blue addressed Ralo pulling out stacks of $100 bills. "The city is ours!!"

Everybody's attention in the club was on Blue, Smiley, and Ralo. They were in V.I.P looking down on the club and any bad bitch they pointed at came running. They popped a bottle after bottle of champagne like they had just won a championship game.

Smiley sat in VIP taking in the scenery. It was just 6 months ago he was sitting in the Silver Foxx with no motion. Now he was at the top with the same niggas he was robbing and starving with. This was the type of shit you see in the movies. But he had said in his mind. Nobody knew his name but now he was a street legend.

"Look at us now!" Blue slurred drunkenly eliciting Smiley and Ralos attention. "It gets lonely at the top and look who here with us, niggas never gone forget us in this town, when it's all said and done, rather we be in the feds or dead, these niggas gone be talking about us the same way they talk about Alpo, Rich Porter and AZ, the difference between us and them, I'll never cross my niggas, I'll do life in the feds before I cross my niggas, let's toast to the good life." Blue finished and they each held up their champagne bottles and clinked the glass bottles together.

Blues words were strong like a prophet. Sometimes you must be careful of what you speak into existence in the universe. Because the feds were indeed in the building tonight snapping pictures. They were fascinated with the center of attention in the club tonight. Also, someone would cross the team. And he was right, the town would never forget the names of Blue, Smiley, and Ralo.

The rest of the night the trio lived up to the saying, "Ball Until You Fall." They spared no expense at tonight's party. They bought the bar out and gave free drinks to the entire club.

While sitting in the V.I.P section Ralo analyzed the entire club. And came to the realization that half of the people who were now in their V.I.P section, were nowhere to be found when they were broke. It was a sad reality of the streets. Whoever played the biggest part that's who the streets followed. He was learning in the streets love don't love nobody. The streets only love what you could do for them at that time. Ralo was now looking at Blue and smiley in a new aspect. He wondered if they ever thought about life without the game. Would the game still love them if they retired. Probably not he thought to himself. Then suddenly he seen a bright flash. He looked over to Blue and Smiley who were drunk entertaining two women apiece. They missed the flash of the camera.

"Aye! I think the police taking pictures of us." Ralo yelled over the loud music.

"Oh yeah! Let me give them something to take a picture of!" Blue shouted and stood up on the couch and V.I.P and begin to rain with $100 bills.

Smiley popped $1200 bottles of champagne and poured them on the crowd below. Smiley grabbed the baddest bitch in the V.I.P. He gave her and her friend enough money to pay their rent and car notes for a few months.

Anybody who was broke when they came to the club that night. They left with a little something in their pockets after. It was like a Robin Hood scene, where the rich riches were given back to the poor.

Sitting outside the club were Chevy, Val, and some goons out of the neighborhood. They were parked in front of the club. They each had on black trench coats and were armed with AK's, that they concealed underneath the trench coat. The black Chevy Tahoe's were parked along the curve of the club.

Club 904 was now letting out, as the DJ's called the last song. And announced last call for alcohol. A beautiful Puerto Rican named Bonnie stepped outside the club doors with her drunken boyfriend Flacko. Flacko stuck out more than the rest of the partygoers. Prolly because he was dripping in diamonds. And each ear he had a karat a piece of flawless diamonds. And around his neck was a 15-inch platinum chain covered in VVS diamonds and for a charm he had a Puerto Rican flag that was encrusted with red rubies and diamonds. Flacko was a brick man from the West side of Jacksonville. He was getting money and decided to step out with his fiancé Bonnie. But he was at the wrong place at the wrong time.

"Look at that Chico." Val nodded his head in Flacko direction.

In a matter of seconds, Chevy stepped to him and grabbed the flashy chain. Caught off guard and feeling the hard steel of the kutta on his back. He thought twice about giving up his chain. Sensing this Chevy began to speak.

"This is a robbery don't make this a homicide O'yae."

Realizing what was going on Bonnie reacted quickly removing her all Chrome 380 from her panties. Before Chevy could blink twice Bonnie had the 380 against his temple.

Soon as the rest seen what was taking place. They up'ed their kuttas in Bonnie's direction. Sensing danger, Bonnie began to speak with her trigger finger wrapped around the trigger.

"I'ma make sure that we all cry." Bonnie spoke in a menacing tone.

"Slow down it's just a misunderstanding. Yall put them guns up." Chevy told the goons.

They complied with what Chevy said. Bonnie and Flacco made their way with the chain. Holding their heads high.

They were true to the definition of Bodiqua (Brave Lords). To them the chain meant more than jewels. It was about the struggle the island went through. The flag represented Puerto Rico (Port of Riches). And the pride they carried for the enslavery of their people by the Spaniards and anyone else who participated in the slave trade.

Blue, Smiley, and Ralo staggered out the club with three women. "What y'all got going?" Ralo asked viewing Chevy, Val, and the goons clutching their assault rifles.

"Nothing much." They all pretended everything was normal.

"We gone take one of these trucks." Blue called out hopping in one of the three Tahoe trucks parked.

Blue, Smiley, and Ralo and three ladies left the club in the Tahoe. Blue drove them across the Main Street Bridge to the Double Tree.

The truck pulled up to the five-star hotel. Stepping out onto the streets. The three women stepped out in a pair of Christian Louboutin's. The three women were friends who attended Edward Waters College (EWC) located on Kings Rd. From the South side of Chicago. When they seen the three ballin like NBA players they decided to go along for the ride.

Blue stepped outside shortly and handed Smiley and Ralo cards to the exquisite suites on the top floor.

They bypassed the front desk and made it to the elevator. Each room held a beautiful view of the city's skyline and the Saint Johns River.

They went to their rooms and enjoyed the ladies. After each one was done with one of the college girls. They sent them to the next room. Until all three of them had a piece of each. Each girl was given some money and sent on about their business.

Chapter 23

(At the U.S District Attorney's Office)

Inside a dark room at the federal building downtown, sat 10 DEA agents. Detective Owens was controlling the projector that was showing pictures. These pictures were showing different drug dealers. But what stuck out the most was the pictures of the three men inside the V.I.P section of Club 904.

"Ladies and gentlemen, this is Blue, Smiley, and Ralo. They are running Jacksonville's cocaine trade. Our goal is to take them down."

The small space was quiet, as each detective read the 30-page manifestos on Blue, Smiley, and Ralo. When the Drug Enforcement Administration came. They came with all the facts. They watched you until they had enough concrete evidence. But these three were moving like no other they seen move in their age range. They could tell and detectives could see that they were on to something. It was something really big. It was something well organized. It was something they wanted a piece of.

First and foremost, they sent the images via e-mail to JSO's drug task force. Usually if the DEA lacked any small Intel or information they needed they contacted local authorities. Who in return would send them the mug shots or better yet, whereabouts of the criminals and interests.

This was a part of the game where a lot of people failed. Every day in the game people became rich. But the only how people knew is if they told someone or begin to show it. And just like the ones before. Either they became a target for robbers or got the attention of the feds. And this was no different.

(At Mr. Brown's Barbershop)

Mr. Brown's Barber shop was a known spot in the Grand Park area. Where you could get the Tea's on anything and anybody. And on this Saturday morning was a packed shop. Everybody was in attendance at the shop, from the boosters to robbers, from the Ballers to the peons.

Sitting in the middle of the shop were three Barber chairs. Nothing could be heard but small chatter as two older men played a game of chess. The remaining noise came from the Clippers and edgers as the barbers went to work. The remaining occupants were either in their phones, reading a magazine, or tuned in to ESPN on the TV.

"I know y'all been hearing about all these bodies turning up everywhere?" The Barber Jake asked nobody in particular. But that was all it took to crank the shop up.

"I heard that's been Blue and Smiley nem."

"Well, I heard Blue was the police and Smiley was the killer."

"They say Blue got like 10 babymommas."

"They also say Blue be fuckin boys."

"I heard he had aids."

"I know one thing; everybody gets served by them either dies or go to jail." Jake the Barber spoke up.

"Facts!"

"He getting all that money I heard that jewelry fake as a muthafucka."

"I know y'all seen that ugly ass donk that he got." Jake the Barber said.

"I'on Like the nigga ass anyways I'on like when he come round."

"So this nigga aint got no type of morals for himself? Huh?!"

It's two things you gone hear all around the jail system and the streets. "That's what they say", or "that's what I heard." But who is they say? And who is I heard? Nobody never knows.

The barbershop continued gossiping about everybody and they momma. When a sixty-eight pulled up with its glistening candy apple red paint. The Chevy was sitting on 22 Dayton's. The dark tint was concealing the driver. Blasting through the speakers was Trick Daddy's "What's Up." The loud pipes from the Chevy's 454 motor and music got everyone's attention in the shop. When suddenly the car shut off and Blue hopped out. Entering the barbershop, you can hear a mouse piss on cotton.

"What they do?" Blue addressed the entire shop.

Everybody who was just gossiping, was now trying to talk at one time. At seeing Blue appear before them.

"Damn I just was telling these boys, how I be seeing you in the club and your jewelry be hittin like a muthafucka."

"Shidd, I just was tellin that nigga, I heard you be fuckin all the stripper hoes at the Silver Foxx."

"I was just telling a hoe how every time you come round you gone turn a dead block to a block party."

"I was just telling that hoe how you got the rawest Donk in the city. I know you dropped about 80 in that bitch." Jake the Barber lied. Like he wasn't just the leader of the gossipers.

Blue sat down and enjoyed the attention. He paid for everyone's haircut. And just to skip the long line paid whoever Was next double the haircut fee. After a quick shape up Blue left to go post back up in Flag Street Apartments.

The hood was swole. It was around the 1st of the month, so the trap spot was jumping. It was a sunny day and fiends were getting their fix. The bad bitches were outside with they hoochie-momma shorts and coochie cutters in full effect.

Blue sat on the bench eating some boiled peanuts. When he noticed Shaq pull up in the 1st lane. The two men embraced and began to kick the shit. Shaq was off the scene for a while and back at it like he never left. They both sat back and enjoyed the project breeze. Shaq was one of the brick layers to the empire that now stood tall. So naturally they both felt the euphoric of seeing everything now come together.

"Man, you heard about Chevy and Val getting jammed up?" Shaq told Blue.

"Yeah, I heard, what about it?"

"I was just asking making sure them boys was straight. You know them boys gone need money on their books for commissary. And a lawyer." Shaq finished.

"That's the type of shit you gotta think about why you out there doing shit." Blue said.

"That's true, but these was the same niggas doing shit for you too." Shaq responded getting frustrated.

"You acting like I put a gun to these niggas head and made them do the shit they did. Them niggas locked up for they own doing. I'll see if they got jammed up on a mission I sent them on. Come on now Shaq? Let's keep it real!"

"I guess you're right, but if that was me I would at least make sure they books good."

"Man, I got damn near 10 kids out here. I gotta make sure my lil ones good. I just buried 500 G's in the ground just in case this all fail. That's niggas problems they living for now. You gotta be able to see 5 to 10 moves ahead. This shit a thinking man's game. It's about who can think the best." Blue preached feeling his phone vibrate.

While Blue took his calls. Shaq sat there pondering on what Blue said. What he was saying was absolutely correct in a sense. A man had to be held accountable of his own actions he committed. But if you were thugging with them on the streets. It's only right you hold them down when they fall. Chevy and Val would end up later catching life sentences. The people they were running with forgot about them. I guess it's true what Plies said. Muthafuckas forget about you when ya bid long.

Shaq seeing blue had a worried look on his face. Begin to question him. "You good my nigga?"

"Something just ain't right. My spirit telling me something going on. And now these crackas wanna meet all of a sudden."

"What crackas?"

"My lawyer wanna meet with me." Blue was throwing Shaq for a curve. Truth was Waldon had called him and told him things were getting ugly. But he wouldn't tell Blue how or what was going on. When you do a lot and did a lot. The not knowing of something could eat your conscious up.

Feeling his phone vibrate again. He looked at the screen and seen it was a play. A eerie feeling came over Blue as he answered the call.

"Yoooo."

"Aight just meet me in front of Flag Street Store in 30 minutes." Blue sat there thinking of his next moves. Today wasn't feeling right. Everything was moving too fast. Instead of him going to meet the play. He was going to send Shaq. His focus was on the bigger picture. He was more worried about Waldon and the phone call he received earlier.

"Shaq you wanna make some money?"

"Hell yeah, what the play is?"

"I gotta play for half-time, take my car they gonna meet you in front of Flag Street Store in 30 minutes. I'm bout to go meet my lawyer." Blue gave Shaq his car keys and jumped in a low low to go meet Waldon.

"You good?" Shaq asked.

"Am I good?" Blue asked him with a quizzical look. "Of course, I'm good. Why wouldn't I be?"

"I don't know you just seem a little off today. Huh, take this." Shaq was worried about Blues well-being. So he gave him the gun off his hip to make sure he was protected.

Blue was now sitting at the Raceway gas station on Pritchard Road. The gas station was full of 18 Wheelers who stopped off of I-10 to get gas.

His brain was racing as he sat there waiting on Waldon to pull up. He was massaging his temples and flexing his jaw muscles. He was eager to hear what he had to say. He was betting Smiley or Ralo had done something to cross him.

A pair of high beams flickered in the corner of Blues right eye. He looked through the windshield and saw a Ram 1500 pulling into the gas station then went around back.

Blue threw the low low in drive and pulled round back. Parking next to the Ram 1500 that was sitting high. He jumped out his low low and got inside the truck.

The windows were rolled down about two inches from the top and the air conditioner was on full blast. It was cold as Alaska inside the truck. But Waldon was dressed like he just left a tennis match, and some small tennis shorts and a V-neck. Only thing was showing he had money was the iced out big face rollie on his left wrist and the diamond studded wedding band on his ring finger.

"You seen the news?" Waldon asked calm in a low voice.

"Nawl, what I missed."

"The feds are in town. And they are sniffing around. They even sent us these." Waldon tossed Blue an white envelope full of pictures of him, Smiley, and Ralo.

Blue shrugged his shoulders. "A'ight, Ain't that's what I'm paying you bitches for."

"You gotta be bullshittin me right now? Waldon looked at Blue sideways. "Do you know what kind of heat is about to come down? I just showed you pictures the feds took of y'all, and you's got the nerve to tell me that's what you pay me for? You've gotta be shittin me right now?" Blues demeanor was unexpected to Waldon making his words come out in a different tone. He could not believe Blue was so naive about something this serious.

"So what's next? You got anymore licks for us. The house you put us on in ocean way had $1,000,000 cash in 25 bricks in it. Let's talk about this muthafuckin money."

Waldon just sat there shaking his head. Stupid muthafucka, he thought to himself, but knew better to say it out loud. "Back seat", Waldon pointed looking out the driver side window. He was so disgusted with Blue he couldn't even stand to look at him.

Blue grabbed the duffel bag in the back seat. He unzipped the large duffel bag and discovered 15 wrapped bricks of cocaine. Blue's eyes lit up like Christmas lights on Christmas Eve, when he seen the bricks.

"Now this what I'm talking bout." Blue cheered by himself.

"Look, since we got the pictures emailed over to us. We built a file on the three of you, as if we already were investigating yall, those 15 bricks are not real, I need you to divide those bricks between three spots, so when we hit, we can come up on something. But after this you must lay low for a while."

"Okay, you heard me though? I'ma need some more licks like the last one. I'm trying to get my chips up. I'm not trying to be doing this forever."

"Yeah, blue I heard you. But I'm telling you now, with all the heat from the feds about to come down, if shit gets too crazy for you, you keep me out of it, you understand?"

Blue frowned at him. "Damn, you on some real disrespectful shit right now. You coming at me like I'm a rat or something."

"I'm just sayin", Waldon replied then he pulled down on the gear shift and put the truck in drive. He was staring straight ahead, still not wanting to look Blue in the eyes.

"Whatever you say." Blue said as he opened the door and climbed out the Ram 1500 with the duffel bag clutched in his hand. He closed the door with his back and began to walk away.

"Aye Blue." Waldon called out behind him.

"What man, what you want?" Blue spoke with an attitude turning back to face his direction.

"The way you are moving, you better keep me outta yo shit."

"So, you still with this rat shit dawg?"

"No, I'm not calling you a rat." Waldon said in a calm voice.

"I'm just sayin." He pulled out of the parking lot, leaving Blue caught up in his feelings.

"Pussy ass cracka." Blue said as he tightened his grip on the duffel bag. He jumped back in the low low and pulled back into traffic.

Meanwhile, Shaq sat in front of Flag Street laundromat. He was backed in sitting in Blues car awaiting on them to pull up. He didn't need his number because he figured he knew Blues car. Besides that, it was supposed to be Blue inside the car anyways.

Observing his surroundings Shaq noticed a smoke Gray F150 with dark tint at the four way stop sign. The truck waited on all of the cars to leave the stop signs and pulled up in front of Shaq. Shaq believing this was the play for the half a brick. He pointed for the truck to pull on the side of Blues car through the windshield. Seeing the car wasn't complying he started to reach for his gun. And remembered he gave it to Blue earlier.

Soon as Shaq felt fishy about the situation. It all explained why blue was acting paranoid earlier. But it was all too late.

A masked man holding a mini 14 rose from the bed of the truck. Nowhere to go Shaq tried to shield himself under the dashboard. But it was no help as the gunman let all 50 rounds loose inside of Blues car.

After the shooting nothing could be smelled but Gunsmoke. Shaq sat in a bullet riddled car with blood leaking from its driver side door. The paramedics arrived and announced him dead on arrival.

The murder of Shaq was sad and not for him. He died but his name will never be forgotten. (Rest Up Shaq)

Chapter 24

The aftermath of Shaq's murder was felt more than heard. The raid of the three spots Blue arranged was to go down tomorrow. He never shared the information with Ralo and Smiley about the feds. He figured everything would be handled. And he didn't know how they would react under pressure.

(Private Location)

All the lights were turned off, and the only thing moving was the two bear-like (Belgian Malinois) also known as Malawa's. Blue had just purchased the two well trained dogs. He had the dogs specifically trained for intruders and protection. His favorite trick was to send them to search the house before he entered. But now they were standing watch for any sign of trouble. Ever since word was spreading, they were getting to a big bag. And they experienced A casualty of war. It was no room for error.

"Love and Happiness!" It can make you do wrong." Al Greene's strong soulful voice could be heard blasting through the speakers of the basement.

The smoke-filled room was damn near dark as the entire house. The only light was coming from the big screen TV that was hanging on the wall. It was playing the movie Belly starring DMX and Nas.

Blue and Smiley was laid back on the leather couch passing a blunt back and forth and loading up banana clips. They were watching the scene where Ox killed everybody just to be killed by Chiquita. The female assassin from Jamaica. Blue was feeling like Nas/Sincere He was up half a ticket and wanted out of the game. Smiley was more like

DMX or Bundy. He was a street nigga and loved the game and what came with it. The murders, violence, guns, was normal activity.

Sitting across from three G.I.T's. They were their young Gangsters, In, Training. They kept their noses fed with cocaine and money in their pockets. All three of them were dressed in black sweat suits, and bulletproof vests that read Police in bold letters on the front. It was their time to put in some work. They had kuttas with soldier straps and ski-masks on top of their heads.

"We done been on that walk, it's y'all turn now. Tonight, y'all gone be put to the test. When we drop y'all off, I want y'all to not leave a soul alive in that house. You understand me?"

The three gits just sat there and taking the words and powdering their noses. The uncut cocaine had their faces numb and their trigger fingers eager.

Ever since the gits linked up with Blue and Smiley a few months back, the three had been extorting nearly every drug dealer in the city. Whoever got down with the get down and accepted the cocaine being supplied by Blue, they were given something like a pass and allowed to operate as a affiliate. But on the rebound, anybody who refused, were robbed or simply killed.

Everyone who refused was now on the hit list. Shaq's killers were kidnapped and murdered the same day Shaq was killed. But once Blue and Smiley had that taste of blood which was an addiction to killers. They said fuck it and kept pressing buttons. Tonight was no different it was time to get richer and do some soul collecting.

Turk was one of the many who refused, so now he had to pay his debt. He had no clue that Blue and Smiley was posted outside his house and that the three gits were tiptoeing through the dark spacious 4-bedroom house in the suburbs.

The gits were strapped each with kuttas and dressed in all black. Each had on ski mask that read JSO and Police across the bulletproof vest.

One of them searched the house. While the other two remained in front of Turk's bedroom door.

When the one searching had found the money and bricks. He approached the bedroom door with the rest and stopped. The only thing they heard were the sounds of Turk beating some bitch back in.

"Ooooooh, Turk! Shit!" His new bitch Paris cried out.

She was bended over the bed with her phat ass in the air and Turk was behind her doggy-style, long-dicking her, pulling her hair. Turk was going pornstar in the pussy, jabbing so hard the headboard was hitting the wall with a loud clap.

Clap! Clap! Clap!

He smacked Paris on the ass and gripped both ass cheeks spreading her so he could get every inch inside her tight pussy.

Paris was performing as well, arching her back and popping her ass matching Turk pound for pound. He was deep in her guts she was feeling him in her stomach.

"Fuck this pussy, Daddy! Just like that. Give me that dope dick. Fuck me, Turk! Fuck me! Aaagghhnn!"

"Wwiiiinnnnne!" Turk went to imitating the rapper B.G'S big punchline.

Her pussy was so tight and moist that every time Turk went deep inside her and pulled back, his dick was becoming whiter and whiter, covered in her cream.

"Gone pop that pussy for a real nigga."

"Like this?" Paris replied making each ass cheek jump and bucking even harder.

"Yeah, just like that. Now, tell me where you want this nut at?"

"All, over, my face. My face Daddy!" Paris shuddered and moaned. "I wanna taste that nut daddy! Shit!"

Turk leaned forward and grabbed her around the shoulders. Staying steady inside her, he gyrated his hips and mashed his pole against the bottom of her tight wet pussy.

"You like when I hit that G-spot?"

"Yes, Daddy, just like that. Keep it right there!" She squeezed her fuck muscles around his pole and popped her ass a few more times. Paris's body begin to shiver, and her eyes rolled to the back of her head. "Oh, My Lawd, Damn, Shit! I'm cumming! I'm cumming! Shit! Uggghhnnnnnn!!"

A watery stream of hot cum squirted from her pussy and splashed on Turk's satin sheets. Totally aroused he jabbed even faster. The headboard was knocking, his chest was heaving, and toes begin to curl. Feeling the tingling sensation in his balls. He pulled out of her wet pussy and began masterbating his manhood.

Soon as Paris felt Turk pull out. She instantly turned around and assumed the position. Ass tooted up in the air, tongue out, she faced Turk. Paris was ready to eat it all like a greedy dog.

Noticing Turk's stomach sucking in, she sensed his orgasm was near. And took over.

Paris put that mouth on him like it was a vacuum. Never coming up for air. She sucked until she could taste his seeds. She grabbed his balls and began to pull and massage them, as she cleaned his manhood of her creamy nectar.

Exhausted the two of them, sticky and wet, collapsed on top the soft satin bed set. The euphoric sensation of Turk catching a nut had Turk riding the wave. Unaware that he was lacking, and death was on the other side of his bedroom door, literally.

"Damn, you fucked that bitch like a porn-star my nigga"

The first git snickered as he crept inside the bedroom with the other two behind him.

"Huh? What the fuck?! Do yall got a search warrant?" Turk shouted. Covering Paris naked body.

They aimed their kuttas at both of their bodies. "Slow down now cowboy."

Turk looked at the three dressed in police garbs and shook his head. He noticed one had a pillowcase filled with his money and bricks. This shit was ugly, and he knew it. By running in his spot and not announcing themselves as police, he knew the three men stood on business.

"Damn! Man! Fuck! Fuck! Fuck!" Turk began to panic seeing he was all out of options.

"Shut up before you wake the neighbors."

"And if you think you're lonnnnellyy nooowww, wait until tonight girl." The sound of two voices singing Bobby Womack's smash hit (If You Think You're Lonely Now).

Then strands of smoke started rolling into the room. Unbeknownst to the entire room, Blue and Smiley crept up a few minutes earlier. And made their presence known by singing. Blue gestured for the gits to finish the job.

Whop! Whop! Whop! Whop! Whop!

The gunshots from the assault rifle were so loud, fast, and unexpected. The entire room closed their eyes for a split second. As everyone's ears began to ring.

"Now what if we were laying on y'all. Yall in here slipping." Blue said as he held a 38. Snubnose in his right hand. And pointed it at the shooters head.

Click! Click! Click!

The sounds of the empty 38. were the only thing heard inside the room.

Pssst! The sounds of gasping could be heard by the three gits.

"Let's move out." Blue directed everybody.

They made it off with the bricks and money. And it was on to the next. Turks body laid their lifeless atop Paris. The white satin sheets were now crimson red. Erased were his thoughts. Blood was leaking from a quarter sized hole on his forehead.

(The Following Morning)

At 6:30 AM a search team led by Officer Waldon filed into the 3rd house on their list this morning. In hand was a no-knock warrant. In the closet of the master bedroom, the team found three bricks of cocaine and $25,000 in cash.

Altogether, they found 15 bricks and $80,000 in cash. The Lieutenant was happy about the drugs and money. But he was vexed about the fact nobody was there. This made him look bad to the feds. Who showed up after the 3rd house was hit.

The DEA agents arrived and began to look inside the back seat of each police cruiser. They were searching for their "three kingpins."

"Where the fuck is our guys?" One DEA agent shouted.

"Nobody was here, nobody was at either three houses. What kind of cops are you? You take drugs without the bad guys. You gotta be fuckin kidding me!! Keep your hands off these three." The DEA agent snapped at Jacksonville Sheriff's Office police officers. Showing them three previous mug shots of the trio.

The city of Jacksonville Sheriff's Office was officially not allowed to deal with any Intel on Blue, Smiley, or Ralo. It was what it was. The three were too fast for the feds, and too cocky for the cops.

For the past year agents of the US Drug Enforcement Administration had been keeping watch on the city of Jacksonville's drug trade. The Miami boys were coming to the city flooding it with cocaine. But the mentality of street niggas and dope boys were different in those times. No snitching was a code honored amongst all. So this made the government really have to do their jobs. Agents believed they knew what was going on. But majority was hearsay.

The DEA first identified Blue, Smiley, and Ralo, as suspected drug traffickers in the late 80s around 89. But back then, they were small fish. They didn't register as big fishes until some years later. That's when they picked up on them. See the difference between the feds and the cops, the feds had enough patience and smarts to build a case on a mastermind. After they got on your trail. They followed you like a shadow.

The DEA kept in touch with JSO who slipped them info about the three. And built ties with confidential informants who gave them little information on the three. But somehow the trail always went cold.

Chapter 25

Cameras were snapping photos as video cameras were rolling. The sheriff of the city of Jacksonville had called an emergency press conference. Every local station regular daily scheduled program was interrupted to broadcast this press conference.

"Uuum Uumm", Sherriff Nat Glove cleared his throat before speaking.

"Last night our city experienced a series of murders and robberies. A survivor has come forward with details, and it has been brought to my attention these individuals were dressed in Police garbs, it seems we have a breech in one of our Sherriffs Office, but we will get to the bottom of this and prosecute them to the fullest extent of the law."

The TV in the break room at the Sheriff's Office was on full blast.

Sitting inside the break room sat a plush red Waldon. His face was turning colors. The heat was coming down and the kitchen was hotter than he expected. Word was spreading quickly around the Sheriff's Office. It was a bunch of dirty cops, and they were on the hit list with a bunch of suspected drug dealers. Waldon had to think, and he had to think fast. It was time to cut ties with the underworld. From that moment he knew the friendship they'd built that came with expensive cars, lavish vacations, and unlimited salaries. Would now have to come to an end.

The following months, several drug dealers' houses and drug houses were raided. With the majority coming up empty. A federal probe started to look inside of JSO's drug task force. As well as the three suspected kingpins.

Investigators convinced a judge in approving a title 3 wiretap on an associate of Blue, Ralo, and Smiley.

After climbing onto several Jacksonville major players. They finally came up with Blues phone number. Blue's phone number was turned over to the DEA. Through listening to Blues calls, the investigators were able to jump onto Ralo's number. Then eventually Smiley's number. To have a wiretap on the three was the biggest progress over the last 10 years.

A dirty cop of JSO had been forced to resign over not following JSO's policies on traffic stops. A citizen reported the officer pulled him over, took keys of coke, then assaulted him. This officer was very close to Blue. And this drove Blues anxiety to an all-time high. The threat against everything he built was inescapable. He didn't doubt for one second that the officer would betray him. He also knew that eventually the feds would come knocking on his front door, and that jail was inevitable.

Not only did he not take heed to Waldon's advice, to stay away from the dope game. But a little over a month ago he met another Cuban connect. He and the Cuban struck a deal that would allow him to have enough coke to expand his clientele to out of town. At the beginning of the month, he was now getting fronted 75 uncut bricks of cocaine. In Blues eyes he had everything to gain and shit to lose. Especially since Waldon cut ties, believing if they kept doing business they would eventually get caught.

"All I need in this life of sin is me and my girlfriend." Blue sung along to Tupac's lyrics as he dropped a stack of money in his money counter.

"Fffddddddd! Beep!

He looked at the digital screen and scribbled the numbers on a small writing pad.

"That's two-hundred and fifty thou-wow. I just counted up. I still gotta drop these bricks off to the hood, and we gone eat good girl." Blue said to his two Malawa's that stood erect on each side of his desk. He zipped the bag up and said something in German. Then the bags of money were dragged by each dog to the hallway.

Watching his surveillance cameras, Blue was thinking about if it all failed. Who would he leave everything to. He had double digit babymomma's. And was still finding out daily he had more kids on the way. Either way it went he had enough money buried in the ground to send every single one to college.

When the dogs returned to the office, blue tossed them each a doggy snack. And they sat back erect on each side of his desk. He was backing away from the desk getting ready to leave when the phone on his desk began to ring.

This was not a regular for him to receive calls. Ever since they've cut ties with Waldon. Blue did take heed not to be the first hand in the mix. He sent everyone to Ralo to grab their drugs. So, he wasn't expecting any calls.

He looked at the caller ID as the phone kept ringing. "Who the fuck could this be calling the spot." Blue mumbled to himself.

The phone stopped ringing and the only thing blue could hear was the bear like Malawas breathing. A part of him was paranoid and somewhat scared. Who the fuck could be calling his house phone? If they were calling his phone, that meant they knew where he lived as well.

Some few minutes later, the phone began ringing again. This time it was a different number. He was receiving way too many calls on his phone today. This time he decided to answer it.

"Yo, who this?" He spoke calmly as possible. Trying to disguise the worry in his voice.

"I just called, why the hell you ain't answer?"

"I didn't make it to the phone in time."

"Okay, well check this out. Take a look at your cameras. Blocka spoke in an urgent voice. "Hurry up and look!"

"For what?" Blue asked in a paranoid voice. "What's going on daddy."

"Just listen! Blocka snapped at him." Now is not the time to be bullshittin. Now, stop asking so many fucking questions, and do as you're told."

Blue walked back over the desk where five security cameras were. He searched the cameras for anything abnormal.

"What am I looking for?"

"I just got word danger is heading your way." Blocka warned Blue.

"Danger!!" Blue began to grit his teeth. "Tell them send their best man, I'ma kill em all."

"Kill who? What the fuck is you speaking about? It's the alphabet boys.

"Well let they ass come." Blue shot back all while grabbing his 2.23.

"Calm your happy go lucky ass down." Blocka spoke in a calm voice. "I know you's a fighter, but this time is different. This time you gotta think your way out of this one on your own. Meanwhile grab anything you not supposed to have and place it across the fence in your neighbor's yard."

Blue removed the 2.23 soldier strap from around his shoulder, and he reached down and chambered a round inside the rifle.

"Son, You still on here?" Blocka asked hearing silence on the line "say something."

"Yeah, I'm here. I need time to process this for a minute."

A part of blue wanted to go out like Tony Montana in the end. Jail wasn't an option. He took his time to build his empire from the ground up. He was almost to his set goal. Where he would be able to leave the streets alone. Visions of his kids ran through his mind. If he fouled out and went out like Tony who would raise his kids?

"This is do or die!" Blocka snapped through the phone getting Blues attention.

"God Dammit!!" Hearing Blues tone both Maliwa's perked up hungry for action. Following Blues' every move, they began to grab duffel bags with Blue. Some were filled with money others were filled with bricks. Blue did as he was told and started to toss them in the neighbor's yard.

260

Making it back to his office, blue picked up the phone. "Hello."

"Yes, son you need to make wudu (ablution) and go wash your hands, face, head, arms, feet, of the sins you've committed. Make two rakats (cycles) or salat (prayer) ask Allah for forgiveness."

"I gotta call Smiley and Ralo, let them know to be on beat."

"At this point it's every man for himself. Salamu alaykum." Blocka ended the call.

Blue made wudu then placed his prayer rug to the direction of the east. A lonely tear crept down his right cheek as he recited Surah (chapter) 3, ayat (verse) 160. "If Allah helps you, there is none that can overcome you: and if he forsakes you, who is there that can help after him? And in Allah should the believers put their trust."

As blue finished reciting the front door of the house came crashing in. Hearing the sound of intruders. The Maliwa's jumped into action. They were shot quickly. DEA agents flooded the house flipping any and everything in their way. The only room they didn't search for some odd reason, was the office. Where Blue sat in prostration with his face at the front of his prayer rug. Hearing footsteps near. He ended his prayer. Walked over to his desk and took a seat in his office chair. He opened up the cigar box and grabbed a Cuban cigar and fired it up. Watching the security cameras as they swarmed the house and his subdivision like a parade.

The office door came crashing and sitting there was Blue, feet kicked up puffin a Cuban Cohiba cigar.

"Let me see your hands. Don't move." Different voices yelled and red laser beams could be seen all over Blue's face. As the officers approached him like he was a ticking bomb.

"It took yall long enough." Blue said behind a large cloud of smoke.

(Back at the Memorial Building)

"I don't got shit to say to none of bitches! Eat a dick!" Smiley screamed at the two-way mirror in the interrogation room. He was handcuffed to the table in the middle of the room, dressed in only a tank top and gym shorts. The air conditioning was on full blast. They were determined to break him. By any means necessary.

"Call my fucking lawyer 904-888-2324!" Smiley continued to snap at the two-way mirror. He had a feeling somebody was on the other side watching him.

Jacksonville sheriff, Nat Glove was boiling hot on the other side of the two-way mirror. His goal was to let his men talk to the three first. And get as much information about any inside dealings with his Sheriff's Office. But things weren't going as planned.

For one, somebody tipped News4Jax off about the three being arrested. By the time they were brought to the memorial building, news cameras were everywhere in the lobby hungry for a breaking story.

Soon after Blue was picked up, so was Smiley then Ralo. On the other end of the memorial building detectives received different results.

"Yeah, I was told I'm being charged with conspiracy to distribute 1.5 kilograms of cocaine and cocaine base."

"That is correct, the amount of drugs we have you charged with is enough to get you a life sentence. You know that right?"

"Yes Sir I do."

"Do you know about any dealings being done with JSO, or any other law officials of Jacksonville?"

"Yes I do Sir. But I would like to have my lawyer present with me. Before I discuss anything further."

"That's fair enough." The detective opened the door to the interrogation room and stepped outside. He walked one room over and tapped lightly on the door.

"Hey Mr. Robins, Blue is what they call you right?"

"Yeah, I guess you can say that."

"Oh okay, Ralo told me a lot about you and how you had police working for you. How many did you have Blue?"

Well, I had at least one officer of JSO working for me."

"Is that right?" The detective stated. He was just about to tear into Blue but was interrupted when the US District Attorney called out from behind the closed door.

"Yes, I just was about to start the interrogation."

"I don't think so, this case is out of your jurisdiction. We'll take over from here."

The detective spun around to face the voice. He noticed right then and there that the US District Attorney was occupied by two DEA agents. Both men were smiling at Blue.

The government has its ways of dividing and conquering. It has been like that before slavery was abolished. And now it was no different. That was the plans of the feds. They kept Blue, Smiley, and Ralo separated while being housed at the Duval County jail. Most likely, to keep communication at a bare minimum. To make matters worse, officers came to question the three about robberies, murders, anything they heard. Ever since they aired them on the news. Everybody who was once scared came out of hiding. Rumors began to spread like wildfire.

On Monday morning, bright and early, the C.O's at the Duval County Jail gathered its inmates for court. Being at the time, there was no federal holding facility in the region. It was inevitable Blue, Smiley, and Ralo would be in the same holding cell. Also, they would be transported together in the patty wagon.

It was a quarter past seven, Blue, Ralo, and Smiley were placed in the same holding cell. Only thing heard in the small space was the chains of the shackles. The three were at an impasse. Ralo had made his mind up already. He wasn't taking 30 years. Smiley had his sights set on putting the law on the law. Only one thing stood in the way. He knew, but he didn't know enough about Blue's political connection. Blue was playing his hand however it was dealt to him.

"What we gone do about this shit?" Blue asked the question that broke the silence like glass.

"I'm gone trade them crackas in for my freedom." Smiley voiced.

"I'm gone keep it solid they only know what we tell them."

"Yeah, that's right; Soon as Blue begin speaking, he was interrupted by the opening of the cell door.

The officer placed two additional inmates in the cell with the three. Then the room continued its silence. That silence would remain a whole decade between the three.

After the first court date, reality set in. Ralo began working with the feds immediately. Blue also did as well. Smiley attempted to, but jailhouse rumor has it Blue sent word he would expose murders. And Smiley fell all the way back.

For sentencing, Ralo received seven years. Blue received twenty-one years. Smiley on the other hand was given a stiff thirty-year sentence. The legend of Blue, Smiley, and Ralo would never be forgotten. A lot of people were happy they were in the feds. They felt as the streets of Jacksonville was safer.

Inside the courtroom, news reporters were lined up to ask the US District Attorney questions.

"Today you all have prosecuted 3 dangerous men, why the different numbers in sentencing?"

"Well, the seven-year was handed down, because he began to cooperate first. He gave us a lot of information we would have known nothing about."

"And why so harshly with the 30-year sentence?"

"Dealing with that individual was very difficult. One minute he was given information, the next was like a light in the room was turned off. So, we felt the thirty-year sentence was well deserved."

"These individuals had police officers working for them?"

"Right now we can't say whether that is true or false. At this moment nothing had been brought to my attention."

"Twenty-one years, why not thirty years?"

Well, his sentencing was a lot different. He gave us a lot of information. But it wasn't solid enough to grant a 5K motion. He's still working with our offices. He may see a sentence reduction in the future. Sorry I can't answer any more questions. Today justice has been served."

Acknowledgements

All praises are due to Allah. Thankful for my best of the best staff at SKYBOXX PUBLICATIONS. All this wouldn't be possible if it wasn't for you!! You are HEAVEN SENT...

My mother and tete for loving me no matter what. I know at times I have been a person only ALLAH could love. Shout out to my O.G for being the type to teach, and not tryna run the game on me. To my bros Wop, E, Dino & Dede I love you forever ever. One time for Durt Face, Pee Wee, 7FIG. Monster & Toetag!! FOUR times for T.Berg!! FIVE times for Grumps!! B is forever love and loyalty. People will never understand you, when you are a rare breed! Everybody from the set FS13, it's too many to name but you know what it is FL!

SIGNED M.SHULA

@I.G MOODY_SHULA

(Ace in the Hole 2)

2009

It's always three sides to a story. And this one is no different. Only Allah knows the truth, eventually you'll hear theirs, but this is mines.

It was a little past noon, when the gates buzzed open to let Blue re-enter society. The year was 2009 a far cry from the 21 years he was supposed to serve. The only thing he left Coleman Correctional Institution with were books and a white envelope Brother Jihad instructed him not to open until he made it home.

The parking lot was filled with families happy to have their loved ones back with them. Some families held cakes, balloons, and presents of different sorts. Blue scanned the parking lot and became angry instantly. His life had turned for the worse the last 10 years. He left the streets damn near a millionaire and came back with nothing. But a house on the west side of Paxon that he owned. Which was destroyed due to lack of up-keeping. Without a ride home Blue settled for a ride home with one of the prisoner's family.

Entering the city limits of Jacksonville. Blue was amazed by how much things had changed within 10 years. With Jacksonville being the biggest city land wise in America. There were a lot of areas that were majority land. But now the city was re-built. Blue stared out the window pondering his next moves. Only thing on his mind were two things. Buy back the hood in real estate. And get in the rap game. He had to try the impossible. While being in the feds he'd met many plugs and had 10 years of planning to use them.

The car came to a halt on 13th and Canal Street. The block was roped off. The entire street was packed with a slew of different cars, motor bikes, and trucks. All of them belonging to JSO. One of the latest shootings had taken place right in the middle of the block. From the looks of things this was a murder. This was the beginning of the Grand Park Vs. Flag Street war. That JSO named "Casualties of War". In this war friends who once played pop warner sports, smoked, gambled, drunk, now became enemies. This was a bad time for Blue.

   Word spread quickly the Legend Blue was free again. All the fake love returned as he expected. Many came to show love and respect. A lot of the little homies that was buying their first packs from him was now grown up doing big things. And wanted to return the favor showing good grace. Majority of them brought drugs, which Blue felt was double hustling. So he advised everyone to go sale the drugs and bring him the money.

   The months that passed by in the Grand Park and Flag Street area were filled with violence. An incident at the club and drinks being thrown left bodies on the pavement on both sides. It was time to forget the body bags and bring out the money bags. "War and getting money is like oil and water it don't mix, never will and never have." He could hear his father's voice inside his head. Blue picked up his phone and called a number.

   "Hello", Black Tony said into the phone.

   "All this shit gotta come to a end. I can't move how I wanna move with homicide detectives everywhere round here." Blue expressed through frustration.

"Niggas on my side saying they will chill. You gotta holla at ya boy Ryan or what yall call him Bossgoon. Tell him I'll give him a brick of coke to ease up." Black Tony offered.

"Ight, I'll let him know. But you gotta tell Marc-Marc to fall all the way back. Them niggas use to be friends I heard this shit gotta stop."

"I'ma do my part you just do yours. We aint gone say to much over the line. One!" Black Tony ended the call.

Blue sat there holding his phone trying to figure out how he was going to get in the head of BG. Bossgoon was a hot head who jumped off the porch a little late. But when he did, he jumped headfirst in the murder game. So it wasn't necessarily about the money. It was the adrenaline and the powder cocaine made it no better. He was a one-man army and ready for only death. Jail was not an option. He made sure to tell the world, "Before he go lay down he'll die."

The brakes were squeaking loudly on Blue's broke down Ford Taurus, in front Zay's house on 14th Street. From the looks of things, it was a normal day. Traffic was coming and going. Zay was the neighborhood weed supplier.

On the porch, was Bossgoon and one of Blue's sons playing Madden. While everybody else watched and smoked discussing hood politiks.

"I like my boy for fifty dollars." Blue challenged Bossgoon seeing an opportunity to build a connection with the young gunslinger.

"I call that Big Dawg", Bossgoon accepted the bet.

Since Blue came home his name was hot. So he switched his name up and beginned calling himself "Big Dawg". The hood accepted the title being he had status of a Big Dawg. It was always speculations he was a rat. But with the case being 10 years old. The streets weren't in tuned enough to get the facts of the case, or the paperwork. So the title was given to Blue. And he proudly accepted it.

Bossgoon and Blue son played the first game. Bossgoon ended up winning, Blue asked for a bet back. On the second game he'd won twenty-one to zero. Which was double. Blue was to pay the sum of $150. Blue didn't bulge a muscle and his demeanor was showing he wasn't paying.

Bossgoon was 22 years of age and heartless. In the streets he was a stone-cold blooded killer with not an ounce of pity. He was good at applying pressure to niggas in the city. With the 357. in his waistline he weighed his options.

Blue on the other hand, was well respected on every side of town. He was feared the most in the same neighborhood that he was having a standoff in with the young killer. Any chance he seen fear in anybody he took advantage of that fear. To his surprise he seen no fear in the eyes of this Bossgoon. But still he showed no sign of paying him.

Bossgoon tossed the controller to the PS3, clutched his 357 looking into Blue's brown eyes.

"You took that Big Dawg." He said as he left the porch.

The silence was the loudest sound at the moment. Everybody knew what Bossgoon was capable of doing. It was evident in the last few months. Only the hood heard about what Blue used to do. And read the news and newspaper articles. But today was a new age and time.

Several months passed by the war continued. Blue made the offer to Bossgoon to squash the beef in exchange for the brick of cocaine from Black Tony. Bossgoon quickly denied and advised him the only way to end it all was through bloodshed. In Blue's eyes he seen it a different way.

On April 1st, 2010

A truck sat unnoticed on Zay's Street with tinted windows, waiting on the correct moment to catch Bossgoon leaving so they could tail him to either his home or his grave. He seemed impossible to catch. Nobody knew where he rested his head. As far as the streets knew, he was a ghost. Today all that was going to change. And Bossgoon was to be remembered as a Monumental Figure. And so were his killers. May they be remembered and freed of bondage.

Bossgoon did not notice the brown truck that pulled up behind him and two others, until it was too late.

The sounds from the kutta and semi-automatic machine gun filled the atmosphere.

Bossgoon smashed his foot on the gas. He tried to escape as the truck pulled up again.

Shots fired; the truck pulled off down Kings Road.

As the shots rang out, Bossgoon could feel the burning sensation of the gunshot wound to his right thigh that punctured his main artery. When people tried to save him and get him to a hospital. He refused the help.

Bossgoon reached for the door handle, but as soon as he did, he felt his soul leaving his body. He couldn't breathe any longer, and his eyes were weaker. He couldn't hold on any longer and let go completely.

Blue felt his heart pounding away in his chest. The gunshots of Bossgoon getting killed echoed throughout the neighborhood. But the last phone call he received almost gave him a heart attack. The caller stated that one of Blue's many sons was in the car with Bossgoon. When he instructed him no matter what he did not to get in the car that day. His son made it out with only a bullet going through his skull cap.

Blue read the text message as a smile crept across his face, and then looked down at the brown paper bag. Suddenly a thought of Brother Jihad flashed inside his head. The jewels Brother Jihad had given him back in the days in a cell in the county jail was still strong. Either you can be a piece on the board, or the hand that pushes the pieces. Pondering, he reached inside the bag and pulled out the white envelope. Brother Jihad had given him the envelope before he left again at Coleman Correctional Institution. Now he was back in society and settled. He decided to open the envelope and read the wise words he was sure Brother Jihad had shared.

Upon opening the envelope, he thought it was a trick at first. Because at first sight he didn't find a letter. But eventually he seen what was enclosed inside the envelope. It was a playing card he remembered seeing every day inside Jihad's window seal in his cell. It was a Ace of Spade Bicycle card. Blue sat there making sense of what Jihad was trying to communicate through this encrypted message. When suddenly a mischievous grin came across his face.

Welcome to the Ace in the Hole Series my reader....

Coming Soon!

Made in United States
Orlando, FL
09 February 2025